DATE DUE

Sage Creek

**Center Point
Large Print**

**This Large Print Book carries the
Seal of Approval of N.A.V.H.**

Sage Creek

JILL GREGORY

CENTER POINT LARGE PRINT
THORNDIKE, MAINE

This Center Point Large Print edition
is published in the year 2012 by arrangement with
The Berkley Publishing Group,
a member of Penguin Group (USA) Inc.

The text of this Large Print edition is unabridged.
In other aspects, this book may vary
from the original edition.
Printed in the United States of America
on permanent paper.
Set in 16-point Times New Roman type.

ISBN: 978-1-61173-305-1

Library of Congress Cataloging-in-Publication Data

Gregory, Jill.
Sage creek / Jill Gregory. — Large print ed.
p. cm. — (Center Point large print edition)
ISBN 978-1-61173-305-1 (library binding : alk. paper)
1. Bakeries—Fiction. 2. Montana—Fiction. 3. Large type books. I. Title.
PS3557.R4343S34 2012
813'.54—dc23
                                              2011041786

To my wonderful sister Peggy
and my dear friend Debbie,
with love and appreciation.

Chapter One

A charcoal and rose dusk streaked above the Crazy Mountains as Sophie McPhee turned her Blazer onto the private gravel drive that would lead her home.

The drive was called Daisy Lane, and the rambling two-story timber house looming a half mile in the distance was the Good Luck ranch house built by her mother's grandfather more than ninety years ago.

Three generations of her mother's family had called it home, and it had been *her* home the first eighteen years of her life. Sophie wondered with quiet desperation as darkness stole over Lonesome Way if it truly could be her home again.

Would this house or this town *feel* like home, after all this time, after everything that had happened? Would any place ever again feel like home?

She swallowed, hoping it would. But the emptiness inside her seemed as if it would never go away, never allow her to feel anything but loss and anger ever again.

Back in San Francisco, friends had told her she wouldn't always feel this way, that things would get better. The platitudes sounded nice and Sophie knew they were well-meaning, but they bounced off her like drops of cold water hitting a sizzling skillet.

Her throat tightened as she neared the head of Daisy Lane and the Blazer's headlights caught the gleam of the big white house and the familiar landmarks of the now empty Good Luck barns and sheds and paddocks. The same-old, same-old words of encouragement weren't doing a thing right now to help her fight the fist of pain squeezing her heart.

She didn't have any idea what—if anything—ever would.

All she'd been able to think to do was to leave her old life with all its tears and mistakes behind, and to start over.

And here in her hometown of Lonesome Way was the only place where she'd imagined having the strength to try.

As the flaming rose sun slipped behind the mountains, and darkness swallowed the foothills, a tiny flicker of hope made Sophie catch her breath. The sage-scented air, the vast miles of rugged rolling land, were familiar. Comforting.

Home.

On that thought, the kitchen window suddenly glowed with a bright, cheerful light. Her mother was expecting her. Sophie had called from the road. Next on was the living room lamp, gleaming with welcome. And then the porch light sprang to life, illuminating the old white wooden swing and her mother's carefully planted rosebushes.

A crystal wind chime tinkled sweetly, swinging in the night breeze, and there were the wide porch steps where she'd perched on countless summer afternoons as a girl, playing jacks with Lissie and Mia.

A rush of emotion filled her as she switched off the ignition and climbed down from the Blazer on tired feet. Even as she grabbed her purse, the front door of the house swung open and her mother appeared in the doorway. Not quite as tall as Sophie, she was thin and angular, wearing a loose blue cotton top and jeans, her feet bare in the summer night.

Diana McPhee hurried out onto the porch. Her chin-length fair hair was peppered with gray, her eyes reflected a mixture of eagerness and concern. Sophie was struck by the fact that nearing sixty, her mother was still a strikingly pretty woman.

"Sophie! Thank heavens. I was starting to get worried."

As Sophie moved toward her, her throat ached with unshed tears.

"I've been holding dinner. Guess you must've hit some major traffic on—"

9

Then her mother saw her face and broke off. Sophie knew how she must look—pale, sad, tired, with the tears that were always close shimmering in her green eyes. She was so sick of the tears. She blinked them back and forced a smile.

"Sorry to keep you waiting, Mom. There was construction, and at one point, believe it or not, I was so distracted that I took the wrong turn and had to backtrack."

"Well, now, that happens. You have a lot on your mind." Her mother's arms went around her, hugging very gently as if she were afraid Sophie would crack in pieces. But her voice was brisk and bracing as she touched her daughter's toffee-colored hair, tumbling in soft curls around a beautiful face with wide cheekbones a model would covet, a generous mouth, and dimples when she smiled. But Sophie was definitely not smiling now.

"You're here, Sophie, that's all that matters." Her voice was overly cheerful. "Leave your bags, we'll get them later. Let's go inside. I've fixed your favorite—meatloaf and biscuits, garlic mashed potatoes, and a big salad—oh, Sophie . . . honey, what's the matter?"

Sophie's feet had frozen on the threshold of the ranch house. Behind her flowed the night, full of stars and a crescent of moon, the buzz of insects, the lone cry of a hawk. The cool night wind rustled delicately through the ponderosa pines. And ahead of her loomed her past, the house of her childhood and teen years, warm and faded yet so familiar it was startling.

She felt herself teetering between two worlds.

She couldn't move, could only stare past the entry into the rectangular living room, with its big chintz-covered sofa and matching love seat, warm maple end tables, and the black walnut TV stand centered along the far blue wall. She took in the massive stone fireplace, the bookshelves, and her father's favorite tan leather chair in the corner beside the reading lamp.

How many times had she torn through this door, or downstairs from her room, to see his long legs stretched across that chair, his feet propped on the footrest, his hooded eyes intent as he watched a football game or devoured the newest Tom Clancy novel—or slanted a stern glance at her as she hovered uncertainly in the doorway, just as she was doing now?

Her father's granite voice seemed to scratch the air around her, blasting his opinion of all the ways she fell short of his expectations.

You forgot your spelling list at school. How do you expect to pass the test? That's just plain irresponsible, Sophie. You're eight years old. I expect more from you than that.

How much time have you wasted talking to Lissie Tanner on that phone? You weren't raised to spend half your day jabbering about nonsense.

All your daydreaming is nothing but foolishness. Stop living in the clouds, Sophie. There's plenty of work around here that needs to be done.

Worst of all, that F in Geometry during her junior year.

Damned laziness. You wouldn't know hard work if it kicked you in the butt. Why don't you use your God-given brain, girl?

She'd never been able to please Hoot McPhee. But then, no one had. Not even her mother, though, somehow, for most of the years they'd been married, she'd put up with him—Sophie didn't know how. And finally, when he stepped way over the line, even her mother couldn't look the other way anymore.

Hoot had perhaps been hardest on her brother, Wes, who'd responded to the never-ending reprimands by leaving for Missoula and the University of Montana at the age of eighteen, and never looking back.

Wes had gone on to law school at the University of Texas, taking out student loans and working two jobs all the while so that he never had to ask his father for a dime above basic tuition. And he hadn't called home or come home more than three or four times in the years after his high school graduation. He hadn't returned to Lonesome Way for Hoot's funeral either.

Hoot McPhee had been gone five years. But for

12

a dizzying instant as Sophie stared into the living room, she could have sworn she sensed her tall, formidable father in that chair.

"It's the first time I've been back . . . since the funeral," she murmured as her mother came up behind her. "For an instant, I could almost see him sitting there—"

Sophie drew a breath and told herself to stop acting crazy. She walked into the living room, her flats clicking across the hardwood floor, and touched her hand to the back of the tan chair.

"Sorry, Mom. I know if he were here, you wouldn't be." After her mother had divorced him, Sophie's father had spent the last few years of his life living alone—or with one or another of a succession of women—in a cabin on Bear Claw Road. "I probably wouldn't be here either," she added with a rueful smile. "I'm just being stupid. Emotional, as he would say."

"No, you're not, not in the least. I don't wonder it seems strange to you to come in here and not see him. But a lot of things are different on the ranch now, Sophie. I've sold all the livestock and leased most of the grazing land. It's not the same as when your father was here, running cattle, running everything." Her mother's gaze held hers. "All the years you lived at home, he was here—we both were, together. So you've barely been in this house without him here—of course it feels odd to walk in and not see him."

Sophie studied her mother. She didn't look the least bit upset. Which was a wonder. Sophie couldn't imagine how her mother could talk about Hoot so calmly, almost dispassionately, as if he hadn't been discovered having an affair with the mayor's wife, Lorelei Hardin, during Sophie's junior year of college—and who knew how many other women he'd cheated with before that?

Sophie was still reeling from finding out about her own husband's infidelity. When would it stop, that ice-pick-to-the-heart pain? After a year—or two—a decade?

It's only been a few months, she told herself. *You won't always feel this rage, this pain. This blinding sense of betrayal. Mom survived. She's a normal, rational human being. You'll become one again too.*

But she knew she'd never trust any man again. Sophie couldn't ever see that happening. No way.

And she would be careful not to share her heart again, much less give it away. To anyone. The pain was too intense. The risk too great. She understood that now.

"You know, Mom," she said quietly. "It's because of Hoot that I tried so hard to make things work with Ned. I always dreaded the possibility of a second generation of divorce in the family. I needed someone different from

Hoot, someone who'd hold to his vows. Who'd encourage me and laugh with me and not tear down the people he was supposed to love. I thought I found him. So I kept trying for so long even after . . ."

Even after Ned became so distant, burying himself in his work. Putting Sophie and their life together on the back burner.

Somewhere along the line, Ned had let go of her and their marriage, and committed himself instead to his drug of choice—his own ambition.

In the end he'd had much more in common with Hoot McPhee than Sophie could have dreamed the day she walked down the aisle in swirls of white silk, seed pearls, and taffeta, making promises to love, honor, and cherish.

But she didn't know that—not until the day she found out about Cassandra Reynard.

"I really thought we'd last. Forever." She turned away from her father's chair. "Which just goes to show how much *I* know."

"There's no sense in blaming yourself. None at all." Taking her hand, her mother determinedly led her into the kitchen, lips pursed and concern sharpening her gaze. "Not one bit of this is your fault. I know Ned told you it is, but he's full of it. Don't let him screw with you any more than he already has. Divorce isn't a family curse, passed on from one generation to another. It just happens. And *he* cheated, not you. You gave him countless chances to keep your marriage together. A damn sight too many, if you ask me."

Sophie had to grin as she carried the wooden salad bowl brimming with greens and tomatoes and peppers to the square table. Her even-keeled mom rarely got so worked up. Obviously, Ned was high up on her shit list.

"Good to know you have my back, Mom."

"Family sticks together." Diana brought over the platter of sauce-laden meatloaf surrounded by garlic mashed potatoes and set it down. "That man better never show his face around here or he'll *really* get a piece of my mind."

The table was set with a robin's egg blue tablecloth and her mother's prettiest blue and yellow dishes. Matching napkins were folded atop each plate. Sophie's gaze was drawn to the bouquet of wildflowers filling an oval white vase in the center.

It all looked so festive and inviting.

Mom's trying so hard to make this easier for me.

But nothing was easy these days.

Sophie needed to lift her own mood, or else fake it, for her mother's sake. Which meant not thinking about Ned or about how she had to find a job, or wondering how she was going to restart her life.

"Everything looks great. You made too much food, though, Mom." *Especially since these days*

I have the appetite of a flea. She slid into a chair, reached for the salad bowl. "How's Gran?"

"Same as always." Diana gave a tiny smile at the mention of her mother. "She still has more energy than a windstorm and still thinks good always wins out in the end. Not such a bad philosophy, I guess. She's coming to dinner tomorrow night. Be prepared, she's planning to tell you how to fix your love life."

"What love life? I'm done with a love life."

"Not if your grandmother has anything to say about it. I give her a week at most before she seriously gets on your case."

"Maybe coming home wasn't such a great idea." Seeing her mother's alarmed expression, Sophie regretted her flip words. She felt a rush of warmth for her mother, for this house, for the Montana night that seemed to enfold them, at least at this moment, in a cocoon of safety.

"I'm just joking." She hugged her mom. "I'd rather be here than anywhere else in the world right now."

And she meant it.

After putting away her clothes and storing her suitcase in the back of her walk-in closet, Sophie gazed around her small, high-ceilinged room brimming with knickknacks and memories. The familiar lemon scent of Pledge, freshly washed cotton sheets, and fresh air wafting through the open window stirred her senses.

With the soft white lace curtains rustling in the breeze, she realized how little these four walls had changed since she'd left the ranch for college. She was twenty-nine now, single again, and staring at the remnants of innocence and childhood.

From the photographs and posters hung on the walls to the peach and yellow quilt folded neatly over her double bed, the room whisked her back through time, to days when she and her best friends Lissie Tanner and Mia Quinn spent almost every minute together, and if not together, gabbing on the phone.

All of her old stuffed animals from kindergarten through senior year in high school, including the huge stuffed lizard Wes had won her at the state fair, still slouched on the top shelf of her oak bookcase, which took up half a wall, and her creaky old six-drawer dresser occupied the other half.

Her mother had told her at dinner that Lissie—now Lissie Norris—was pregnant. And that Mia was throwing her a baby shower a week from Saturday.

I'll look for a gift in town tomorrow.

She was thrilled for Lissie and Tommy—they'd been together since high school and had been trying to have a baby for over a year.

But suddenly, the hollowness inside Sophie

became a hard, tangible ache in her chest. So many of her friends were pregnant or had babies now. She'd gone to all of their baby showers. Watched them hug and feed and bathe their infants, bundling them into tiny coats and hats, strapping them into strollers and car seats, caring for them with a joy and total intensity that Sophie could only yearn for.

Soon, Ned had told her, over and over. Be patient. We'll start trying soon. In six months. Then it was another six.

Then a year.

The timing needed to be perfect, according to him. And that meant after his career was firmly on track, rolling along in the ideal groove. After he landed a cable or network job and could cut his ties with the local affiliate crap Ned felt was so beneath him.

Her ex-husband had been a local news producer on WBBK in San Francisco, and he was good at his job. Damned good. Under his direction, the nightly news ratings had climbed from third place to number one in just under a year. But Ned had wanted more, a whole lot more. He wanted to become executive producer of a cable or network news show, one that was big and important and would get national attention—and that would thrust him into the big time.

With the big budgets, he'd told Sophie, pacing across the bamboo floor of their Potrero Hill condo, wound up the way he used to get before a final exam in college. *Not to mention big players, big media attention—and big money.*

Sophie wasn't sure exactly when the cute, brown-haired guy with the serious eyes and a cleft in his chin, with the perfect manners and a double major in journalism and business, the guy she'd studied with in the library, gobbled pizza with at Dewey's, lived with in a tiny studio apartment off campus their senior year, and married ten months later, had morphed into a man with tunnel vision—burrowing straight ahead toward his career goals and forgetting the life and family and home he'd promised to build together with her.

Maybe it was sometime after her own small bakery business, Sweet Sensations, had taken off, becoming as popular as her cinnamon buns, which flew off the shelves every morning and were gone by noon.

Sophie had gradually expanded the offerings in her shop beyond baked goods and coffees. She'd added a couple of soups and a handful of sandwiches and several unique gourmet salads to the menu, and eventually, at the suggestion of her friend Rosa, she'd begun taking on some catering jobs.

Somehow, over the next few years, the orders ratcheted up until she had to add staff and take out a loan for more equipment and supplies.

Sophie Sinclair's Sweet Sensations soon earned a designation as one of San Francisco's top three go-to caterers for upscale corporate events. Her business had grown beyond her most optimistic daydreams. Written up in local gourmet magazines, in newspaper food columns and online reviews, Sweet Sensations had flourished, and the clients had poured in.

But all along, Sophie had been prepared to hire managers and as much staff as were needed to take over, just as soon as she and Ned got pregnant.

She'd been craving a baby ever since she turned twenty-five. Day after day, she'd found herself smiling at every infant and toddler she encountered at the grocery store or the movies, or being swung by the hands by his or her parents down the street, and the ache of wanting a child of her own filled her with a pang that was almost physical.

But things hadn't gone the way she'd hoped. They'd originally planned to start trying for a family early in their marriage, but Ned had changed his mind, persuading her that they should get more established in their careers first. So they'd put it off.

By Sophie's twenty-eighth birthday, her biological clock was in full racing mode, turning her yearning for a child into a longing that reached into the deepest parts of her heart.

But by then, Ned's head—and a lot more of him than that, Sophie reflected bitterly—was fixated elsewhere.

Cassandra Reynard, to be exact.

The vice-president of the cable network that was tops on his list, and that had been considering hiring him for months, was carrying Ned's child. The baby Sophie had longed for.

And to top it off, Ned was enough of a bastard to blame her for the destruction of their marriage.

"You caused this, Sophie," he'd had the nerve to tell her on the phone two weeks after she accompanied a pregnant friend to the obstetrician, only to find her own husband seated in the waiting room, holding hands with another woman.

Cassandra Reynard, a red-haired, Julia Roberts look-alike, had still been nauseous at the beginning of her second trimester.

"All you could think about was what *you* needed—a baby. You couldn't let up on the pressure, Sophie. You didn't give a damn about my needs, my goals. Just because your stupid bakery took off like a firecracker, you thought it should be easy for me too. You have no idea what I've been going through to give us a shot at the life we wanted—"

"I definitely know what you've been going through, Ned."

"Don't—"

"Sleeping your way to the top must be terribly hard work. Pure torture."

"I was doing this for *us,* Sophie. Things just got out of control. It doesn't mean I don't love you."

"Is that what you call it?"

"Sophie, look, I gotta go. Cassandra's beeping in, I'll get back to you."

Her hands were shaking so much as she punched off her cell that she dropped the phone on the floor.

For a moment, she'd struggled to fight back her sobs, then had given in to them and let the tears burst from her. She'd snatched up her leather notebook and a pen as tears streamed down her cheeks, and had sat down to scribble an addition to her list.

Imagine Ned as a football. In the center of the stadium. And it's kickoff time at the Super Bowl.

A sound somewhere between a laugh and a sob escaped her throat. A counselor at a group divorce session she'd attended at the library a few days before had suggested the participants keep a list of thoughts that made them feel good—or bad—so they could get in touch with their inner selves as a way to relieve stress and deal with anger toward their former spouses.

"How's that for being in touch?" Sophie had wiped the tears with the back of her hand and shakily stuffed the notebook into her tote bag.

She wasn't sure how, but somehow she'd held it together through the next few months. Packing up the condo, listing it with a Realtor, meeting with lawyers.

Yesterday, she'd signed her name to a contract officially selling Sweet Sensations to the Cramer Restaurant Group, and faxed it, and her divorce agreement, back to her attorneys.

Then she'd rolled her luggage into the hall and closed the door forever on the chic San Francisco condo where her marriage had begun—and where it had ended.

Catching Ned with Cassandra had shaken her out of the dream that they could somehow save their marriage and have the life she'd thought they'd been building. She'd been fooling herself for much too long, ignoring the truth.

That was over now.

Grabbing an old comfortable hoodie, Sophie hurried into the hall and down the old stairs. Softly, so as not to wake her mother, she eased open the front door and stepped out into the Montana night.

The gentle movement of the porch swing did little to soothe her. Pushing the swing with her foot, she breathed in the chilly late-summer air sweeping down from the mountains and forced herself to focus on right now. The sweet tinkling of the wind chimes, the sage-scented breeze. There were insect sounds and mysterious animal scurryings coming from the darkness surrounding the cottonwoods, and a hawk flew high in the night.

Gradually, she felt the tension in her shoulders ease. She got lost in the beauty of the dark sky and wisp of moon, in the wink of stars above.

But the familiar gliding motion of the swing soon stirred more memories.

All of the times she'd sat out here doing homework, struggling to complete extra credit in Geometry so she could eke out more than a D from Mr. Hartigan, the geometry teacher from hell.

Whispering secrets to Lissie and Mia on the phone.

And, when she was even younger—eleven and twelve—curled on this swing, foolishly daydreaming about Lissie's oldest brother.

Rafe.

A faint grimace touched her lips at the memory of Rafe Tanner. She'd never looked twice at Lissie's other brothers, Jake or Travis, even though both of them were closer to her age and as handsome in their own right as Rafe. But Rafe was seventeen when she was twelve—and not only impossibly older and out of her league, but wildly sexy. At seventeen, he was already six foot three. Lean, dark, and reckless. With eyes so dark a blue they reminded Sophie of a wild indigo sea.

And like a wild sea, the heartthrob of Lonesome Way High had definitely seemed more than a little bit dangerous.

There wasn't a football he couldn't catch, a horse he couldn't tame, or a girl he couldn't get.

But he was far too mature and cool for skinny, gawky twelve-year-old Sophie. Still, she'd barely been able to speak whenever she was over at Lissie's house and Rafe came barreling through the kitchen door.

Of course, that was all before her last encounter with him—that humiliating moment on a hot August day when she was fifteen. An immature and impulsive fifteen—who'd made a complete idiot of herself in Rafe's beat-up old truck.

A rush of mortification still swept her whenever she thought about it. Fortunately, she didn't think about it much. And she hadn't laid eyes on Rafe Tanner since.

Sophie couldn't even begin to picture him as a grown-up. She leaned back against the swing, shaking her head wryly in the darkness just as, out of the blue, a cell phone chirruped.

The sound wafted down from one floor above. Her mother's bedroom. The window must be open. *But, who's calling this late?*

Worried that something might have happened to Gran, her feet suddenly hit the porch and she stopped swinging. She was about to rush inside when she heard her mother's voice, calm and faint above the wind.

"No, no, I haven't told her yet."

Then, surprisingly, what sounded to Sophie like soft laughter. "Yes, we had a nice dinner. Everything's fine. She's going to be just fine. I didn't have an opportunity to mention anything to her. . . ." A sudden gust of wind drowned the next words. Then: "I know, but there's no rush. . . ."

Uncomfortable, Sophie pushed off the swing and slipped inside. She didn't want to eavesdrop. But as she hurried up the varnished stairs, she wondered about what she'd heard.

Had that been Gran on the phone? Or Wes? Or one of her mother's friends? And what didn't her mother have the opportunity to mention to her yet?

They'd spent the entire evening together, and she could have brought up anything on her mind while they were clearing the table, tidying up the kitchen, and having coffee in the living room for almost an hour before Diana invited her out to the old barn—which was now her mother's workroom—to show Sophie her latest project.

While Sophie was growing up, most of her friends' mothers had hobbies like reading, knitting, or gardening, but for as long as Sophie could remember, her mother had made things. All sorts of things. Beaded jewelry, fabric

27

purses, decoupage frames and mirrors, scented soaps, and potpourri.

Now though, Diana had thrown herself into crafting wind chimes.

The one tinkling from a hook on the porch was one of her newest creations—a pretty, delicate thing made of dangling copper tubing and nuggets of stained glass, shells, and colored beads.

There were a half dozen others on her worktable, some constructed of sleek metal tubes, others of wood. With pride, her mother had shown Sophie the finished pieces, each one unique. She'd explained that she planned to sell them at the upcoming fund-raiser for the Lonesome Way Public Library, which was badly in need of renovation.

But she hadn't *mentioned* anything out of the ordinary during the entire evening—so what was that phone call all about?

By the time Sophie sank into bed, she was too tired to wonder anymore. Except for bathroom breaks and fast-food runs and five hours' sleep in a dingy motel outside Salt Lake City last night, she'd driven nonstop almost two days straight from San Francisco to Lonesome Way.

For the first time in months, the moment her cheek touched the pillow, she sank into sleep.

Chapter Two

"Sophie, look at you. It's not fair—you're as gorgeous as ever. And I'm . . . a cow." Lissie Norris laughed as she threw her arms around Sophie's neck and held her close in the wide paved drive of the colonial house on Old Creek Drive.

"I've missed you, Soph. Your mom said you were due in last night. It's a good thing you called first thing this morning or I'd have come hunting for you."

Lissie didn't look to be in much shape for hunting anything besides a dish of ice cream topped with pickles. Her belly was huge, and she was glowing, her dark hair swept into a ponytail and off her pretty oval face. She wore maternity jeans and a big floaty white lace top, with red sneakers on her feet, and her lilting laugh was just as rich and warm as ever.

She looked beautiful.

Sophie hugged her back, taking care not to spill the basket of home-baked muffins she'd brought with her. "When is this little munchkin due to make an appearance? In the next hour?"

"No such luck. Still twelve weeks to go—can you imagine? I'll be the size of a truck." Lissie grinned. "Come on in and tell me everything. I can't believe you brought banana walnut muffins. I've been craving them for months. I was going to ask your Gran to make me some, but I couldn't bring myself to bother her. What did you do, get up at dawn?"

"Something like that. But I always do anyway." It was true. Sophie hadn't slept all the way through a single night since the day she found out about Ned and Cassandra.

Today it had felt good to wake up early, tiptoe down to the ranch kitchen, and bake. To be alone with the mixing bowls and muffin tins, the sun peeking out over the foothills in a burst of glimmering amber.

She'd put on a pot of coffee and slipped joyously into the ritual of measuring out flour and sugar and baking soda, of mashing bananas and adding walnuts and cinnamon, milk, an egg, and salt.

She'd had precious little chance to do much baking these past few years, even though it was her passion for baking—thanks to Gran—that had inspired Sweet Sensations in the first place. But the business had grown so much, so quickly, it had become just that—a business. *Work.*

Sophie had found herself so consumed with the need to hire more staff, her time so eaten up meeting with managers and accountants and suppliers and corporate clients that she no longer had time to do any hands-on baking in her own company's kitchens. She hadn't baked so much as a coffee cake in months, much less anything fancy like her lemon mascarpone layer cake, or pumpkin orange cheesecake with sugar-dreams frosting.

In Lissie's bright cherrywood kitchen, Sophie set the table and poured coffee for herself while decaffeinated green tea steeped for Lissie. Lissie took out cream and sugar, then whisked a sky blue platter of muffins onto the table, moving gracefully despite her bulk.

"So this is me, Soph. Spill." Leaning back in a kitchen chair, Lissie stretched out her legs and popped a bite of muffin into her mouth. "How are you *really* doing?"

"Trust me," Sophie said with a grimace. "You don't want to know."

"That bad, huh?"

She mustered a smile, which might have fooled anyone except Lissie. There was no sense hashing over how stupid she'd been, trying to hang on to something with Ned that had apparently been gone for a very long time.

"I can't let Ned and his baby mama ruin the rest of my life. That's all I know. I won't let them."

"Good." Lissie's brown eyes were soft with sympathy. She hesitated. "I know how horrible this whole thing must have been for you. I'm sorry."

No, you don't know, Liss, Sophie thought. *You might think you do, but you can't imagine what it feels like. And I hope you never do. Seeing your husband with his pregnant mistress. The shock of your heart blowing up. The pain, tearing everywhere. Like shrapnel.*

Sophie pushed back her chair and paced across the kitchen. She stared out the window at the patio and Lissie's pretty, airy garden. In the distance, lavender gray mountains gleamed against the cobalt sky. But she saw instead a doctor's waiting room. The man she loved holding the hand of a woman whose belly was rounded with new growing life.

She squeezed her eyes closed a moment, trying to block the image.

It's too bad there isn't a recipe for happiness, she thought. *I'm a whiz at following recipes.*

When she turned back toward Lissie, the old cheerleader gleam had entered her friend's soft brown eyes and Lissie spoke with determination.

"You're going to get through this, Soph. You're going to be happy again. Things will be better than you can even imagine."

"Liss, I don't need a pep talk—"

"Just you wait and see." Lissie sailed on as if she hadn't spoken. "You're going to meet a wonderful man and have a beautiful family and all of your dreams and wishes are going to come true—"

"I hate to interrupt you, Fairy Godmother, but right now I'd settle for getting through the next forty-eight hours without throwing something." Sophie grinned wryly and returned to the table as Lissie held up both hands.

"That's okay. Just give me fair warning so I can duck." She plopped another muffin onto Sophie's plate.

"How's Tommy?" Sophie seized the chance to change the subject. "He must be counting the seconds until the baby."

"You have no idea. Poor guy's up to his ears in work, trying to get as much out of the way as possible before she makes her debut. It's a girl, you know." Lissie smiled mistily. "I mean, *she's* a girl. We've decided to name her Molly—or Caitlin. Depending on which one we think she looks like when she finally makes her appearance—oh!"

Lissie paused as they heard the sound of a truck door slamming in the driveway.

"That must be them."

"Them who?" Sophie took another sip of coffee.

"Rafe. And Ivy. His daughter."

Sophie set the cup down with a slight rattle just as a girl's voice rang out and the screen door creaked. "Aunt Liss, it's me."

"Come on in, honey bun, we're in the kitchen." Lissie seemed too comfortable to hoist herself from her chair.

"I'm hanging out with Ivy today," she explained quickly as rapid light footsteps echoed through the airy house—and Sophie went very still at the table. "She starts sixth grade in a few weeks, and it's a very big deal, if you remember. I promised to take her shopping for new school clothes. Rafe has to drive to Helena for a horse auction and won't be back until suppertime."

Sophie felt a ridiculous flash of electricity under her skin as she braced herself for Lissie's oldest brother to come through that door.

You're not an infatuated twelve-year-old anymore—get over it, she reminded herself. *You have bigger things to think about than the one that got away . . . hell, the one that never got close.*

"Hey, Aunt Liss." A coltish young girl of eleven or twelve burst through the doorway. Tall and thin for her age, Ivy Tanner had a shoulder-length mop of wavy auburn hair and delicate features, which Sophie suspected would soon bloom into startling beauty. Her arms seemed too long for her narrow body, her ink blue eyes almost too big for her heart-shaped face. She peered in surprise at Sophie, then her gaze shifted shyly away to Lissie.

"Dad said to tell you thanks."

"What do you mean? Where is he?" With a frown, Lissie glanced at Sophie, then away. Her lips puckered. Sophie immediately recognized that peeved expression, and a sudden horrifying suspicion dawned on her.

Oh, Lissie, please don't tell me that's why you wanted me here by ten o'clock. I'm so not ready to be pushed into the path of any man—and I won't be for a long time. And especially not your big bad brother.

"I don't see why he couldn't have come inside this house for one little minute," Lissie complained.

The platter of muffins was attracting Ivy's interest. "He said he was running late for the auction and that I should tell you he'll be back to pick me up by six. I have a sleepover tonight at Shannon's."

Lissie didn't appear the least bit satisfied with this explanation, but she quickly introduced Ivy to Sophie.

"It's nice to meet you, Ivy." Sophie smiled at the girl, who was trying to unobtrusively study Sophie's sleek dark jeans, her scoop-necked yellow top, and low-heeled sandals. "I bet you were named for your grandmother."

Ivy's head bobbed. "Yeah, but I don't really remember her that well. She died when I was a little kid. My dad showed me pictures though."

"I knew her." Sophie smiled at Lissie, who had lost her mom seven years ago. "She was a wonderful woman. And it's a beautiful name."

"Sophie knew Grandma Ivy because we've been best friends since first grade," Lissie explained. "Exactly like you and Shannon."

"Oh." Ivy looked at Sophie again, quickly, this time with a dawning realization. "You're *that* Sophie—Sophie McPhee. The one who just moved back here. I heard about you yesterday."

"You did?" Lissie's brows rose, but Sophie wasn't all that surprised. Lonesome Way's legendary gossip hotline had apparently been activated.

"From who?" she asked.

"A bunch of us were over at Mary Kate's house. Her mom was talking on the phone about the library. You know, the fund-raiser."

Lissie grimaced. "Mary Kate's mom is Georgia Landry—Georgia Timmons now," she told Sophie with a grim look. "I'm sure you remember her."

Sophie did. In their high school yearbook, Georgia had been crowned Most Likely to Take Over the World. There was no committee she hadn't headed, no major student office she hadn't run for.

"How in the world did Georgia know I moved back already?" Sophie began, then realized there were a hundred interconnections that could account for it.

Her own mother might have told Martha Davies, owner of the Cuttin' Loose beauty salon, and Georgia could have come in afterward for a blow-dry.

Or Gran might have told one of her friends, who mentioned it to Lila Benson at Benson's Drugstore while Georgia was in line buying hand cream and breath mints.

Word got around in Lonesome Way. Often faster than it took to click and send an e-mail.

"So what did she say?" Lissie probed, as she plucked a muffin on a plate for Ivy and shuffled to the refrigerator to pour her niece a glass of milk.

"Something about . . ." Ivy hesitated.

"Tell us, Ives," Lissie coaxed, grinning. She set the glass of milk down on the table in front of her niece. "It's okay, we want to know."

"Well . . ." Ivy took a breath. "She said something about how Sophie McPhee"—she glanced at Sophie apologetically—"better not think that just because she's run back to Lonesome Way with her tail between her legs that she's going to get to take over as refreshment chair for the fund-raiser."

Finally, a giggle escaped Ivy as Lissie and Sophie looked at each other and burst out laughing.

"She also said if you wanted to bake anything to help raise money for the library, you'd have to bake what *she* told you to bake, nothing more, nothing less. You've probably figured out," Ivy added, "that Mary Kate's mom is in charge of refreshments. And she's pretty bossy."

"You think?" Sophie grinned. "Liss, remind me, no matter what happens, not to volunteer."

"It's too late for that." Lissie lowered herself back into the chair. "I heard something from Minnie Cole, who's on the crafts committee, that your mom already volunteered you. You're stuck."

Sophie's grin evaporated. "Kill me now," she muttered with a sigh.

"So you baked these muffins?" Ivy had already devoured the first one and was reaching for a second. "They're really good. I think *you* should be in charge of refreshments."

There was a natural sweetness about Rafe's daughter, Sophie realized as she refilled her coffee cup and poured more hot water for Lissie's tea. One day soon, Ivy Tanner was going to turn into a very stunning young woman. She didn't know it though—hadn't a clue. There was unaffectedness in those incredible dark blue eyes, the same dramatic shade as Rafe's.

That's where any obvious similarities ended though. Ivy's eyes were soft and childlike—innocent. While Rafe's . . .

Well, there'd never been anything soft or innocent in the eyes of the wild and handsome young cowboy Sophie remembered.

And she remembered quite a lot. Especially all the times she and Lissie—when they were nine, ten, even eleven—had followed Rafe around Sage Ranch, annoying the daylights out of him as he did his chores and took care of the horses. And then there were the other times—when they'd spied on him, trailing him like little unseen ghosts as he led this girlfriend or that to out-of-the-way places around the ranch for make-out sessions.

They'd had to smother their hands against their mouths to keep from giggling aloud when they followed him and his latest girl to the barn or one of the sheds or even out into the pasture, one of Rafe's favorite make-out spots. They hadn't dared get too close, but had dropped down to the ground and crawled, their hearts pounding with the fear of giving themselves away. They'd considered it exciting and fascinating and funny to huddle there, silent as mice, spying, and scarcely daring to breath while Rafe sweet-talked Angie Cook or Linda Rae Simkins or one of his other girlfriends into sneaking off alone, locking lips in the hayloft or the deep grass or even on the banks of the creek that ran through both the Sage and Good Luck properties.

How many times had she and Lissie shaken with silent laughter as Rafe and some girl teased and kissed and tussled and tickled each other in a nest of straw or summer grass?

It had seemed uproariously funny at the time. Until Lissie would sneeze or a giggle would escape Sophie or one of Rafe's brothers, Jake or Travis, would suddenly stumble upon them and demand in a shatteringly loud tone, "Hey, what are you two brats up to *now?*"

Furious, Rafe would chase them off while they shrieked and ran for their lives. Sophie thought it was a wonder he hadn't killed the both of them for the way they'd tormented him. She seemed to remember that the girlfriends had been even more livid, screeching in outrage.

Only because we interrupted all their fun, she reflected wryly as she sat in the Norris kitchen listening to Rafe's daughter tell Lissie that her father had given her a credit card to use today and had called over to the Top to Toe clothing store on Main Street to be sure they let Ivy charge what she decided to buy, up to the amount he'd set for her shopping spree.

"Oh! Well, here we go again." A beatific smile suddenly spread across Lissie's face, and she gazed raptly down at her belly.

"She's kicking again?" As Ivy sprang from her chair, her face lit up like a Christmas tree. "Can I feel?"

"Sure. Come here." Taking the girl's hand, Lissie guided it to the left side of her stomach, rounded beneath the ruffly white top.

Wonder filled Ivy's eyes. "She's really trying to get out of there, Aunt Liss. Even more than last time."

"Don't I . . . know it." Lissie grunted after a particularly hard kick. "She already seems like a pretty determined little thing, doesn't she? But she's going to have to stay put for a while. Especially since you and I have big plans for today."

"And I should be letting you get to them." Sophie hoped no one would notice the slight catch in her voice as she stood up. She fought back a twinge of longing, wondering how it would feel to have her baby kicking inside of her, knowing that in a matter of weeks and days, she'd be holding a tiny new life in her arms. For an instant, the intensity of her sadness almost made her dizzy.

She reminded herself that she was happy for Lissie and Tommy, and for their little girl, who was going to have two phenomenal and loving parents.

Parents who both wanted her with all of their hearts.

"Sophie, why don't you come with us?" Lissie drew in her breath at one particularly ferocious kick. "We'll scout out all the cute preteen tops and jeans first, and then grab some lunch at Roy's. You'd better come—you won't have too many more chances."

"What are you talking about? Chances for what?"

"To eat at Roy's. Didn't your mom tell you?"

Lissie shifted position in the chair. "Roy's is closing next week. Roy and Lil are retiring, moving to Wyoming to be closer to their kids. As I remember, you thought their fried chicken was the best in the west."

"It is. It was." Roy's Diner was a Lonesome Way institution. It had been in the same location on Main Street ever since Sophie could remember. She and Lissie and their other friend, Mia Quinn, had hung out at Roy's after school almost daily.

"What will Lonesome Way do without Roy's?"

"Well, there's still the Double Cross Bar and Grill and the Lucky Punch Saloon. And the drive-throughs, but . . ."

Lissie shrugged, and in her head, Sophie finished the words she hadn't spoken aloud.

But it won't be the same.

Sophie could picture the small round tables in the front half of Roy's Diner. The black vinyl booths in back. The white-tiled floor and homey pictures of old cabins, cattle, and horses on the green walls. Roy's Diner served breakfast, lunch, and dinner. Its menu was extensive, from pancakes and sausages to hamburgers, milk shakes, chicken pot pie, and blueberry crumble.

"So? You coming?" Lissie winked at Ivy.

"Wild bears swarming up Main Street couldn't keep me away. But I'll drive. Your job is to sit back, relax, and count the baby's kicks." She turned to Ivy.

The girl had looked surprised when Lissie invited her to join them.

"You don't mind if I tag along?"

"It sounds great. If Aunt Liss gets tired, then you two can go over to Roy's while I finish shopping. Sometimes it takes me a while to try clothes on and decide and stuff."

"Now that sounds like a plan." Sophie remembered all too well the importance of back-to-school clothes. Particularly the seemingly momentous choices that would help determine one's social standing in middle school. Ivy seemed to feel she had her work cut out for her.

"What are we waiting for then?" Sophie began loading the plates in the dishwasher with quick efficiency, then wiped down the table with a pink dishrag. As Lissie held out a hand, Ivy helped her rise off the kitchen chair.

"I'm only worried about one thing." Lissie smoothed her top down over her bulging belly. "I hope you two can keep up with me."

Chapter Three

Ivy's cell phone rang while she was in the dressing room zipping up the cutest pair of black jeans she'd ever seen. Even before she grabbed the cell, her stomach started to hurt over what the caller ID might show.

But it was just her dad, so her heartbeat slowed down and the pain in her stomach eased away.

"Dad, did you get the mares?"

"One of them so far. She's a beauty, Ivy. The other one's coming up for bidding later."

Joy rushed through her. A new mare. Maybe two mares. She could hardly wait to see them. "And what about the gelding, the one Mr. Henry said was skittish?"

"Got him too, baby. We're going to have our work cut out for us."

"Yeah, Dad, right. You mean, your work." He never let her actually train the horses, not the difficult ones. She got to feed them, brush them, muck out their stalls and stuff, all the boring work, but she didn't get to start them or ride them until her dad had finished what he called "working out the kinks."

It sucked.

She was eleven, not a little kid anymore, and

she knew almost as much about horses as he did. And was just as good a rider. It wasn't fair.

"Are you bringing him home today? I can see him tonight?"

"I'm bringing the mares back, honey. Shiloh will be delivered in a few days. You leave any clothes on the hangers, or have you bought everything in the store by now?"

"Very funny, Dad. Aunt Liss bought me a really cool shirt as a present, and I found khakis I can wear to Val's party. And Aunt Liss's friend Sophie spotted this pink top on sale—it's sweet, the best top ever, and it costs ten dollars less than when I saw it online the other day."

It had been kind of nice, actually, having Aunt Liss's friend come along with them to town. Sophie was really pretty and sophisticated, like a model on TV, and her clothes were cool. She'd hand-picked a few other tops Ivy really liked too, before she and Aunt Liss went over to Roy's for lunch.

Ivy was supposed to meet them there. But she still had lots more clothes to try on. Getting super-cute new clothes for school was way more important than eating lunch.

"Good deal, Ives. Listen, I'll be bidding on the second mare at three, then I'll head back," her father said.

"Dad, don't forget. I told Shannon's mom I could come for supper. That's still okay, right? I don't have to eat supper at home with you, do I?"

The moment Ivy said the words, she knew they came out wrong. It's not that she didn't like eating with her dad. It was pretty fun, most of the time, unless he started asking too many questions, trying to find out if any of her friends were smoking or getting into drugs or anything like that. But she and Shannon had stuff to discuss tonight. Important stuff. Like school, and what to wear the first day. And Nate Miles.

Ivy had liked Nate since last spring. But she'd only gotten up the nerve to talk to him once, when she ran into him at the beginning of June outside the hardware store while her dad was inside buying lightbulbs or something.

"I mean, if you want to have supper together, that's okay—" she backtracked, feeling guilty.

"Are you kidding? Without you around, I can be a slob, eat with my toes, and use my shirt for a napkin."

"Dad!" She wanted to sound annoyed, but she couldn't help it; she laughed. A rush of relief ran through her.

"You don't ever have to worry about babysitting me." He was using that serious voice now, the one that he used just before he planned to make a lame joke. "I'm busy too. Got myself a hot date getting a couple of really cute mares settled into their stalls."

"Hilarious, Dad. If it wasn't so pathetic."

He had to go then, so she stuffed her cell back in her purse and tried to concentrate on how she looked in the jeans, but she just couldn't get into it now. She kept having this feeling her cell was going to ring again, and this time it would be the call she was waiting for—and also dreading.

Maybe she wouldn't answer it. She hadn't answered last time. That was two days ago. And so far, no more tries.

Maybe there would *never* be another try.

Then how would she feel?

Her stomach started to hurt again. She might have already lost her chance.

So what, she thought, hauling the jeans and a heap of other clothes from the dressing room, approaching the crowded sales counter with her arms full. *I don't care. If I cared, I'd have answered the last time, right?*

But sure enough, just as she gave Erma Wilkins the credit card her dad had told her to use, her cell rang again. And it was the phone number she'd been watching for.

"Call back in ten minutes, okay?" She hadn't even said hello, and she didn't wait for an answer but snapped the phone closed, her throat dry.

Ivy glanced around, feeling like everyone in Top to Toe was staring at her. Like everyone knew who she was talking to.

But Erma Wilkins was smiling her slight, crooked smile, handing back the credit card, and thrusting the big shopping bag at her over the counter.

A few feet away, Liza Craig and her mom were sifting through a table of neatly folded cable sweaters. Some other girls she knew from school were modeling jeans and pullovers for their moms in front of the big mirror.

No one was looking at her. No one was paying any attention.

"You say hello to your daddy for me, Ivy, all right? Tell him Erma said hey."

"Yes, ma'am."

Outside, she glanced around, then ducked toward the alley behind First Street. She didn't want to meet Aunt Liss and Sophie at Roy's until after the call.

But now she'd have to wait. Eight more minutes.

Her stomach roiled. She felt like she might throw up. But she told herself to stop acting like a baby.

The trouble was, when the call came—*if* the call came—she had no idea what she was going to say.

Chapter Four

Sophie breathed in the delicious smells of the old-fashioned diner. Fried chicken and blueberry pie. Beef gravy and mashed potatoes. Burgers and onions crisping on a grill.

The big cozy diner with its antique cash register, curving display counter for pies and baked goods, and weathered booths was so intrinsic to Lonesome Way that a hard little jolt had twitched through her when she'd seen the sign in the front window with her own eyes.

SPACE FOR LEASE.
CONTACT HOGAN REALTY.

"I still can't believe Roy's is closing," she murmured.

"Believe it, girl." Lil Waller strode past with two tall glasses of sweet tea in her work-roughened hands.

She was a big-boned woman, almost seventy, with a chin like a shovel and a smoker's rasp, even though she'd given up her Camels ten years back.

"We're headed to Laramie in six days—count 'em. And I can hardly wait. It's time we lived closer to our kids. Me and Roy have had enough."

Lil handed Sophie and Lissie setups just as Roy himself trudged from the kitchen bearing two large white plates piled with burgers and pickles and French fries. Roy Waller was tall and thin as a scarecrow, wearing his grease-splattered apron over a chambray shirt and jeans, as well as a frown so perpetual that when Sophie was younger she'd wondered if he was born with it.

"Enough? Enough don't begin to cover it," he tossed out as he headed toward the front of the diner. "We had a good long run, but now we're kicking back, as you young people say. Anyone got any objections, they can take it up with me at the fishing hole over in Laramie. So long as they don't scare away the fish."

Lil rolled her eyes. "The man claims he's going to do nothing but fish five days a week—and take the grandkids to the movies. I'll believe it when I see it. Me, I'm gonna join a book club, knit when I'm not reading, and put my aching feet up for a change. Nobody better try'n stop me."

"No one deserves it more than you do, Lil," Sophie said warmly as Lil grabbed a couple of menus and handed one to her and one to Lissie.

"Everyone in town's going to miss the both of you. Except this little one." Lissie placed a hand across her belly. "She'll never get to taste your hash browns, but at least the poor thing won't know what she's missing."

"There you go." Lil Waller patted Lissie's shoulder, then turned her shrewd gaze on Sophie.

"Haven't seen you around these parts for far too long." Her gruff voice softened with affection. "I heard all about you going through a rough patch back there in San Francisco. Don't let it get to you, you hear?"

Sophie pasted a smile on her face. Was there one person in this town who didn't know every inch of her business? She did *not* relish being guest of honor at a Lonesome Way pity party. Unfortunately, that old saying of her father's was true—if one person in Lonesome Way told a joke, the whole town laughed.

"I'm doing fine, Lil, honest. Don't worry about me."

Lil shot her a look that plainly said she knew Sophie was lying through her teeth, but just this once, she'd let her get away with it.

After Sophie and Lissie ordered grilled chicken sandwiches, carrot and raisin coleslaw, and a heaping platter of Roy's special thick French fries on the side, Lissie ran down everyone who was coming to the baby shower.

Sophie tried to listen, but she was distracted, caught up in the familiar sounds and memories of the diner, in the smells of seared meat, fried onions, and the warm fresh-baked pies cooling on the counter along the back wall.

Her own recipe for cherry rhubarb pie had been acquired right here—scribbled down for her on an order pad by Lil more than a dozen years ago. For Sophie's money, it was still the best cherry rhubarb pie she'd ever tasted.

Of course, when it came to her famous cinnamon buns, the ones that had first put Sweet Sensations on the map, that recipe was all Gran's.

There were only a dozen people in Roy's right now—some ranch hands in boots, T-shirts, and jeans; a couple of high school kids, including a boy and a girl laughing and throwing French fries at each other; and a thin, tired-looking blond woman feeding bits of a grilled cheese sandwich to a toddler.

Across the aisle, Sheriff Teddy Hodge, who'd been Lonesome Way's sheriff for as long as she could remember, was drinking a cup of black coffee and working his pencil across a crossword puzzle in a thin booklet. A trio of hikers were engaged in energetic discussion, their heads bent over a map.

Probably on their way to the Half Moon Campground off Big Timber Canyon Road, Sophie thought.

Her mother had mentioned that more tourists were discovering Lonesome Way as they wove their way through the state headed either toward or home from one of the national or state parks, monuments, or campgrounds.

Suddenly, Sophie saw something that made her blink. One moment she was sitting in Roy's with its picture windows and old vinyl booths, and everything looked just the same as it always had. Then, in an instant, another image flashed through her mind.

She glimpsed something fresh in this old, familiar western diner. A flicker of air, color, light, smells.

A possibility. Something new. Something *hers.*

Then, as quickly as it had flickered in her mind, like a firefly, it was gone.

"Look who's here." Sophie was yanked back to the familiarity of Roy's as the bell over the door tinkled and Mia Quinn stepped in. She swooped toward their booth with a grin.

"Well, take a look at you!" Mia hugged her excitedly. "I was planning to call and see if you wanted to head over to the Double Cross for a drink tonight. You too," she told Lissie. "Except for the drink part."

"I'll have you know I'm rocking decaf sweet tea these days," Lissie retorted. "Although by the time I get home and throw supper together tonight, I think I'll have spent my daily quotient of energy."

Sophie slid over on the seat so Mia could sit beside her.

"How can I help with the baby shower?"

"Let me count the ways. Starting with baked goods for the brunch. We can figure out the menu and other stuff later when a certain someone isn't here." Mia glanced pointedly at Lissie. She was a fifth grade schoolteacher now, but at just a smidge over five foot three, her figure was still as voluptuous as a stripper's, and her short blond hair framed an adorably kittenish face. She waited as Lil arrived with Sophie and Lissie's lunch, then ordered the tuna salad platter.

"We need to brainstorm games, theme, and decoration," she told Sophie, ticking them off on her fingers. "I have a few ideas, but we can work out the deets at the Double Cross later."

"Hold on a minute," Lissie protested. "This shower isn't a secret. Why can't we talk about it now? Nothing needs to be a surprise."

"Well, the sex of the baby isn't a surprise, not these days—and certainly not in your case, so *something* has to be," Sophie pointed out.

"It'll be more fun this way," Mia added as her root beer arrived in a cool frosty brown glass.

When Ivy came in, they waved her over.

Everyone wanted to see her purchases, and she produced them dutifully, but she was quiet, Sophie noticed. Much more quiet than she'd been this morning.

"Everything okay, Ives?" Lissie asked at one

54

point as Ivy silently chewed a bite of her burger and washed it down with a gulp of Coke.

"Yeah, why?"

"For someone who just scored all these great clothes, you don't seem too happy."

Two spots of color tinted the center of the girl's golden cheeks. "I'm fine." There was a hint of defensiveness in her tone. She picked up her burger again, then set it down. "I'm just thinking about all the homework I'm going to have this year. Susie Tyler told me there's going to be *tons* of homework."

"If you ever need any help, call me," Mia offered.

"Okay. Thanks." A halfhearted smile, then Ivy ducked her head. Lissie and Sophie exchanged glances.

"Did something happen over at Top to Toe? I thought you were looking forward to sixth grade," Lissie murmured.

"I was. I am." Ivy pushed her plate away. "I'm not really hungry right now," she muttered, not looking at anyone. "Can I wait outside, please, Aunt Liss?"

"Sure, honey bunch. Unless you want some dessert—"

But she was already scurrying toward the door, clutching her shopping bag. The bell above the door chimed once more as Ivy escaped onto Main Street.

"Oh, boy, here we go." Lissie sighed. "The

dreaded teenage years. She's not even twelve yet, and already the moodiness is creeping in. Poor Rafe."

Poor Rafe. Sophie couldn't begin to picture Rafe Tanner raising an eleven-year-old daughter. She tried to remember what had gone wrong between him and his ex-wife, but it had all happened while she was busy with her own life—married to Ned, living in San Francisco—and the details were vague. Something about the wife—Lynnette? Lynelle?—running off, abandoning him and their daughter.

How could any woman leave her own child? Sophie wondered. *Or was it Rafe she was running from?*

She had no idea what kind of man Rafe had become. In high school, he'd roamed from one girlfriend to the next like a horse grazing in a well-watered field. Immature and pleasure-seeking.

She'd seen him only that one time after he'd graduated from Lonesome Way High, the time when she was fifteen and trudging home from Cougar Rock in the heat of summer, wearing shorts and a tank top, sweaty and furious as she headed toward the main road and home.

She'd broken up with her high school boyfriend up at Cougar Rock that day, and he'd been such a jerk about it that she'd refused to get in his truck and let him drive her home.

He'd roared off, angrier than a grizzly with a

sore tooth, and Sophie had begun the walk home beneath a broiling sun. It was only five miles, no big deal, but the sun was strong, and sweat trickled down her forehead and between her breasts, and she suddenly was thirsty. She'd lifted her hair off her nape for a cooling moment as she reached Squirrel Road, angling downhill finally—and had dug out a red plastic hair band from the pocket of her jeans, pausing a moment to secure her hair high off her neck.

She'd walked another two miles before Rafe Tanner sped past in his pickup. He blasted by in a blur, then, just as suddenly as he'd passed her, he slammed on his brakes and backed up.

"Sophie? What the hell are you doing out here in the middle of nowhere? You all right?"

"I'm fine. I like walking." She brushed the sweat from her eyes with the back of her hand, wondering why it had to be Rafe instead of anyone else who happened upon her out here, a sunburnt, sweaty mess. He, on the other hand, looked more handsome than ever. Lissie had told her he was home on break from college. But what were the odds he'd be on Squirrel Road right now?

When she was twelve, and he'd gone off to college, she'd dreamed of running into Rafe when she was older, not a kid anymore. She'd seen herself wearing a sexy, low-cut top, snug-fitting jeans, and killer red heels.

Now instead of the annoying child who'd spied on him and his girlfriends, he was seeing a weird, sweaty girl whose nose was probably red and peeling, whose pale peach lip gloss had all but melted away, and whose faded blue top was sticking to her chest.

Go away, Sophie thought miserably. *Just go away.*

He was leaning out the driver's side window, frowning at her.

"Get in, Soph." Rafe reached over, pushed open the passenger-side door. "Come on, don't argue. It's hot as hell out here. I'm taking you home."

"I like walking. It's not that far."

"Are you nuts? It's another two miles to your place. You're my sister's best friend. If you think I'm leaving you out here in the middle of nowhere, you're dead wrong. Get in."

Those midnight blue eyes had pierced right through her, dissolving all of her willpower, and so she had. She forced herself to stare straight ahead as he put the car in gear and took off to the sound of Clint Black's voice blasting from the radio.

If it had all stopped there, it wouldn't have been so bad, but she'd made the situation worse. Much worse.

Rafe had driven her all the way to the Good Luck ranch, cruising up Daisy Lane until they were twenty feet short of her front door.

He'd only asked her one more time what she was doing all the way out there alone on Squirrel Road, and when she hadn't answered, he'd let it go.

If she'd just climbed down from the pickup with a simple thank-you, it wouldn't have been so bad.

"See you around, Sophie." His voice had been easy, calm. And she'd made the mistake of looking at him just as he reached across her and opened the passenger-side door.

Something wild and daring broke loose inside her. Maybe it was all those fantasies she'd had about him when she was younger, but all Sophie knew was that the way she felt at that moment was not the least bit childlike.

She was intensely aware of Rafe beside her, of that long, sinewy, powerful body, and the clean grass and leather scent of him. Dark stubble fringed his jaw, and his dark hair was just long enough to brush the collar of his faded old black T-shirt.

But it was his eyes that drew her in, breaking down all her common sense and natural defenses.

They cut through her like blue razor wire. Later, she was certain they'd hypnotized her, because without thinking, she did the craziest thing she'd ever done in her life. She leaned over and kissed Rafe Tanner on the mouth.

For one surreal instant, his lips molded warm against hers. She felt lightning sizzling through her skin. And she could've sworn he felt it too. Then he must have remembered the age difference between them, or what a brat she'd been all the years he'd known her.

His entire body tensed and he jerked back suddenly, as if she'd burned him with her mouth, staring at her as if she'd dropped down through the roof of his truck, an alien from a faraway planet. His big hands gripped her arms, holding her at arm's length and so tightly there was no chance she could move even an inch closer.

"Whoa, Sophie. What are you doing? That was real nice and all. But you're fifteen. You're just a kid—"

Mortification seared through her. She didn't wait around to hear the rest. What she'd just done, and the expression of baffled sympathy on his face, brought her crashing back to reality, and she wrenched free, backward, scrambling out of the pickup so quickly she fell onto the gravel and scraped her knee.

She couldn't remember later if she'd ever thanked him for bringing her home. She only remembered running, her legs pumping like pistons as she darted across the dirt, not looking back as she stumbled up her porch steps and burst into the house.

It was cool and quiet inside, and she was

grateful with every fiber of her being that no one else was home.

No one would ever need to know what a fool she'd made of herself by kissing Rafe Tanner.

Except Rafe.

Now Sophie studied Rafe's daughter as she dropped down onto the sidewalk outside of Roy's, her shoulders hunched, her shopping bag from Top to Toe beside her, and her knees drawn up.

"Where's Ivy's mother?" she asked Lissie suddenly.

A dark look entered Lissie's usually sparkling eyes. "Who the hell knows? Or cares?"

"Does she ever see her?"

"Not since the day Lynelle left." Lissie stabbed the last of her coleslaw with her fork. "And for Ivy's sake, let's hope she stays away."

Sophie wondered what had happened. Lissie was the kindest person she knew. The split must have been pretty ugly to get this kind of reaction.

It was none of her business though, she told herself. Rafe Tanner, his daughter, and his ex-wife were not her concern. Lil came up with their bill just then, and the moment was gone.

Chapter Five

It was Sophie who spotted the dog.

Lissie was tired by the time they drove home, and Ivy was quiet, locked in her own thoughts. Sophie had just turned the Blazer onto Thunder Ridge, only a half mile from Lissie's house. She'd been thinking about Roy's Diner closing. And about needing a job.

And was musing over the possibility that had come to her in a momentary flash.

Thanks to California's divorce laws, she'd had to give Ned fifty percent of the money from the sale of Sweet Sensations.

There was enough left to last her for a while, but not forever.

She needed to work.

But not just for the money. She missed baking and she missed the little shop she'd opened years ago, all by herself. Sweet Sensations had evolved into something much bigger and very different by the time she sold it. It had been so long since she'd talked to customers, learned their names, actually fed people, instead of dealing with contracts and managers.

She missed the cozy warmth of a place where people came to meet and relax or to buy themselves a treat before going to work or school.

She wanted that again. The smell of fresh dough and chocolate and cinnamon. The hustle and bustle, chatter and laughter.

Something more and bigger in her life than the sum of her own problems.

That's when she saw the dog.

He was small, a black and brown mutt with white feet and a sad little stump of a tail, walking all alone. His head was hanging down as he trudged aimlessly down the center of the road.

She eased the Blazer to a halt. At the same time, Lissie leaned forward.

"Oh, no, look at that poor little thing. I wonder if he's lost, or if some idiot just left him."

"One way to find out." Sophie already had her door open and was springing down. Behind her, she heard the back door creak and Ivy's feet hit the ground.

"Hold on a minute, Ivy, let's make sure he's friendly. We don't want to converge on him and scare him away."

Sophie approached the dog slowly as the girl reluctantly hung back. The mutt turned toward her, his eyes and his body language wary.

"Hey, there, peanut." In response to her quiet voice and whatever other vibes his instincts picked up, the mutt's tail began to wag with a hopefulness that twisted at her heart.

Equal measures of eagerness and caution shone in the dog's eyes.

"Come on. Over here. Don't be afraid." When she knelt down only a few feet away, he finally took a step forward.

"There you go. Come on, only a few more."

The closer he got, the more his pathetic little tail wagged.

Ivy crouched beside her. "I've never seen him around here before. He doesn't have a collar or anything. I wonder how long he's been out here alone?"

The dog looked at her as she spoke, as if to say *too long.*

He was bedraggled, dirty, and painfully thin. But he kept inching right up to Sophie, and as she slowly extended her hand, he nuzzled his head against it and his tongue shot out, giving her fingers a grateful lick.

"Well, now, it's a pleasure meeting you too," she murmured.

"Look how skinny he is." Ivy reached out to stroke the dog's head. "I wish we had some leftovers from Roy's to give him."

"He'll be okay just as soon as I get him home," Sophie told her cheerfully as the dog nestled closer, his wariness forgotten. He gazed happily into Ivy's face, his tail wagging harder as she stroked his matted fur.

"I'll feed him the minute we get back to the

ranch. A home-cooked meal, a bowl of water, and a quick bath, and this little guy will be just fine."

"I wonder if he has a chip?" Lissie called from the car.

"Doc Weatherby should be able to tell me that tomorrow. But from the looks of him, he's been on his own for quite a while."

Sophie gently scooped the dog into her arms. He stared at her rapturously.

This poor creature had known hard times. *Maybe his entire life has been hard,* she thought, her throat tight. She held him close, but carefully, aware of how thin and frail his body felt. She hoped he wasn't sick. She didn't even want to imagine what he'd been through.

"But all that's behind you now," she muttered as she carried him to the car. "Don't you worry about a thing. We're going home."

Ivy was practically hopping with excitement behind her.

"Can he sit in back with me?"

"Absolutely."

After Sophie started the engine, she glanced in the rearview mirror at the girl in the backseat. The dog was now sprawled across Ivy's lap, trying to lick her hand as she pet him. "You have a dog, Ivy?"

"We had two, but Leggo got old and died last spring. We still have Starbucks though. He's nine."

"You're good with this little tidbit."

"You should see her with the horses," Lissie said. "She has a way with them, just like Rafe."

"Back in California, they'd call that good energy." Sophie smiled into the rearview mirror.

"My dad says I take after him." Ivy was focused on the contented stray in her lap. "I just *get* animals. So does he. It's hard to explain. I'm going to be a vet when I grow up. Can I . . . come visit him if you keep him?" she asked suddenly as Sophie pulled up in front of Lissie's house.

"Anytime you want."

After Lissie and Ivy had gone inside, Sophie reached around and scooped the little dog up front, onto her lap.

Tidbit curled up in a ball with one long sigh, then slept all the way to the Good Luck ranch.

Chapter Six

Sitting in his truck, Rafe watched Ivy do that still-a-little-girl-at-heart half run, half skip toward the porch of Shannon Gordon's house.

It always made him smile. She wasn't grown up, not yet, not by a long shot, and that was a big relief.

As always, she whirled around and sent him a

hurried wave when Shannon opened the screen door, then vanished inside the small gray frame house surrounded by old cottonwoods and a meticulously groomed garden.

She'd been in a pretty good mood when he got home—chattering about a stray dog she, Lissie, and Sophie McPhee had found on the way home from town. She was even more excited about the dog than about the clothes she'd bought, and had begged him to let her go over to the Good Luck ranch one day to visit it.

Unfortunately though, her upbeat mood hadn't lasted. By the time they'd headed out to the Gordon place a short time later, it had disappeared like the sun when rainclouds drifted in across the Crazy Mountains.

And as usual when it came to his eleven-year-old daughter's moods, Rafe had no clue why.

As he was backing out of the drive, Kate Gordon, Shannon's mom, stepped onto the porch. "Rafe, how about joining us for supper?"

"Thanks, Kate, can't tonight. 'Preciate the offer, though."

He actually could have stayed for a meal and would've had a helluva better one than what he was planning at home. But for some reason, Rafe wasn't in a mood for making conversation. He felt out of sorts, restless—"itchy," his dad would have called it—and wanted to fix himself some hot dogs and beans on the stove, open a beer, and try to get a handle on the ranch books for a few hours.

He figured he needed to start getting himself accustomed to Ivy being gone more and more. Up until lately, she hadn't slept out that often—when she was younger she'd never wanted to—and he was used to having her around most of the time when she wasn't at school or the library or a friend's house.

He loved every moment he spent with her and always smiled to himself when he heard her laughing as she watched *Wizards of Waverly Place*. He even liked being with her when she was moping about having to make her bed every day or complaining about a teacher giving too much homework.

Most of all he loved when she hung out with him in the barn or the corral, working with the horses, brushing them, talking to them in the animated way she had whenever she was around them.

Tonight she'd been delighted by Bretta and Bonfire, the two broodmares he'd bought today. She'd asked him a million questions as she leaned against the white pasture fence and watched the mares explore their new stomping grounds, eager to hear all about the auction and the gelding that would soon be delivered.

But on the drive over to Shannon's, her mood had changed again, quickly, as it so often did these days.

He'd offered to bring her along next summer to the horse auction in Great Falls, but she'd just shrugged and fallen silent, responding to everything he said after that in monosyllables.

What was going on inside that head of hers? He knew he wasn't likely to find out.

That's what happens when your daughter's entering the sixth grade, he told himself. His cousin, Decker, whose kids were all in high school now, had warned him about the powder-keg moods and the pulling away that went on in the tween and teen years.

At the time Rafe hadn't been able to picture Ivy ever pulling away from him. But now he saw the future written in her sighs, in her closed bedroom door, in the rolling of her eyes when he said the wrong thing.

Which lately happened at least once a day.

Driving down the deserted back roads toward Sage Ranch, Rafe couldn't help but grimace, remembering the wildness of his own teen years. How he'd been fearless, not to mention reckless.

He'd thought he was invincible and life a joy ride. He had to shake his head now over how he'd let everything his parents tried to tell him whistle through one ear and out the other.

Sort of the way his youngest brother, Jake, was now, and Jake was thirty.

Becoming a rodeo star must have done something to Jake's brain—he never got tired of living life hard and fast and on the edge. There was no risk he wouldn't take, no bronc he wouldn't ride, no woman he couldn't tease into his bed.

By now Jake should have grown up, settled down, but he was too much the way Rafe had been as a teen—living life just the way he wanted, tough and wild as the broncs he rode, no ties to anyone or anything except the rodeo, always the rodeo. And the women and beer and risks that were as much a part of that life as the bulls and horses and chutes.

Travis, on the other hand, had gone the other route. After majoring in criminal justice in college, his middle brother had gone on to law school, eventually becoming an assistant prosecutor. Then, two years ago, he'd joined the FBI.

And here I am, Rafe thought, catching sight of a doe and her fawn darting through the trees up ahead. *Going home to pour kibble into a bowl for Starbucks, fix my own supper, and spend a thrilling night balancing the ledgers.*

The saneness of it actually made him chuckle and wonder what his parents would think if they were still alive and could see their cocky, hell-raising oldest son now.

The wildest Tanner boy of them all was running the family ranch, breeding and training horses, and raising a child on his own. And he wasn't one bit sorry for it.

The most important thing in the world to Rafe now was taking care of Ivy. Then came his love of the Tanner land, which belonged equally to him and his brothers, and seeing to the dogs and horses that had shared life on Sage Ranch with them over the years.

The ranch house and its outbuildings, and every inch of lush Montana meadow, foothills, and creek stretching to the farthest corners of Tanner land was as much a part of him as the brothers who'd ridden off on their separate ways, following their own paths. Maybe Jake and Travis would come back someday, maybe not. That was up to them. It had taken him a while, but after both his parents died in that small plane crash, and after Ivy was born, it had hit him.

This was what mattered. The ranch and his daughter, doing his best for her, keeping her safe, happy. And trying to keep her from missing her mother too much.

He knew Ivy didn't understand why Lynelle left. And especially the *way* she'd left.

He sure as hell didn't understand it either.

But deep down it always worried him that Ivy might think *he'd* leave her one day too—just abandon her and disappear like Lynelle had. So Rafe had made it his job every single day to show her that that was never going to happen. That he'd always be here, taking care of her, looking after her, loving her, no matter what.

Quite a change from twenty-odd years ago—high school. Back then, Rafe had studied just enough to get by. He hadn't buckled down until he went to college and decided to major in accounting so he'd have something to fall back on financially besides the ranch.

But during his teen years, girls and sex had dominated his thoughts the way school should have, and the same had been true for all his friends.

Which made him all the more apprehensive now about Ivy.

He despised the idea of any boys thinking about Ivy that way, the way he'd thought of girls when he was in high school. It kept him up nights, more and more, as he realized she was physically maturing, making him wonder with a panicked feeling in his gut about how he was going to prepare her for what was ahead.

He'd talked to her about some things, and Lissie had helped out by discussing others. But now Lissie was going to be busy with her own baby.

What Ivy needed was a mother. . . .

But she didn't have one. At least, not one who cared about her enough to stick around. Or even to call or visit.

And Rafe would sooner saw off his own foot than trust Lynelle for thirty seconds alone with their daughter ever again.

Turning into the drive leading up to Sage Ranch, Rafe wondered where the hell his ex-wife was now. He'd last heard from her two years ago—a short letter that had come a week before their daughter's ninth birthday, in which she'd asked him to buy Ivy a new dress and tell her it was from her mama. She'd mailed a birthday card to Ivy the same day.

I love you, baby girl. You're getting so big. Send a picture of yourself to Aunt Brenda in Forks Peak so I can look at your gorgeous little face. She'll see that it finds me.

It was no easy feat finding Lynelle, Rafe thought as he entered the ranch house, switched on the lights, and headed across the hardwood foyer to the kitchen.

He had no idea whether she'd ever received the photograph he'd helped Ivy send to her Aunt Brenda. He only knew there'd been no card for Ivy on her tenth birthday or on her eleventh.

No phone call or e-mail either.

There was no way of knowing if Lynelle was somewhere in Montana, or in Reno, or Laramie, or down in the Texas Panhandle, from where the last note had been mailed.

It didn't surprise him one bit that she hadn't been back. There'd only been a scattering of communication since she abandoned their seven-year-old daughter in town, outside the Toss and Tumble Laundromat. Lynelle had left Ivy all alone with nothing but her stuffed. giraffe and a bag of Doritos.

I just can't bear being tied down in any one place too long, she'd written a week later. *It makes me feel like a pig in an ant bed. Don't hate me, Rafe, but I had to leave.*

Starbucks raced in from the living room to greet him, the old dog's tail wagging as if Rafe had been gone for weeks and not under an hour. But that was Starbucks's way, especially these past few months since Leggo had died. The two dogs had been inseparable.

Now every time Rafe or Ivy came home, Starbucks acted like he'd thought never to see them again. The nine-year-old black lab–golden retriever mix—a half-starved mutt Rafe had found huddling outside the barn as a puppy—sat on his haunches as Rafe ruffled his ears.

"Time for some grub, pal. It's just you and me tonight."

As the sun sank in a deep violet sky, Rafe set a cast-iron pot on the stove, removed a package of hot dogs from the fridge and a can of beans from the pantry.

It was a pretty good dinner, even better when accompanied by a cold bottle of beer. His stomach was satisfied. But the rest of him . . . wasn't.

He checked his e-mail, then he and Starbucks headed out the kitchen door. His foreman, Will

Brady, and the wranglers who worked for him had all gone home to their own lives and families. The sky bled pale pink and purple, the encroaching dusk creeping in silence but for the rustling of the pines. A wind foreshadowing the chill of autumn lashed their leaves and branches.

Rafe couldn't shake his restlessness as he forked hay, fed the horses, checked the barns, made his rounds. Every single thing on this ranch was settled down. Except for him.

Maybe it was because Leggo was gone, not side by side with Starbucks, the two of them trotting after him together as they always did.

Maybe he and Ivy should head over to the shelter one of these days and pick out another companion for Starbucks.

Maybe it was just too damn quiet here tonight.

Rafe felt something flicker like a low-burning fire through his skin. *Itchy.*

He washed up his few dishes, put everything away, and by then, the moon was up, the first stars incandescent in the vast Montana sky, and night cloaked the mountains.

Suddenly, he knew he had to get out. Be around people, if not make conversation with them. The pool table at the Double Cross Bar and Grill fit the bill.

And it was calling his name.

Chapter Seven

"Has she told you yet?"

Sophie's grandmother spoke in a whisper in the living room of the Good Luck ranch. She had just settled into the rocker near the fire with a mug of tea cradled in her thin, spider-veined hands.

"Has who told me what yet, Gran?"

They'd finished dessert moments before—a still-warm lemon-frosted banana nut cake Gran had whipped up while Sophie was upstairs bathing the dog, who was now sound asleep on the rug, inches from Sophie's feet.

"Oh, dear. If you have to ask, then she hasn't. I'm talking about your mother, of course."

Gran pursed her lips. Her white hair, pure as a snowfield, trailed down her back in a sweeping braid. She looked almost spry enough, Sophie thought, to leap on the back of a horse and gallop off toward the mountains. In her day, Ava Louise Todd had been a renowned horsewoman.

"I just don't know what she's waiting for," Gran fretted. "You're bound to find out sooner or later and it would be much better if . . . oh, hush, never mind."

Hastily, she took a long noisy sip of tea as her

daughter entered the living room carrying her own buttercup yellow mug—this one filled with sugared coffee—and curled up on the love seat across from the couch.

"Did I miss something?" Diana glanced back and forth between her daughter and her mother, her eyebrows raised.

"Only the creaking of my bones as I settled into this chair."

Gran's eyes, the color of very old green glass, met Sophie's, imploring her to keep silent. "I'm about to foist an old lady's opinions on Sophie." Her gaze softened on her granddaughter's face. "If you don't mind, dear."

I'd rather know the secret that you—and Mom—are keeping, Sophie thought. Worried, she fought against the urge to ask her mother right this very moment. The only reason she *didn't* was because she didn't want to get Gran in hot water.

"Go ahead, Gran. Shoot." She braced herself for the lecture she knew was coming. For all of her sweetness and gentle ways, Sophie's grandmother, who'd grown up in this house, was a force to be reckoned with. Like a marshmallow-covered bulldozer.

At this rate, Mia would definitely beat her to the Double Cross.

Not that Sophie really minded. She didn't feel much like driving into Lonesome Way and plunging into the raucous tumult of the bar. But she didn't have much of a choice. They did need to plan Lissie's baby shower, and she'd promised to meet Mia there.

The chill air seeping beneath the cracks of the doors and windows in the old ranch house brought with it a breath of the autumn and winter soon to come. But the warmth of the dancing flames in the fireplace touched even the farthest reaches of the sage-and-cream-painted room.

Tidbit, curled up a dozen feet from the stone fireplace, sneezed suddenly, and woke himself up.

"I've been talking with Martha and Dorothy." Gran took another sip of tea. "And we all agree."

"No surprise there," Diana murmured.

Martha Davies, owner of the Cuttin' Loose beauty salon, and Dorothy Winston, a former elementary school principal, had been Gran's closest friends for more than sixty years. The three women were thick as thieves. But actually, Sophie thought, they were more like a trio of determined, would-be fairy godmothers, always itching to tinker with someone else's life. In a good way, of course.

She secretly thought of them as Bippity, Boppity, and Boo. "As I was saying," Gran continued, pretending her daughter hadn't spoken, "we're worried about you, Sophie. It's high time you get on with your life. You know, spur it forward. Like a horse."

Gran set her teacup down on the side table with a clink. "And that means finding something to take your mind off your troubles. Now, my eyes might not be what they once were, but I can see the hurt still in your face. And so can your mother."

It's that obvious? Sophie glanced in dismay between her mother and grandmother.

"When you don't think anyone's looking," Gran said, as if reading her mind, "the people who love you can see."

Sophie felt her throat thicken. Tears pricked at the back of her eyes. "Don't worry about me," was all she could manage to say.

"Well, now, it's our job to worry about you." Easing off the rocker, Gran moved to sit beside her and patted her arm.

"So here's what I think. First off, find something to do. Something you love—and throw yourself into it."

"As a matter of fact—" Sophie began, but her mother interrupted.

"For heaven's sake, Mom, give her time. She's only just come home." Diana McPhee swung her feet to the floor and sat up straighter. "Sophie has barely unpacked."

"Don't you think I know that?" Gran shot her an impatient glance. The only person in the world Gran didn't easily get along with was her own daughter. "But Sophie's marriage ended months ago. Three months, to be exact. The sooner she gets her mind wrapped up in something besides Ned and her divorce, the better off she'll be. So what is it you'd like to do, Sophie? Think, quickly now, what springs to mind? What would you love more than anything?"

A baby. A husband who loves me. A home of our own.

But she couldn't bring herself to say that out loud.

"I'm going to—"

"Bake for the library fund-raiser," her mother supplied. "Sophie's helping out with food and refreshments. That will definitely keep her busy for a while."

So will pulling my hair out over taking orders from Georgia Timmons, Sophie thought. The fund-raiser was set for late September. There was to be a townwide celebration all day and a huge dance on the grounds of the high school in the evening. Several local bands were scheduled to perform, as well as a country singer from Bozeman—Lee Ann Hollows, who had once opened for Brad Paisley and was volunteering her talent and donating autographed CDs to be auctioned off, as well as a cowboy hat Paisley had given her after the tour.

"Well, that's a fine start." Gran looked pleased.

On the rug, Tidbit stretched, got to his feet, and

peered anxiously at Sophie as if reassuring himself she was still there. Since she was, he promptly settled himself down again, right where her feet would have been if she hadn't just tucked them beneath her.

"But you need something more, dear," Gran added. "Something to keep you from thinking about that no-good ex-husband of yours. Martha says somebody ought to take a switch to him, and of course, she's right. But that's neither here nor there—"

"Gran," Sophie interrupted, "don't worry about me. I've got a plan."

"Do you now?"

"What is it?" Diana asked quickly.

Sophie took a breath. "I'm opening a bakery in town. Inside Roy's Diner—just as soon as he and Lil close up. I decided today, and I'm hoping to sign a lease tomorrow."

Silence.

But at least Gran had stopped talking about Ned.

Ava Louise Todd stared at her granddaughter for a long moment before a pleased smile creased her face.

But Sophie's mother shot her a look of concern. "A bakery? Honey, are you sure? Do you really want to jump into a brand-new business so soon? You just sold the other one."

"And I have to share half the profits from the

81

sale with Ned. Community property laws—California, remember?"

"Well, that's not right." Her mother frowned.

"It's the law, whether we like it or not. So I need to work, to make a living. But that's not the only reason I want to do this." She glanced back and forth between her mother and grandmother, searching for the words to explain.

"I miss the part of me that started Sweet Sensations. My work hasn't been about food and baking and customers in a very long time. It's been phone calls and paperwork and meetings. I . . . I feel like I've lost something along the way. A part of *me*. And I want it back."

Gran was nodding, and understanding flickered in Sophie's mother's eyes.

"I know that some people in town might think nothing can replace Roy's, but I'm going to offer them an alternative. It won't be anything fancy, just a simple little bakery-cafe, which is something I know how to do. People might like it," she said hopefully.

"*I* like it." Gran was beaming now.

"*I* think it sounds lovely," Diana stated.

"I'm going to need some help. If either of you know of anyone with baking or restaurant background who's looking for work, I'm planning to hire two or three people—"

"Me. I'll do it." Gran beamed at her.

"You'll do what?"

"I'll do the baking. For you. *With* you. Whatever you need, Sophie." She chuckled at her granddaughter's astonished expression as Diana McPhee looked on, bemused.

"Who was it who taught you everything you know?" Gran asked smugly. "I can't think of anything that would be more fun than to be part of your new bakery. And I live right in town, only a few blocks away. It'll be a snap for me to get there first thing in the morning and get everything started for you."

"Gran, are you sure you want a . . . *job?*" Sophie asked. "At this stage of your life?"

"You mean because I'm seventy-six? Well, Martha still owns the Cuttin' Loose and works six days a week, and she's older than me. Dorothy had to retire from the school district, but she still tutors kids. And I bake most days at home anyway. Don't you want me, Sophie?"

There was a hurt look in her eyes.

"Of course I do," Sophie said quickly. And she did. Gran had taught her everything she knew about baking. Her grandmother knew by heart and instinct nearly all of the recipes that would be the mainstay of the bakery.

"It would be wonderful to have you work with me. But if it gets to be too much for you, promise you'll tell me and we'll cut back your hours to whatever's comfortable for you."

"No need to cater to me. What do you think,

I'm some fragile hothouse lily?" Gran sniffed and waved a hand dismissively.

Diana finished the last of her coffee and set it down on the small walnut table beside the love seat. "Who else are you going to hire?"

"I'll need someone to help out at the counter, with orders and serving and cleanup. Once I'm within a week or two of opening, I'll put a help-wanted sign in the window."

"Sophie, don't you forget that work is never the end-all and be-all." Gran reached over and squeezed her hand. "There's something else you need to do."

"Gran, don't start—"

"Hear me out, young lady. You need to get back out there." Gran waved her arm vaguely, as if not quite sure where "there" was. "It's time for you to meet some new men. Recharge your love life."

"There's plenty of time for that." Sophie forced a smile.

She didn't have the energy to explain to her grandmother just how little interest she had in dating. She'd given her whole heart away once— to Ned. And he'd stomped on it. She wasn't looking to try that again anytime soon.

If ever.

She'd be an idiot to risk giving any part of herself away again. Especially now, when all she wanted was to forget what it felt like to be lied to and cheated on. What it felt like to believe every day she was getting closer to having a baby, having a real family with Ned, and all along she was alone in her hopes, a wishful idiot who'd been incapable of seeing the truth.

What kind of a woman was she? Where was her feminine radar, her instincts? She'd missed all the signs.

Maybe she'd wanted to miss them.

Maybe she was to blame, like Ned kept telling her.

She had a crushed heart, and even worse, a crushed spirit. Her chest ached every day as if an anvil was wedged inside it. She had to force herself to smile. She was in no shape to go out on dates with men, much less consider letting any man get close to her again.

"Time has a way of sneaking past you, Sophie." Gran's faded eyes held hers, giving Sophie the impression she knew exactly what was going on inside Sophie's heart. "If you wait too long, your time is gone. You're dead."

"Mother!" Diana shook her head. "That's enough. Give her some room to breathe. If she says it's too soon, it's too soon. That's the end of it."

"How about letting Sophie decide for herself? She hasn't even heard what I have in mind yet."

On the words, the doorbell pealed, and Tidbit leaped up with a woof worthy of a German shepherd.

"There they are now." Gran was beaming as her daughter and granddaughter stared at her in surprise. "I invited Martha and Dorothy to stop by so we could tell you together."

"Tell me what?" There was a sinking sensation in the pit of Sophie's stomach as her mother hurried toward the door. She didn't have a good feeling about this. Especially when Gran didn't reply to her question, pretending not to hear instead.

"Hope we're not too early," Dorothy Winston said perkily. In her track suit and sneakers, she looked almost exactly the same as Sophie remembered her—petite and round-shouldered, with squirrel-like cheeks, soft gray hair that wisped around her face, and a surprisingly authoritative voice honed by years of announcements intoned over grade-school loudspeakers.

"Did you tell her yet, Ava? Did you mention John?"

Though Martha, the owner of the Cuttin' Loose beauty salon, was pushing eighty, she was still taller than both Gran and Dorothy, a spare, dramatic-looking woman whose thick short hair was a bright and improbable red. Sophie remembered that Martha had always loved to change her hair color the way most women changed nail polish. She wore purple hoop earrings, a mood ring, and a bright paisley shawl over her turquoise silk blouse and jeans.

"I'm talking about my grandson, John," Martha explained to Sophie before Gran could respond. She sank down beside Dorothy. "He's a sweet, sweet boy. I mean, man," she added with a chuckle. "He'll be forty in November. A *widower*," she added. "And quite handsome. You two would have such pretty children—"

"Martha, I haven't told Sophie any details yet," Gran interrupted. "Stop jumping the gun."

Details? I don't want to know details. Dismay flashed through Sophie as she gazed at the three beaming faces arrayed before her.

To no one's surprise, it was her grandmother who took charge. "It so happens, Sophie, that Martha and Dorothy and I have put together a list of eligible men right here in Lonesome Way. Men we know personally and who we can vouch for."

"Mom." Diana's voice was low. "I'm not sure this is the best time—"

"Nonsense, of course it is. What's the point of waiting? Sophie needs to move on."

"And the sooner the better," Dorothy put in earnestly. "It's not as if we want her to go on some Internet dating site or something like that."

"These are men we *know*." Martha leaned forward in her chair. "Like my grandson."

Sophie gazed from one eager face to the next, feeling dazed.

Gran, what have you done?

"Don't forget my nephew, Roger." Dorothy smiled at Sophie like a chipmunk with a cache of nuts. "Roger Hendricks. Perhaps you remember him, dear? He was a year ahead of you in school. He played football."

Sophie remembered Roger. In grade school he'd been a schoolyard bully, who enjoyed shoving several of the smaller boys every day at recess until one afternoon Jake Tanner noticed and asked him if he wanted to pick on someone his own size. Roger hadn't—and had made sure he was on his best behavior after that, at least whenever Jake was around.

"Roger was divorced almost three years ago. He's lonely and ripe for the picking. I'd love to give him your phone number," Dorothy continued. "I think you two would hit it right off."

"But I've already *told* John about you," Martha put in triumphantly. "And he *wants* your phone number."

Gran gaped at her, a frown settling over her face. "Martha! You didn't!"

"I . . . You . . . *What?*" Dull red color flushed Dorothy's puffy cheeks. "We *agreed* we'd wait until *after* we talked to Sophie. I can't believe you *cheated*."

"Ladies," Sophie interjected hastily, "you're all very sweet to think of me, but I'm not in the market for a man—or even for a date. Not yet."

"It's true. Sophie needs more time to adjust to her divorce," her mother said.

"But how much time does a body need?" Martha shook her head, bewildered. "Meeting new people will *help* you to adjust, Sophie. Sometimes you just have to push yourself, honey."

"That means going out of your comfort zone," Dorothy added.

Gran pointed a thin finger at her. "What did you learn, Sophie, when you were five years old? That time Cloud reared up and threw you in the corral? You flew right off his back and hit the ground. I swear, you yelled so loud and cried so hard they probably heard you in Missoula. But your father made you get right up and get on again and ride Cloud around the corral three times. Well, it's the same thing when love throws you as when a horse does it."

Not exactly. The horse doesn't also kick you in the teeth. And get some slutty mare pregnant.

"Gran, I just need some more time. Another month or two."

Or twenty.

"In the meantime," she told Martha and Dorothy, before either of them could argue further, "please don't give my phone number to *anyone*. Not until I say so. And right now, I'm sorry, but I have to leave."

She jumped to her feet, startling Tidbit, who

also scrambled up and gazed at her worriedly. "I'm due to meet Mia at the Double Cross to plan Lissie's shower," she explained.

"Well, then. We'll simply need to table this discussion for another day, won't we?" Gran smiled ruefully at her friends.

"Just remember," she told Sophie, "that when you're ready, we have a *list*. And there are others on it, besides John and Roger. Good men, every one of 'em. Only the best for my granddaughter."

Great, just what I need. Bippity, Boppity, and Boo in charge of my love life.

After brushing a hasty kiss on her grandmother's cheek, Sophie rattled off good-byes to Martha and Dorothy, then shot a short, speaking glance in her mother's direction and made a run for it.

Tidbit trotted at her heels as she made a beeline for the front hall.

"No, Tid, you can't come this time. Stay here," she told him distractedly, tugging her leather jacket from the closet, grabbing her handbag, and yanking open the door. Then she let out a muffled scream at the sight of the man standing on the porch.

Tidbit barked maniacally, dashing forward, ready to defend Sophie and the house with his life.

"Stay, Tidbit! Down!" Sophie ordered automatically, staring at the man standing before her, not quite able to accept he was there.

His shoulders were hunched against the wind, his right hand lifted, poised to knock. He took a step back, because of either her or the dog, she couldn't tell which. She only knew he looked every bit as startled as she felt.

"Mr. . . . Hartigan? What . . . are you doing here?"

"Taking matters into my own hands."

Her former geometry teacher stood five foot ten. He was still as wiry and tough-looking as a seasoned ranch hand, but his hair was streaked with gray now, and one clump of it fell over his brow as he regarded her warily from deep-set brown eyes that had always reminded her of dried-out plum pits. There were crow's feet at the corners of them, and deep lines scored his forehead.

But there was something in his stern, caustic face she'd never seen before when he'd lectured in class, handed her back a paper with a big red *F* scrawled across it, or told her that no, she could not retake the test.

He looked nervous. As nervous as she'd felt every day in his classroom.

"There's something you need to know, Sophie. If no one else is going to tell you, well, uh, I will." Doug Hartigan cleared his throat. He looked past her into the living room and then spoke in a voice loud enough to be heard by everyone in the house.

"Your mother and I are dating. Each other," he clarified quickly. "And that's not all."

Through the shock that slammed her, Sophie was aware that his Adam's apple was quivering. Mr. Hartigan took a deep breath and swallowed hard.

"We're not just dating. We've fallen in love."

Chapter Eight

Sophie had no memory of driving into town. During the entire stretch of time she'd steered the Blazer over rough country roads, her mind was spinning.

Her mother. And Mr. Hartigan.

Brain freeze set in every time she tried to imagine it. She had no idea how the two of them had gotten together or even how long it had been going on—this dating business—and hopefully it was no more than that, despite what Doug Hartigan had said.

She hadn't waited around to discuss it with him *or* with her mother.

She'd simply stepped aside to admit her former teacher into the house, taken one good look back at her mother's flushed, distressed face, and fled, shell-shocked, toward the Blazer.

Now she found herself cruising at a snail's

pace down Main Street, passing Roy's Diner, the Cuttin' Loose salon, and Benson's Drugstore.

Her stomach was roiling as she turned first right and then left toward the Double Cross Bar and Grill, parking in the gravel lot in back.

She could hear Johnny Cash's "I Walk the Line" blasting from the jukebox. Waves of energy pulsed outward through the crowded lot.

The Double Cross would be jam-packed. She needed it to be. Despite her earlier reluctance, she now needed to escape her own thoughts, to be surrounded, engulfed by people and noise and chatter—enough to crowd out the image of her former geometry teacher walking into her house.

Mr. Hartigan had tormented Sophie for an entire year of high school. She'd hated him, hated her life that entire year. All because of him.

She hadn't been able to master geometry, she just hadn't. Not that she hadn't tried. Every night her mind twisted around the problems, trying to make sense of them.

Hartigan, though, had never cut her any slack or given her an inch for trying. Even all the extra credit she labored over, trying to boost her grade, only earned her a pathetic D.

Which was at least better than an F.

Her father had expected straight As from both Sophie and Wes in every subject. But even Hoot had finally learned to just grit his teeth over geometry and accept less than he wanted.

Despite the tutor her mother had hired, Sophie could never wrap her head around isosceles triangles and supplementary angles and vortexes.

And Doug Hartigan had seemed to take personal affront at her confusion. Hoot had finally been forced to accept that she simply could do no better in that particular subject, but he growled like a grizzly if she didn't ace every other course.

She leaned her forehead against the Blazer's steering wheel as she realized that now the conversation she'd overheard while on the porch swing made sense.

It was *him*. Pressuring her mother to tell her about their—what was it? A relationship? An affair? The very idea made her queasy. But her mother had kept silent. She hadn't been able to bring herself to tell Sophie what was going on.

And why was that?

Because she knew I'd want to barf, Sophie thought. *Or else, she has her own doubts about him.*

Diana McPhee was a smart woman. She'd already lived with one difficult man. What could she possibly see in a stern, gloomy geometry teacher who'd serially threatened to flunk her own daughter?

Switching off the ignition, Sophie stared blindly out at the star-studded vastness of the Montana sky.

Gran knew Mom was dating Mr. Hartigan. Did everyone else in town know too?

Everyone except her?

She slammed the door of the Blazer and headed toward the Double Cross with long, quick, angry strides.

Rafe lined up his cue stick and considered his angle shot. He ignored his cousin Decker's open skepticism that he'd make the difficult shot, and focused on the eight ball and the invisible line he saw in his head, the one going straight into the pocket.

Eyes narrowed, he leaned in, took the shot. The eight ball glided across the table and sank. Smooth as wind on water.

"Damn it. That makes three in a row. Man, are you having a helluva night." Decker tossed back a swig of beer. "I need a break. Let's grab some food."

"You always were a sore loser." Rafe grinned as he handed off his cue to a short guy in a checked shirt waiting for a turn at the table.

The Double Cross Bar and Grill was crowded tonight, its low-lit, cavernous space and long curving mahogany bar teeming with people and noise. A few dozen tourists were mixed in with the locals, enjoying the chance to rub elbows with real Montana cowboys.

Laughter, conversation, and heated discussions

simmered in nearly every corner. Waitresses in tight red shirts, jeans, and high-heeled red cowboy boots raced back and forth with trays loaded with rib eye steaks, burgers, pizzas, and drink refills as Martina McBride's "This One's for the Girls" blared and couples danced, arms wrapped around each other as they gyrated their way around the square wooden dance floor.

As Rafe and Decker worked their way toward the dark booths in the rear, he noticed a commotion at the table closest to the double doors.

Some ranch hands were engaged in a heated argument. He recognized the lean man with dishwater blond hair who seemed to be at the center of the shouting match.

Buck Crenshaw.

It figures, Rafe thought, his eyes narrowing on the cowboy. He'd hired Crenshaw part-time a year ago to fill in for a few weeks when Rowdy Jones, one of his wranglers, had been laid up with pneumonia. He'd needed an extra pair of hands, and Crenshaw, new to town, had been looking for work.

But Rafe had fired him less than a week later. It hadn't taken long to see that Buck Crenshaw was no good with horses. In Rafe's estimation he was probably no good period. He was rough and abrupt, always in a hurry—just his scent spooked the horses—the dogs too. Rafe had picked up on that right away.

Crenshaw had been careless as well. The last straw came when Rafe made his rounds and checked the barns one snowy December night to find Crenshaw had failed to repair a loose floorboard in one of the barns and had left a push broom lying across the aisle of another. Keeping the aisles free of clutter and all repairs in order were cardinal rules for horse-barn safety. He'd had no choice but to fire the man when he showed up for work the next morning.

Since then, Crenshaw had worked for two other outfits that Rafe knew of. Neither job had lasted more than a few months.

Since he was sitting with a bunch of hands from the Hanging W, Rafe guessed he must have recently landed there.

But not for long, based on the way all the other wranglers seemed to be glaring at him.

"Holy crap, look what just walked in all alone," Decker muttered, coming to a dead halt as they wound their way toward the booths. "I swear, if I wasn't a happily married man—"

Rafe followed his glance. A few feet ahead, a tall, long-legged beauty in a leather jacket, jeans, and boots had just swept into the Double Cross. She was gorgeous, a knockout, her rich tumble of caramel hair tousled by the wind, her walk swift and graceful, like she knew exactly what she wanted and where she was going.

Only she didn't.

She paused five feet inside the door and scanned the booths, obviously hunting for someone.

A lucky someone.

And it was then that Rafe realized with a thud of shock who she was. Not a supermodel or Hollywood actress from one of the fancy mountain homes celebrities were building all the hell over Montana. No, she was his kid sister's pesky best friend. Sophie McPhee.

All grown up.

And how.

He recognized the perfect oval shape of her face, the wide-set eyes, and the delicate nose. The coltish gate he remembered from that young girl was now a graceful, lusciously female stride.

"Hey, isn't that Lissie's friend—Sophie? Sophie McPhee?" Deck recognized her a fraction of a second after Rafe did. "Heard she was back in town. Divorced." He dug an elbow into Rafe's ribs. "That means she's available. You should go for it, you lucky dog."

He and Deck were actually angling toward her as they slipped into a slim opening in the crowd. Sophie was moving too, edging deeper into the cavernous room—at the exact moment one of the Hanging W ranch hands—Wade Holden—shot to his feet, fists clenched, with Crenshaw doing the same. Crenshaw surged up from the table so violently he sent his chair tumbling backward.

In an instant, he and Holden were charging at each other, their fists swinging. Crenshaw slugged Holden in the jaw and sent him spinning on a path that led straight toward Sophie McPhee.

Rafe leaped without thinking, jumping between them. He took the brunt of the collision, which barely seemed to touch him as he shoved the off-balance wrangler aside.

Rounding on Buck Crenshaw, Rafe's gaze was flinty in the dimly lit glow of the bar. "You and Holden want to fight, take it outside, Crenshaw. Now."

"You heard the man." Deck was right beside him, ready to rumble. "Get out."

"I don't take no orders from you—either one of you." Crenshaw's brown eyes locked on Rafe. "Not anymore."

The fool's drunk. Rafe recognized the boozy braggadocio and overbright glare in Crenshaw's stare. He was swaying slightly on his feet and looked like he wanted nothing more than to hurl himself in uncontrolled fury straight at Rafe.

"Bad move, buddy. Don't even think about it," Rafe warned quietly. He had four inches and twenty pounds on the man—Crenshaw would have to be as drunk as a skunk to even consider taking him on.

"Get the hell out of here while you can still walk. Don't make me toss you out that door myself." His voice was low, meant for Crenshaw only, but his face was as hard and unflinching as iron.

"Best not to force him to say it again," Decker drawled.

Crenshaw wavered. Fear warred in his eyes with drunken pride. Suddenly Big Billy Watkins, the owner and bartender of the Double Cross, strode up, 225 pounds of muscle, fat, whiskers, and wild mustang tattoos.

"You heard 'em, Crenshaw. You too, Holden," he boomed with a glance at the ranch hand Rafe had shoved aside, who was just now staggering to his feet. "I want the both of you outta my place. *Now.*"

Wade Holden headed for the door, head down. But Crenshaw glared like a bull from Rafe to Decker to Big Billy, and suddenly seemed to slink into himself.

His shoulders hunched and his chin shot out.

"Even the beer here tastes like crap anyway," he muttered, and veered around Deck to push his way through the double doors.

Sophie let out her breath. She'd jumped back after Rafe intercepted the man who'd been tumbling right at her. She'd watched the entire confrontation while glued in place, her heart stuck in her throat.

All around her, the spectators let out their collective breath. Big Billy sauntered back toward the bar, the crowd parting to let him through.

People returned to the enjoyment of their steaks and pizzas and beers, and the chatter in the room surged, drowning the tension. A cowboy wearing a black shirt punched in a Waylon Jennings song on the jukebox.

There was, if anything, an extra buzz in the air as the music and the excitement of the almost-fistfight circled through the place, but Sophie's attention was focused completely on Rafe Tanner.

He'd come out of nowhere. Protected her from getting knocked down, perhaps seriously hurt. She still felt shaken, thinking about what could have happened.

"You all right, Sophie?"

"I'm fine. He never touched me. I . . ." She couldn't help the tiny shiver of reaction that swept over her now that it was over. "Thank you."

It was a miracle she got the words out without stammering. Rafe Tanner could have that effect on a woman.

He was standing so close to her she could see the black irises of his midnight blue eyes, the solid outline of his jaw. In his charcoal T-shirt and jeans, with a sexy bit of five o'clock shadow across his chin, he was enough to make a woman swoon.

How was it possible he could look even sexier now than the last time she'd seen him when she was a fifteen-year-old in shorts and a tank top, shocking the hell out of him by kissing him in his pickup truck?

The intervening years had hardened him. An aura of toughness clung to his muscular six-foot-three-inch frame. But there was something more than sinewy strength and magnetism now. A quiet maturity. Confidence. Very different from the cocky recklessness of the boy she'd daydreamed about night and day when she was twelve.

The next moment she noticed that his mouth—oh, God, that firm, sensual mouth—was curved upward in a hint of a smile.

And what was so amusing? As embarrassment swept through her, she wondered if he was remembering the last time he'd come to her rescue? That day on Squirrel Road. That stupid kiss.

She felt heat rush into her cheeks and hoped she wasn't blushing. Her chin lifted. "I don't usually need rescuing these days," she said tightly.

Rafe's smile widened. Now it reached his eyes. *Damn it. He remembered.* Or if he didn't, she'd just reminded him.

"I'm just glad I was in the right place at the right time," Rafe said, his voice easy. "We'd better move out of the way before we get trampled."

He snagged her arm, and a jolt of electricity quivered through her skin where his hand touched it. He eased her back a few steps as a family of tourists barreled past them.

"Nothing like a little excitement to welcome you back to town, Sophie," Deck said heartily beside them.

She hadn't even noticed Lissie's cousin before now, but once he spoke, she immediately recognized him.

"I wouldn't exactly call what just happened a welcome," she replied with a rueful smile.

So he gets a smile, I get nothing. Rafe was partly amused and partly irritated. He heard Deck say something about going on ahead to hunt up a booth, but he couldn't seem to tear his gaze or his attention away from Sophie McPhee long enough to respond.

The annoying little pest had transformed into a gorgeously sexy woman. Beneath the leather jacket, she was wearing a silky coral tank top and low-cut jeans. Rafe had to quell an impulse to stare at her breasts and those enticingly rounded hips. The top of her head didn't even reach his chin, but her face was upturned to his and he felt himself getting lost in smoky natural beauty, the tilt of a shapely nose, the glimmer of cool green eyes. He'd have bet a dozen of his best quarter horses that the strands of her honey-colored hair would feel like a silken river flowing through his fingers.

Good thing he'd given up his old ways, dedicated himself these days to being Ivy's father. Because for the life of him, at the moment, his mind was a blank and he couldn't come up with a single smooth, funny, seductively charming thing to say to her.

"Ivy told me about her shopping trip today," he heard himself saying. Lame. "She said you were a big help."

"Not really. Ivy didn't need any help, she knew exactly what she wanted."

"She's a Tanner. We usually do."

Sophie felt the pull of that slow, engaging grin. Was Rafe Tanner flirting with her?

No, that was crazy. It was all in her imagination.

Get a grip. After everything that's happened, the last thing you need is to think about a man. Any man.

But especially this man.

Not that she was *thinking* about Rafe. She was so over him. Still, no sane woman could help feeling a little lightheaded when he was standing this close in all his handsome cowboy hotness.

Go find Mia, she told herself, and forced herself to look away.

To her relief, she spotted Mia Quinn hurrying

straight toward them. Rafe noticed her the same time Sophie did.

So that's who she came here to meet. The other part of the triumvirate. Lissie, Mia, and Sophie.

Mia hadn't hung around the house as much as Sophie had, at least not while Rafe lived at home. She probably had been over sometimes when she dated Travis while they were both in high school, but Rafe had been away at college by then. Mia had never teamed up with Lissie and Sophie as they tormented him, dogging him whenever he wanted to sneak in some private time with a girlfriend. That was strictly Lissie and Sophie's game.

"I was in that fourth booth back there, Sophie, watching for you. I saw everything that happened," Mia exclaimed, giving her a hug. "Rafe, you were awesome. Want to join us? We're planning Lissie's baby shower."

"Baby shower?" His eyebrows shot up. "Uh, no, Mia, don't think so." He chuckled. "As fascinating as it would be to discuss . . . whatever women discuss when they're planning baby showers . . . I'll have to pass. Decker's waiting for me. He's down in the dumps with Leigh out of town, and someone has to keep him out of trouble."

"You're sure now?" Mia teased. "You're missing out. This shower is going to be the talk of Lonesome Way."

"Not only that," Sophie heard herself saying. "You could help us decide between playing Baby Bingo or Baby Bottle Guess."

Rafe's gaze locked on hers. "You're evil, you know that, don't you?"

"Just being polite," she told him sweetly.

He couldn't seem to stop staring into those intoxicating green eyes. Especially now that they'd turned teasing. She'd been a cute kid, but oh, man. All grown up, Sophie McPhee was one luscious woman.

Keep your distance, he told himself. *For a whole slew of reasons.*

"I really hate to miss out on all the fun, ladies, but something tells me you're going to do my little niece-to-be justice just fine without any help from me."

"Chicken," Mia called after him as he strolled off across the dance floor.

"What was that all about?" Decker asked a moment later as Rafe joined him in the booth near the dart board. "Were you hitting on Sophie McPhee? You get anywhere? Man, she looks like one of those chicks on the cover of *Sports Illustrated*. What were you two talking about?"

"You don't want to know." Rafe leaned back in the booth as a spiky-haired brunette waitress rushed up to their table.

They ordered beer and nachos.

"Yeah, I do want to know." The moment the waitress rushed off, Decker picked up right where they'd left off. "I'm a happily married man—I can only live vicariously. You need to get out there again, start seeing someone on a regular basis. You know, a relationship. She's perfect."

"Not gonna happen."

"You take a vow of celibacy or something?" Decker joked and Rafe laughed. He spent time with his share of women—not running around like he had in the old days, before he married Lynelle, of course, but he did find time to date, just not seriously. And just so long as the women he spent time with knew the score. No relationship, no romance, nothing serious. Just good times and sex. Light and easy. No strings on either side.

Sophie McPhee wasn't the no-strings type. For one thing, she was his sister's best friend, and though he hadn't paid much attention, he did remember Lissie telling him that Sophie had been devastated recently by the end of her marriage. He didn't know the details, but he knew her husband had cheated on her. That alone made her way too vulnerable for his brand of dating.

All might be fair in love and war, but devastated women were off-limits.

Besides, if he ever went out even once with Sophie, Lissie would find out. And she'd get all kinds of crazy ideas, probably start expecting them to get married.

And if he *stopped* going out with Sophie, there might be hurt feelings. And Lissie could end up caught in the middle between her brother and her best friend.

Last—but definitely not least—there was Ivy.

Rafe had no intention of bringing any new woman into her life—into their lives. Not after what Ivy had already been through with her mother. Which was primarily the reason he didn't date anyone long term. He didn't want Ivy growing close to someone he was seeing, and then being disappointed when things didn't work out. Having a string of women in and out of her life was not something he'd do to his daughter, not after what Lynelle had pulled.

He couldn't put Ivy through that, not after everything she'd already gone through. Hell, she still missed her mother. He knew she did, though she rarely even mentioned her name. But he'd seen the longing in her face when she was with her friends and watched them joking, hanging out, even arguing with their moms.

He could always tell when she was thinking about Lynelle.

There was that sadness in her eyes, similar to the hollow expression he sometimes noticed when she fed or groomed or exercised Misty Mae, Lynelle's mare.

Before Lynelle deserted them, she and Ivy had often ridden together—Ivy on sweet old Duchess, and Lynelle on Misty Mae, the spirited thoroughbred filly Rafe had bought her in the first year of their marriage.

Rafe had recently been considering the idea of selling Misty Mae. Enough time had passed that he thought it might be easier now for Ivy to part ways with such a tangible reminder of her mother. But when he'd casually mentioned selling Misty Mae one Sunday morning after breakfast, his daughter's eyes had filled with tears so quickly, his heart had clenched.

He'd known in that instant, that no matter what she said to anyone—to the therapist he'd taken her to see after Lynelle left, to Lissie, to him—a part of Ivy still believed Lynelle would return, ride Misty Mae again, be her mother again.

It was like a shotgun blast to his heart every time he thought about it.

He hoped Ivy didn't feel responsible, that she didn't think Lynelle had run away from *her*. He'd talked to her about it over and over, but how could a kid so young understand that her mother had run out on them because of her own problems, not because of him or Ivy?

Lynelle had run because Lynelle was Lynelle. Immature, irresponsible, and as restless as a tumbleweed.

These past few years, he'd worked his ass off

trying to give Ivy back the sense of stability Lynelle had nuked the day she left town. Now the two of them had a great life together—everything rolled along on a pretty even keel, smooth and familiar.

So Rafe wasn't about to introduce any new, potentially rocky complications.

"You should date Sophie," Decker said in between bites of nachos and guacamole.

"You should brush up on your pool." Rafe saluted his cousin with his beer bottle. "Before I kick your ass again."

But that night as he drove home from the Double Cross, Rafe couldn't help remembering the sizzling summer afternoon Sophie McPhee had kissed him in his truck a stone's throw from the Good Luck ranch. She'd been only a kid then, fifteen—much too young for him—and he'd hightailed it out of there, hurting her feelings, no doubt, but she'd scared the hell out of him.

It had been a damned good kiss, he thought with a smile. Somehow it had packed quite a wallop, seeing as he still remembered it.

And he wasn't sure why. Probably just because she'd taken him by surprise.

Turning into the ranch, he couldn't help wondering what it would be like to gather the woman Sophie McPhee had become into his arms, carry her up to his bed, and try that kiss—

and a few other things he could think of—again.

Not going to happen, he told himself, staring at the single lonely light ablaze in the living room window, hearing Starbucks give a welcoming woof from within the big, empty house.

He shut off the engine, got out of his truck.

Not. Going. To. Happen.

"Rafe likes you," Mia said thoughtfully as Sophie took a sip of her wine in the booth near the back of the Double Cross.

"You're crazy. He doesn't even know me."

"Didn't you see the way he was looking at you? Don't tell me you didn't notice."

"I'm not in the business of noticing men these days." Sophie took a full-out gulp of wine this time and hoped she didn't choke on the lie. How could she *not* notice Rafe? She might be a mess, but she wasn't blind and she wasn't dead. Rafe Tanner was a god of all things sexy and dangerous. And those muscles . . .

"I'm trying to forget men exist on this planet, not pick one up in a bar. Besides, Rafe and I have known each other forever."

"And you've had a crush on him forever. At least you *used* to have a crush on him," Mia amended, grinning as Sophie glared at her.

"I *used* to be married too, and I'm not anymore."

"Let's drink to that." Mia lifted her glass, and

with a grim smile touching her lips, Sophie raised hers.

Just as they clinked, a waitress rushed up to their table. Sophie recognized the woman with the pale, faded hair who'd been feeding her toddler grilled cheese in Roy's this afternoon. Tonight she was wearing makeup, but she still looked tired.

No wonder, if she's waitressing in this place nights and taking care of a child during the day, Sophie thought with a stab of sympathy.

"Angela's gone on break," the waitress explained quickly, brushing one stray wisp of hair from her eyes. "I'm taking over her tables. What can I bring you ladies?"

They ordered the stuffed mushroom appetizer to share. After the waitress rushed off, Sophie asked the question that had been on her mind since she left the Good Luck ranch.

"Did you know that my mother is dating Mr. Hartigan?"

Mia looked like she'd been struck by lightning. "You're joking, right?"

"I wish." If Mia didn't know, no one knew. Except—until tonight—Gran.

How on earth had her mother and Doug Hartigan managed to keep it a secret?

Of course now that Martha and Dorothy both knew, the news would ripple all through Lonesome Way by morning.

"Are you sure about this, Sophie? I mean . . . *Why?*"

"Obviously my mother has taken leave of her senses."

"Brainwashed." Mia took a sip of wine. "Hartigan was always good at that—making kids feel like they were stupid for not grasping that geometry was the end-all and be-all of life."

As music blared through the Double Cross and couples swayed on the dance floor, Sophie struggled to come up with an explanation for her mother secretly dating the teacher from hell.

"She's probably lonely." Mia set down her wineglass. "That has to be it."

"*He* claims they're in love." Her teeth hurt just saying the words.

"Barf. What does your mom say?"

"I haven't talked to her about it yet." She explained what had happened on the porch tonight.

Sophie knew they needed to get down to the business of planning Lissie's shower, but how could she concentrate now?

She needed to talk to her mother. And she needed to forget she'd seen Rafe Tanner and that he was more dreamy than ever.

Turning her head a fraction, she could still see the booth where Rafe and Decker had been drinking beer only a dozen feet away. Only Rafe's profile had been visible, but her heart had jumped just the same. He'd always had this effect on her. It was depressing. Why hadn't she gotten past it by now?

As Mia pulled a printout of baby shower games and favors from her purse, Sophie forced her attention back onto the shower plans.

But she knew one thing now she hadn't known when she'd awakened this morning in her old familiar bedroom.

Coming home wasn't nearly as easy as it was cracked up to be.

Chapter Nine

Ten days later, Sophie parked the Blazer across the street from Roy's Diner and studied the activity under way inside the old place.

A tiny flutter of excitement surged through her.

Roy and Lil had packed up and left for Laramie only four days ago, but her father's old friend Sam McDonald and his shy forty-five-year-old son, Denny, had made tremendous strides since then. They'd been working on her renovations nearly around the clock.

Sam McDonald owned a small construction company and did construction and handyman work year-round. She'd handed him a key to the place the same day she signed the lease and applied for her local bakery and food-handling licenses.

He and Denny had been hammering and sanding and painting for ten—sometimes twelve—hours a day, transforming Roy's inch by inch into Sophie's vision of Lonesome Way's first bakery-cafe.

Watching them painting through the plate glass window, pleasure washed over her. The worn old booths had been torn out, and the old wood floor refinished, sanded, and stained to a dazzling gleam. Today, the father and son were painting the ceiling a pale lavender and the walls a rich sage green with almond trim. Tomorrow they'd hang the new light fixtures and install new deep purple leather booths.

Denny would hang the ceiling fan as soon as the paint was dry. Her beautiful glass display shelves were being shipped. And she'd find just the right spot for the portable gas fireplace she'd ordered online to warm and brighten the bakery when winter arrived.

Sophie had decided to keep the antique cash register, but she'd bought two additional stone-fired baking ovens, rolling racks, and a huge modern stainless steel refrigerator from a contact of hers who dealt in restaurant equipment. Everything was scheduled to be delivered the following week, well before the grand opening.

But now she had to make the biggest decision of all.

Beside her on the seat of the Blazer, Tidbit gave a little whine, as if to say, *Are we going to sit here all day?*

"Shhh," she murmured, stroking the soft fur behind his ears. "I'm thinking."

No one had claimed the dog, or even inquired about him. He'd had no chip, and according to Doc Weatherby, looked to be four or five years old and in good health, despite what he'd been through.

"My guess is he hasn't had a home in a long time, not a real one. If he ever did," the vet had added.

"He has one now." She'd scooped Tidbit from the examining table and made a silent pledge into those soft, trusting eyes.

As he yawned on the seat beside her and lay down again, his head resting between his paws, Sophie continued to sit with the window rolled down, contemplating the bakery as Denny McDonald methodically rolled paint across the ceiling.

People hurried up and down Main Street. Next door to the bakery, Martha was finishing up a perm in the Cuttin' Loose. Several young girls— around Ivy Tanner's age—burst out of Benson's corner drugstore, laughing and talking excitedly as they swiped on lip gloss. At the corner of First and Main, two ranch hands hustled sacks of feed out to their truck.

Then Georgia Timmons sashayed right past the Blazer, headed toward Top to Toe, her shoulder-length dark hair and frosted pink mouth shimmering in the sunlight. Sophie jerked upright and held her breath, relieved Georgia hadn't noticed her. She'd already had one annoying phone call from the woman, informing her about a mandatory meeting for the library fund-raiser.

"You heard that I'm in charge, didn't you, Sophie? All volunteers in every department need to be at the library next Monday night at seven o'clock sharp. If you want to participate, you *must* attend."

It had been difficult, but Sophie had resisted the almost overpowering urge to un-volunteer herself on the spot. She only refrained because her mother had already committed her to the cause—and because she'd seen for herself that Lonesome Way's library really *was* in dire need of refurbishing.

She'd stopped by the other day to browse the fiction shelves and was shocked at how small and shabby the place looked. There was only a single computer for patrons' use, just two small shelves of rental DVDs, and the women's restroom had broken locks on the stall doors and cracked sinks. Even worse, the children's section was marred by badly stained and frayed carpeting, as well as a dearth of new picture books.

So even Georgia hadn't been able to deter her from helping. But the former head cheerleader and chief hall monitor hadn't been satisfied to merely tell her about the meeting. She'd weighed in on the bakery too.

"Well, you know, that place will *always* be Roy's for a lot of us here in Lonesome Way." Georgia's voice had flowed through the phone like thickly honeyed whiskey. "You should know for your own good, Sophie, people are wondering why you were so quick to take over and change everything. There's some who're miffed about that. They even think you were . . . oh, what's the word—*predatory* in moving so fast."

"Predatory, Georgia? You're kidding, right?"

"Oh, not everyone, mind you, but there's been some talk. I only hope you know what you're doing. Not that I want to put a damper on your big plans. But I don't have to tell you how people can be. There are some in town who swear they won't set foot in some fancy bakery. They're saying how much they're going to miss all the good wholesome food at Roy's."

"Then I guess they'll have to track Lil and Roy down in Laramie and invite themselves to supper, won't they?"

Sophie smiled with satisfaction as she remembered that for all of ten seconds, Georgia had been speechless.

Sophie had pounced on the opportunity to say a quick good-bye and end the call.

Now as she watched Georgia disappear inside Top to Toe, she glanced back at the bakery and made her decision.

"Guess what, Tidbit, we've got a name."

Several potential names had been floating around in her head ever since *the possibility* of the bakery had first come to her. But the one she was going with had sprung into her mind as she and Mia planned the menu for the baby shower.

She'd volunteered to bring raspberry muffins, cupcakes, a chocolate fudge cake with cream cheese icing—and cinnamon buns.

Cinnamon buns were her specialty. They always had been, ever since Gran first gave her the recipe and showed her how to make them.

She wanted them to be the centerpiece of the bakery.

A Bun in the Oven.

"I like it," she thought, a little quiver going through her, as if telling her she'd made the right decision. Somehow, settling on the name made the bakery seem more real than the fresh paint and new booths did. She was actually moving on with her life. Taking a step forward.

That meant one step further away from Ned and the mess of her marriage.

She found it helped a lot being busy. When she was planning her menus and ordering her supplies and equipment, she didn't have time to remember that Cassandra Reynard was now nearing the end of her second trimester. Or that Cassandra and Ned were no doubt shopping for cribs and car seats now, and batting names back and forth over their breakfast table.

She had her own name to think about. *A Bun in the Oven.*

She tried to envision the bakery a month from now—fresh and pretty and brimming with cakes and pastries, soups and sandwiches. Fragrant with the aromas of dough and chocolate and cinnamon, and crammed with eager, happy customers.

She didn't want to think about what would happen if people stayed away, upset that Roy's was gone and that she'd taken over the space so quickly.

Pushing the worries away, she hooked the leash she'd bought Tidbit onto his new collar. Scooping him into her arms, she stepped onto the street. Then bit back a groan.

Talk about bad timing.

Doug Hartigan had just turned the corner of Spring Street and was headed down Main straight toward her.

Lovely. She'd already endured another in a series of awkward breakfasts with her mother this morning. And now this.

Things had not been comfortable between Sophie and her mom since the night Hartigan had materialized on her front porch like the ghost of high school past. And now . . .

"Sophie." He called to her just as she started toward the bakery, hoping to avoid speaking to him. She had no choice but to turn as he approached.

Hartigan stopped directly in front of her. Just looking into his stern face made her feel like she'd just downed a glass of spoiled milk.

"About the other night," he said quickly. She remembered how slowly he used to speak in class. Slow and distinct, with an edge of sharpness that today was missing. "I . . . just want to say, I'm sorry." He cleared his throat.

"I shouldn't have come by like that unannounced. Or told you about your mother and me. I should've waited until she had the chance to tell you about us herself."

"You obviously didn't care about her wishes, or you would have."

"That's not true," he protested. Then he caught himself. Drawing a breath, he spoke deliberately, his eyes lowered beneath her gaze. "I jumped the gun by blurting it out that way. It was wrong. I just wanted to get everything out in the open."

"Why?" Sophie wasn't buying his humble act. And she wasn't a frightened high school girl anymore, intimidated by the teacher who brought the disapproval of her father crashing down on her. She stared at him, suspicious that he didn't seem to want to meet her eyes. What was he up to?

"I don't understand your hurry, Mr. Hartigan. Exactly what is it that you *want* from my mother?"

His eyes did meet hers then. He looked startled. "I . . . I want to make her happy!"

"I don't think you made her happy when you showed up uninvited the other night. When you told me something that was her choice to tell me, not yours."

She waited for the anger to spark in his eyes. She remembered Mr. Hartigan's anger clearly. Sometimes he'd lashed out verbally, embarrassing her in front of the class. Other times he wrote "loser" or "failure" on her geometry papers.

Shape up, Sophie, or we'll be doing this same dance again next year, was one of his favorite sayings as he walked past her desk and gave back her graded test. It was only because of the tutor her mother had hired that she hadn't had to endure a second year of torture.

Now he didn't look angry—only uncomfortable. He shifted from one foot to the other as she stared him down.

"You're right. I got carried away the other night. I was waiting for her to tell you, so everything could be out in the open, and suddenly, I . . . I just wanted you to know. It was a spur-of-the-moment thing, coming over there like that. Don't be angry with your mother on my account."

"I'm not angry with her. I'm worried about her. I don't want to see her make any mistakes."

"You think I'm a mistake. I understand." Hartigan took a breath. "I'm asking you to give me a chance to prove you wrong."

Like you gave me so many chances, Sophie thought. He had to be after something. She just didn't know what it was. *Yet.*

But she'd find out.

"It isn't up to me." Tidbit was tugging on the leash, spotting a patch of grass at the end of the block he no doubt wanted to pee on. Too bad he didn't want to pee on Hartigan's shoes. "It's up to my mother. But if she asks my opinion, you'd better believe I'm going to tell her."

She turned away, starting toward that patch of grass, then gripped the leash tighter and turned back. "I don't trust you, Mr. Hartigan. And I love my mother. I'm going to be watching out for her, so whatever you have up your sleeve, it's not going to work."

"Up my sleeve . . . ?"

"If you hurt my mother, you'll have to answer to me."

"You should give me a chance, Sophie."

"Like you gave me a chance?"

"I'm not that man anymore," he said quietly. "I know you have good reason to dislike me—"

"Dislike?" Sophie managed to keep her tone even with an effort. "That's one way of putting it. And don't forget distrust."

"I'd never hurt Diana."

She stared at him. He actually sounded sincere. His forehead was creased with distress, and he gave every indication he was struggling to be nice. But nice and Doug Hartigan didn't go together. Not in her experience.

"I'm going to do my best to make sure you don't," she said evenly.

She walked away, allowing Tidbit to rush toward his patch of grass at the corner.

Hartigan couldn't be trusted. Hadn't he already ridden roughshod once over her mother's wishes? There was no reason to believe he wouldn't do it again whenever it suited him.

What in the world does she see in him? Sophie wondered in dismay. Her mother had already endured years of marriage to one difficult, demanding man. Now she was dating another. A man who'd made her daughter's life hell.

When she looked back toward the bakery, Doug Hartigan was nowhere to be seen. She headed back again, but this time, it was Martha

Davies who intercepted her, hurrying from the Cuttin' Loose.

"Got a minute, Sophie?"

Not if this is about my dating your grandson.

Today Martha's short hair was a glossy brown. Her tall, spare frame was encased in khaki pants and a bright tangerine sweater. If it hadn't been for the deep lines etched around her eyes and in the folds of her throat, she could have passed for a woman twenty years younger.

As a brisk wind whipped down from the mountains, hinting at the chill of autumn, Martha bent over to scratch Tidbit behind the ears.

"I've been meaning to talk to you about that help-wanted sign in your window. I happen to know a gal who might be perfect for the job."

"Anyone I know?" Sophie had posted the sign only yesterday, and so far had only received calls from a few teenage girls who were looking for part-time work after school. She might hire one of them later, after she saw how things were going, but right now, she really needed another pair of hands working with her and Gran from eight to five.

"Her name's Karla Sommers." Martha straightened. "Worked for me—shampoo girl—when she first came to town last year, and I can vouch for her being a hard worker. But she had to switch to waitressing five nights a week at the Double Cross because the money was better.

125

She's single and has a three-year-old son to support. See, Karla really wants to work days so her little boy can go to daycare and have a chance to play with other kids, then she could be home and with him at night."

Sophie suddenly remembered the waitress who had served her and Mia at the Double Cross the other night. The one who had been in Roy's with a little boy. "Does Karla have blond hair? Thin build?"

Martha nodded. "That's her."

"Who watches her son while she's working at the Double Cross?"

"Well, you know, that's the problem. It's not the best situation. Karla's paying a friend with three little ones of her own to keep him at her house every night while she's at work. Then she picks him up at two in the morning after closing up at the Double Cross, has to cart him out to the car, take him home, and tuck that child right back in bed again."

She paused to wave at one of her longtime customers who was stepping out of Benson's Drugstore.

"Usually little Austin, bless his heart, is up and raring to go by eight in the morning. So poor Karla's pretty much running on empty. And you know how much energy little boys that age have."

No, Sophie didn't. Not from personal

experience, anyway, much as she would have loved to. She swallowed down a pang and opened her purse, pulling out a notepad with a border of tiny mixing spoons at the top and bottom.

"Here's my cell number." She scribbled it on the pad and handed it to Martha as Tidbit barked at a pickup full of teenagers thundering down Main Street, music blasting.

"Tell her to give me a call. She's welcome to bring Austin to the interview if she'd like. I'll try to work something out."

She spent the next half hour with Sam and Denny discussing the floor plans and to-do list. By the time they'd reviewed everything and Sam had promised her the shop would be ready in time for the opening, she decided to take Tidbit for a long walk around town, and maybe even pay Gran a visit.

But a young girl's voice called her name as she started toward Spring Street and she turned to find Ivy Tanner racing toward her. Tidbit's tail started wagging a mile a minute.

Behind Ivy, Sophie saw Rafe, crossing toward her with long, easy strides.

It was a struggle not to stare at him like a teenybopper spotting a celebrity on Rodeo Drive. In his white polo shirt, Stetson, jeans, and scuffed boots, he looked every inch a rugged, sexy cowboy, as wildly gorgeous in daylight as he'd been in the dusky shadows of the Double Cross Bar and Grill. The white short-sleeved shirt not only set off his sun-browned skin but revealed biceps that stirred something seismic inside her. He moved with a lean, powerful grace that made it almost impossible for her to tear her gaze from him as Ivy skidded to a halt in front of her, grinning.

"I heard from Aunt Liss that you kept him! I wanted to come over and visit," Ivy panted, kneeling to pet the overjoyed dog. "But my dad's been busy working with our new horses and didn't have time to bring me. So he didn't have a chip?"

"No chip." Sophie watched as Tidbit licked Ivy's face and the girl giggled. "I named him Tidbit," she said inanely just as Rafe walked up.

"Tidbit. You *look* like a Tidbit!" Ivy told the dog, giving him a hug. He was still greeting her like an old, favorite friend, enthusiastically licking her face, her fingers, even her knees.

"So this is the wanderer I've been hearing about."

"Isn't he cute, Dad? I think we should go over to the shelter and adopt a new dog too. Starbucks is lonely. So can we?"

"We'll talk about it," Rafe said, his brows knitting. Sophie McPhee had barely glanced at him when he walked up. Much less said hello.

She seemed wholly intent on Ivy and Tidbit, as if he wasn't even there.

It was almost insulting.

He'd been trying to forget about her for more than a week, but the whole town had been buzzing about her and the bakery she was opening. Some were in favor of the bakery replacing Roy's, some against. No surprise there.

What did surprise him was that, if possible, Sophie looked even prettier today in her tight-fitting baby blue T-shirt and jean shorts than she had at the Double Cross Bar and Grill.

He tried not to stare at her breasts. Or at her long, tanned legs. Or at her mouth, soft and full as a summer-ripe peach.

Her hair was swept back in a ponytail, showing off a long slender neck that seemed made for a man to nibble on. When the sunlight revealed an unexpected dusting of freckles across her nose, he found her even more irresistibly sexy.

"When's the grand opening?" He nodded in the direction of the bakery. As she met his gaze, he felt his blood stir with an instant heat.

"A week from Monday, just a few days after Lissie's shower. I hope." She smiled, uncertainty flickering in those bewitching green eyes. "There's a lot of work to do before that."

"What's the name?" Ivy wanted to know.

"A Bun in the Oven."

A smile spread across the girl's face. "Cool."

Rafe's cell phone rang. "Tanner," he answered, without checking caller ID. And then something in his face changed and his entire body went still.

"When?" he said, and a frown settled over his face. "Okay, we're on our way. Ivy's with me— so we'll meet you there. Tommy, everything's going to be fine."

"That was Uncle Tommy? What's wrong?" Ivy stared at him in sudden alarm as Rafe ended the call. "Is Aunt Lissie okay?"

"She will be. She slipped in the kitchen and fell down pretty hard. And now she's having some problems."

"What kinds of problems?" There was panic in Ivy's eyes.

Sophie felt a thin finger of fear slide down her spine. Her gaze was locked on Rafe's face.

"Spotting. And . . . she's having some contractions."

No, Sophie, thought. *Oh, please, no.*

"You mean . . . the baby's coming? Now?" Ivy grabbed at his arm. "But, Dad, she can't. It's not time yet!"

Responding to the alarm in his daughter's face, Rafe pulled her close. He looked calm, but Sophie noticed the tension in his broad shoulders as he held his daughter. "Listen to me, Ives. Aunt Liss is going to be just fine. The baby too."

But as his gaze met Sophie's above Ivy's head,

the stark look in his eyes belied his reassuring words.

"It isn't *that* early, is it?" he asked her quietly, as if she should know about babies.

"No, no, not these days." Sophie gulped, thinking hard. "I think she's twenty-nine weeks now. The doctors will handle it either way, and maybe they can even slow things down."

But Ivy was growing paler by the second. As Rafe released her, Sophie reached out instinctively to touch her hand.

"The doctors will take excellent care of her and the baby, Ivy. They'll know exactly what to do."

"Sophie's right." Despite Rafe's even tone, Sophie saw the muscle clenched in his jaw and she knew he was as worried as she was.

"Aunt Liss and Uncle Tommy are headed to the hospital now. They'll be there soon. And that's where we're going too." He looked at Sophie. "Want to come with us?"

"I'll have to follow you." She glanced down at Tidbit. She couldn't leave him alone in her car in the heat, especially since she had no idea how long she'd be at the hospital.

"I'll catch up with you as soon as I drop Tidbit somewhere."

She kept her tone as level as his for Ivy's sake. "Hopefully at my grandmother's apartment."

Rafe nodded and caught Ivy's hand. Sophie watched them race toward his truck, Rafe slowing his steps to keep pace with his daughter.

Yanking out her cell, Sophie punched in her grandmother's number with shaking fingers.

Relief flooded her when Gran picked up.

"It's a good thing you called, Sophie dear. I can't find my recipe for Aunt Lucy's cherry pinwheels anywhere. Do you still have that copy I gave you? Darned if I didn't used to know it by heart, but now I just don't recall if she used a cup and a half of brown sugar or two cups and—"

"Gran, I can't talk now, but I promise I'll look for the recipe later. Can I bring Tidbit over to stay with you for a while? It's an emergency."

"Well, of course you can, but what kind of emergency?" Gran's tone rose a notch. "Are you all right, Sophie? Is your mother—"

"We're fine, but Lissie isn't." She explained what had happened as she lifted Tidbit back into the Blazer and then drove the half dozen blocks to Gran's apartment building, a few blocks south of Lonesome Way's town square.

Ten minutes later she was hurrying through the hospital, asking where Lissie had been taken. She found Rafe and Ivy in a visitors' waiting room on the second floor.

Rafe was staring down the hall, his expression grim. He'd bought Ivy a Coke from the vending machine, but she hadn't taken a sip as far as Sophie could tell. She was slumped in a chair at the small, square table, her bright curly hair tumbling over her eyes, the untouched Coke before her. Like Rafe, she was desperately watching the hallway for any sign of her Uncle Tommy—and news.

"Tommy's still in with Lissie and the doctor," Rafe explained as Sophie paused in the doorway.

"You haven't had a chance to talk to him at all? Or to anyone?" she asked quietly.

He shook his head. "They were already in the ER when we arrived. Then they moved Lissie to a room, but no one's been able—or willing," he added grimly, "to tell us anything except her room number yet. All we know is that the doctor is with her."

Sophie turned, peered down the hall. "What room are they in?"

"Two-oh-four."

She studied it, foolishly willing Tommy to come out with a relieved smile on his broad face, to tell them that Lissie and the baby were perfect. But, of course, he didn't. The glum, beige hallway was deserted, save for a nurse reading a patient chart outside a room at the end of the hall.

Ivy looked ready to burst into tears as Sophie slipped into a chair beside her. "Everything's going to be all right, you know. This might not be anything serious at all."

"Do you really think that?" Ivy's eleven-year-old eyes peered into hers, searching for truth.

"Or are you just telling me that because I'm a kid and you don't want me to cry?"

"There's nothing to cry about yet. And hopefully there won't be." Sophie kept her tone positive. "My friend Rosie went into premature labor with her son, Oliver. He was born a month early, but he was perfect. And Rosie was fine. Want to see a picture of him?"

As Ivy nodded, a gleam of hope in her eyes, Sophie flipped through the photos on her phone. Rosie had been her manager at Sweet Sensations, and her son, Oliver, was now two.

"He's so cute!" Ivy stared at Oliver's eighteen-month picture. The little boy with the stick-straight black hair and dark eyes was perched on a miniature red truck, a toy football clutched in his chubby hands.

"Your little cousin's going to be every bit as cute." Sophie tucked her phone away. The longer she kept Ivy talking, the less time the girl would have to worry. "Did you get her a shower gift yet?"

"I can't decide what to buy."

"Walmart carries some adorable mobiles. Or you can order one online. There's a great website called BabyBaby you should check out. I'll write the addy down for you." She dug in her purse for her note pad and pen. "I bought one for my friend Susan. It had ten tiny painted-wood puppies dangling from it. If that's not cute, I don't know what is."

She's good, Rafe thought, watching as he leaned against the wall near the magazine rack. He'd wanted to comfort his daughter, but he hadn't known the right things to say. Sophie seemed to be getting it right. *Reassure and distract.* She did it effortlessly.

She'd succeeded in talking Ivy down from full panic mode. Hell, she might even have calmed *him* down too, except that he'd heard the fear in Tommy's voice on the phone, along with Lissie's muffled sobs in the background. A knot of worry tore through his gut.

It tightened painfully as Ivy suddenly looked down, and he saw her lips trembling.

"Ivy, don't forget how tough your Aunt Lissie is," he said quickly. "She had to be, growing up with me and Uncle Travis and Uncle Jake for brothers."

"Aunt Liss promised I could babysit when I turn thirteen." Ivy's voice sounded muffled. "But right now I don't even care if she lets me. I just want to *have* a baby cousin. I want her to be born and to be okay." She stopped, drew a ragged breath.

"She will be okay," Sophie said. "She'll be great. Scares like this happen, they're not all that uncommon. And everything usually works out fine. Little babies—and their mothers—are much stronger than most people think."

"They are?" Ivy searched her face again,

135

doubtful. Then peered at her father. "Really?"

"Oh, yeah." Rafe cast about frantically in his mind. "Did I ever tell you about Uncle Travis, when he was born?" Easing into a chair at the table across from her, he covered Ivy's small hand with his big one. "He was two months premature. He came out a tiny, wrinkled, bawling little squirt no bigger than my fist, and he had to stay in the hospital a spell before they'd let him come home. But he toughed it out. And look at him now."

"He's as big as you, Dad."

"Almost as big as me," he corrected, with a grin. "He's only six-one, the runt of the litter. But we kept him anyway."

Ivy laughed through the tears glimmering in her eyes.

"Girls can be tough too," she said shakily.

"Don't I know it." Rafe spoke lightly, but Sophie heard something more in his voice—tenderness. And she realized as he looked across the table at his daughter that he was talking about her. *Ivy's* toughness.

Ivy had toughed out her mother leaving her. Leaving them both.

What must that have felt like? she wondered with a wrench of her heart. Her own father, despite all of his strictness and demands—and his cheating—had loved his family in his own hard-ass way, stayed with them, and would have continued to stay with them even after his infidelity was uncovered, if her mother had allowed it.

And her mother . . . Well, her mother had always been there for her and Wes, a gentle buttress, offering a soft smile and steady, encouraging words) whenever Hoot's expectations seemed impossibly harsh.

But to have one of them leave? On purpose, and not come back?

Sophie knew what it felt like to be left. The pain of what Ned had done to her still ripped through her like a hawk's claws—and she was an adult.

Ivy had been a young child when her mother vanished from her life.

She couldn't even begin to comprehend that kind of shock and loss.

But fortunately for Ivy, she had Rafe. He was a very different sort of father than Hoot had been to his children. As worried as Rafe was about Lissie right now, his entire focus was Ivy. Reassuring and encouraging her, trying to take her mind off what might be happening in room 204.

She took a breath, saying a silent prayer for Lissie and the baby. And she said more as another hour passed.

Why hadn't anyone come out to tell them what was happening? She was trying not to read too much into that when she looked up and saw Tommy striding down the hall toward the waiting room. Sophie's heart constricted at the raw tension in his face.

"Lissie's doing okay," he said immediately as they all jumped to their feet.

"The baby?" Rafe asked.

"Fine—for the moment." He swallowed hard. "The doctors think that damned fall might have brought on early labor. They've given Lissie some meds, which they hope will stop it. We'll see. We'll know more in a few hours."

"When can Aunt Liss go home?" Ivy asked in a small voice.

"Maybe in a couple of hours, honey, once the meds start to work. With any luck, sometime tonight. She's going to need a lot of bed rest though."

"I'll come and help," Ivy said quickly.

"So will I," Sophie added.

"What about that fall she took?" Rafe still looked worried. "She break anything?"

"Only her pride." Tommy drew a breath and grinned with the look of a man who'd been through a meat grinder and came out in one piece on the other side. "Don't be scared," he told Ivy. "It seems like the docs have this under control."

Sophie felt relief as powerful as a northern gale sweep through her. It was all she could do to hold back tears of gratitude and relief.

"When can we see her?" she asked.

"Now. But only two at a time, that's what Doc Laughlin said. She's worn out, her hip is bruised, and she needs to rest. She . . ." He shook his head, and sighed. "I've never seen Lissie look so drained. But I know it'll do her good to see all of you."

Ivy bolted toward the door. "Come on, Dad, what are you waiting for?"

But Rafe held back. He glanced at Sophie. "Why don't you go in first. I'll wait and take the next round."

The unexpected kindness took her by surprise. But it wasn't right. He and Ivy should see Lissie first—they were family.

"Go in with Ivy." Her eyes met his. "Now that I know Lissie's all right, I can wait."

He nodded but didn't follow Ivy immediately. He held her gaze for a moment, and Sophie felt a rush of warmth. She was the first to turn away, picking up her purse and slinging it over her shoulder.

Her emotions were running too high. She needed to get herself under control. When she looked up, Rafe had joined Ivy in the hall and they hurried toward Lissie's room.

Sophie thought she was fine, but when she looked at Tommy, and no one else was around, suddenly the tears that had been threatening sprang to her eyes.

"Go ahead and cry." Tommy hugged her. "I'd cry too, but if Lissie sees me bawling, she'll think something more is wrong and that I haven't told her the whole deal. So I gotta hang tough."

Sophie blotted her tears with her fingers. "You're doing better than me. Thank God they're both all right." She hugged him back. "Tell you what—I'll come by later tonight and bring supper for the two of you. And I'm available tomorrow to keep her company and make sure she stays off her feet. Whatever you need."

"You don't have to do that, Sophie."

"I want to. I'm going to leave now so the three of you can visit more with her. Tell Lissie I'll see her tonight."

"But—"

"No buts." Sophie was already out the door. She turned and sent Tommy a watery smile before heading for the elevator.

Riding down to the first floor, she thought again about Rafe telling Ivy about Travis's birth. She had to admit that despite all of her reservations about him, he was a great father. He was impressively attuned to Ivy's moods and needs, as much as any father could be with a girl on the verge of adolescence. And he was a good brother to Lissie too, she reflected as she raced outside to the hospital parking lot.

Which suddenly made her think of Wes. He'd moved away so long ago, she barely remembered what it was like to have a brother. Wes had come in for her wedding to Ned, but it had been touch-and-go up until the last minute as to whether or not he'd really show, since their father had been attending, and Wes couldn't stand being in the same room as Hoot.

And she hadn't seen Wes since that day. He popped her an occasional e-mail. Very occasional. But he wasn't exactly in her life and didn't seem to care that she wasn't in his.

He called their mother about once a month, she'd heard. And that was it.

Sophie shook off the sense of loneliness that suddenly enveloped her as she remembered things were strained with her mom right now too. As she put the Blazer in gear and headed toward the parking lot exit, she reminded herself that Lissie was okay, the baby was okay, and that was all that mattered at the moment.

So what if her own family was a mess? They'd always been a bit of a mess. Whose family wasn't?

But she kept thinking back to the gentleness Rafe had shown toward Ivy. She could still see the tenderness she'd glimpsed in his eyes as he spoke to her.

That tenderness didn't fit with the image she'd always held of him. Not at all. Even though she'd been revising that image slightly ever since the night in the Double Cross, the discrepancy unnerved her. So he wasn't the same reckless, immature boy who'd seduced every girl in sight and chased her and Lissie out of the barn with ferocious threats years ago—that didn't make him Prince Charming. It didn't make him someone she ought to be thinking about—even as a friend.

He was kryptonite—at least, he was for her. She'd always had a crush on Rafe Tanner and maybe she always would.

Which was why she needed to stay far away from him.

And she promised herself she would.

Buck Crenshaw tossed a glowing cigarette butt out his window as he waited for the light at Main and Third to change.

He'd been sent to town to buy feed and lumber for the Hanging W ranch and had taken a little detour to grab a beer at the Lucky Punch Saloon on his way. No one needed to know how long his errands had taken. So what if he was blowing off an extra hour of work? They weren't paying him enough for all the crap he did in a day.

So he was in the right place at the right time to see Sophie McPhee's Blazer cruise through the green light while he waited on the red.

She was headed toward the south edge of town.

Hoot McPhee's stuck-up daughter never even noticed him. *Why would she?* He was a nobody, a lowly scumbag ranch hand. She was the rich, snotty brat of a man he loathed even more than his own father.

On impulse, he jerked the steering wheel sharply and followed her. Not too close—it wouldn't be a good thing for her to see him. But he was curious where she was going.

He tapped out another cigarette and squinted at his watch. No one would know he was following the McPhee bitch on the Hanging W's dime. It sure as hell beat going back to that dammed ranch and doing shit work along with all the losers on that crew.

The truth was, he'd never meant to shove Wade Holden into the McPhee woman that night at the Double Cross. It had been a total accident—and he hadn't even recognized her until afterward.

But did Rafe Tanner give him the benefit of the doubt? No way. Just like Tanner hadn't given him the benefit of the doubt before cutting him loose from Sage Ranch.

Maybe he'd made a couple of mistakes, but who didn't? So he'd left the dammed push broom lying across the barn floor. Nobody died. The horses were all fine. And even if some horse did get hurt, have to be put down, Tanner could afford it. He'd just buy another one.

The thing was, Tanner had it in for him.

Well, payback time would come. Tanner would pay one of these days for firing him, and for what had happened last week at the Double Cross.

But how do I pay back a dead man? Buck wondered sourly, taking a deep drag on the cigarette. His fingers drummed on the steering wheel. He'd been too young back when Hoot McPhee was alive to kick his ass. He hadn't been stupid enough to try.

But now . . .

He was old enough to stand up for himself and kick some McPhee butt. Only Hoot wasn't around.

But his pretty little daughter sure was. And if Hoot McPhee was watching from his private little spot in hell, he wouldn't like it one bit. And there wasn't a damned thing he could do about it.

Buck pulled into a space half a block back when she parked near the Lonesome Circle apartments and sashayed her way inside the front entrance without so much as glancing around.

When opportunity knocks, you answer it. Isn't that what his ma had always told him?

With the cigarette dangling from his lips, he waited, watching until old Hoot's girl came out of that apartment building again. Now she was holding the leash of some stupid little dog.

He waited some more, thinking, thinking hard. He sat there until she got in her rig and drove away. Then he flung the butt out the window and grunted.

Hoot, old man, payback starts now. And it's a bitch.

Chapter Ten

Sophie found a note from her mother on the kitchen table when she arrived home.

Having supper in Bozeman. Pot roast in fridge. Won't be late.

Sophie knew exactly who she must be having supper with in Bozeman. But her mom still couldn't bring herself to mention Doug Hartigan's name to her.

That says something right there, she thought, and tossed the note in the trash.

Unloading the groceries she'd bought for Lissie and Tommy's supper, she realized that they'd need to hash this whole thing out sooner rather than later. But it wouldn't be an easy conversation. She had no right to dictate to her mother who she could or couldn't date, but it was impossible to understand what her mom saw in that stick-up-his-butt geometry teacher —or how she could have any kind of feelings for a man who'd made Sophie's junior year of high school a raging hell.

Her mom knew everything she'd gone through trying to pass Geometry. And she knew just what a rock and a hard place Hartigan had placed her in.

He hadn't shown any sympathy for her struggle to master his favorite subject, and her father had for a long time refused to accept her nearly failing grade as evidence of anything but slacking off.

Sure, her mom had hired a tutor to try to help her get by. She'd even gone to school to talk to Hartigan about how hard Sophie was working—not that it had done any good.

Was that when this all started? she wondered suddenly, going still as a stone as she was about to pour kibble in Tidbit's bowl. Had her mom become attracted to Doug Hartigan all the way back when Sophie was in high school?

No, it couldn't be. Bad enough her father had cheated—her mother wasn't the type. Diana had been the peacemaker in the family, the one who tried to balance out the rough edges and soften the harsh standards of a demanding husband and father.

Despite all of Hoot's flaws, including his relentless toughness, he'd loved them all—her mother, Wes, and Sophie. And her mother had loved him back. Sophie had seen that, seen the love between them.

But what the hell did her mother see in Doug Hartigan?

Sophie's brows knit in frustration as she tossed together a salad for Lissie and Tommy, then spooned a light Dijon sauce over chicken breasts before sliding them into the oven to bake alongside a pan of rosemary potatoes.

She didn't linger long after delivering the meal. She stayed only long enough to reassure herself that Lissie was all right. Tommy told her the meds were working, and the contractions had stopped. Lissie looked wan and exhausted in the big king-sized bed, but she'd managed a tired smile when Sophie hugged her and smoothed her hair back from her face.

Still, it was dark as she headed home, Tidbit on the passenger seat beside her, only a misty half-moon swimming in the star-studded vastness of a purple sky. Night had brought shockingly cold air sweeping down from the Crazies, a biting reminder that summer was on its way out the door.

Sophie didn't know if her mom would be back from her date yet, but if she wasn't and hadn't already lit a fire, Sophie intended to do that straight off, before getting to work.

Her to-do list was nearly as long as Squirrel Road and included writing up a final menu for the bakery's opening week, checking on delivery of all her ingredients and the additional bakeware and mixing bowls she still needed, interviewing Karla Sommers, and a dozen other tasks. She was so engrossed in reviewing everything that still had to be done that she didn't even notice anything wrong until there was a jolt that made her hands tighten on the steering wheel.

She felt one side of the Blazer sag, even as the front end almost swerved out of control.

Damn it. A flat tire.

Quickly, she managed to steer the rig to the side of the road, then grabbed the flashlight she kept in the glove compartment and hopped out, shivering in the frosty night.

Exactly as she'd expected, the right rear tire splayed against the gravel. With a sigh, she pulled out her phone to call Tommy and ask if he could come help her change it. At the same time, headlights swarmed up the road toward her.

Blinded, she waited for the oncoming truck to pass by, but instead, it pulled right over, coming to a sudden halt.

Sophie whipped the flashlight up in the silent darkness—and there was Rafe striding toward her.

"Easy. Do you really have to shine that thing in my face?" he asked as he stopped in front of her.

"Sorry." Sophie turned the illumination toward the ground. "I was just about to call Tommy and ask him to give me a hand. I've got a flat."

"Yeah, you sure do." He frowned, bending down to get a better look at the tires. "More than one."

"What?"

He circled the Blazer. "Both of your front tires are low."

"I thought it was the back one."

She whipped the flashlight beam toward the front tires, one after the other, and realized he was right. Both were deflated, though not flat. *Yet*.

"Give me that thing for a second." Rafe held out his hand for the flashlight. He crouched beside the left rear tire, shone the light. Then moved to the right one and did the same.

Tidbit stood on his hind paws, watching through the side window as Rafe and Sophie huddled in the darkness.

"Two flat, two more than halfway there," Sophie muttered. She hugged her arms around herself as a sharp gust whipped down from the mountains and chilled her clear through, despite the thick sweater she'd thrown on before leaving for Lissie's. "That can't be a coincidence."

"Someone let the air out. There was a narrow puncture on each tire. The type that could've come from the tip of a knife blade." Rafe handed her back the flashlight. "Do you know anyone who'd want to do that?"

Sophie could only blink at him for a moment as a different kind of chill blew through her. "No. I don't have any enemies in Lonesome Way—or back in San Francisco, if that's what you mean. My ex is a jerk, but he's not the type to come down here and let the air out of my tires, or hire anyone to do it. Besides, I'm the injured party; if anyone was letting the air out of someone's tires, that would be *me*. This doesn't make sense."

Rafe said nothing.

"It could have been a kid, pulling a prank. Some teenager in town, maybe while we were inside the hospital. Or when I was picking Tidbit up from Gran's apartment."

His eyes narrowed in the darkness. "Could be. But I think you should call Sheriff Hodge. This needs to be reported."

"What's the point?" Sophie drew a breath. "There's no way he'll be able to figure out who did it. Besides, I think it must have been random. Just some bored kid wanting to make mischief."

But even to herself, her words lacked conviction. She had a strange feeling about this, and she couldn't explain it.

Her stomach plummeted as she realized she wouldn't find a tow truck or gas station open at this hour. And she had only one spare tire. Which meant she'd have to leave the Blazer here tonight, get it towed in the morning.

Rafe studied her in the darkness. "You all right?"

"Fine. A little freaked out, that's all." She forced her shoulders to relax. "Where's Ivy?" She was suddenly aware that the two of them were all alone out here in the vast charcoal shadows of the mountains and the endless night sky.

"Shannon's parents invited her to go with them to the movies over in Livingston. After everything that happened today, I thought it would be good for her to go out and have some fun."

"And you were on your way to visit Lissie and Tommy," Sophie guessed. "I'm sorry. It was nice of you to stop. If you want to see them—"

"It can wait until tomorrow. You're shivering."

He reached out and snagged her hand in his large one.

A different kind of shiver stole through her. Electricity thrummed beneath her skin as his strong fingers closed around her hand.

For a moment she clung to him, to his big calloused palm, the broad knuckles, the warmth and strength of his grip. A thread of fire flowed through her fingers, up her wrist, straight to her heart, and she was stunned by the burn. It nearly made her jump. At least it knocked some sense back into her, and she quickly drew a breath and slipped her hand away.

"Any chance I can hitch a ride home with you?" She hoped the question sounded casual and would distract him from noticing how flustered she'd been at his touch.

"I'm not about to leave my sister's best friend standing out here by the side of the road."

He said it with a smile. Almost the exact words he'd spoken that long-ago day when she was fifteen. Sophie felt color flooding her cheeks and was grateful for the darkness.

"I owe you," she said lightly and turned away.

Keep it cool, Rafe told himself as she hurried toward the passenger side of her car. He beat her there and opened the door for her to lift her dog from the seat. As Rafe slammed the door shut, he reminded himself that he needed to be careful. Sure, Sophie was beautiful. And warm. And sexy as hell.

But that was no excuse for taking her hand, wanting to look into those stunning green eyes. Or trying to picture her in his bed.

You shouldn't have touched her. She's a complication. A complication your life doesn't need. Ivy doesn't need.

But maybe she was what he needed. . . .

The thought popped, unbidden, into his mind.

He didn't want to go there. Didn't want to explore the buried loneliness he'd learned to ignore. The longing sometimes in the middle of the night to hold a woman he loved in his arms.

Despite all the women he'd known and taken to his bed—or to his hayloft, the backseat of his car, or Larkspur Point, Lonesome Way's favorite make-out spot—he'd never loved any of them.

Not even Lynelle.

Oh, he'd thought he'd loved her. He'd loved

the way she looked and the way she smelled and the way she flirted with him when he met her in that bar in Bozeman the first time. He'd loved the carefree abandon she exhibited in everything she did—but he hadn't loved her.

He'd married her impulsively and she'd gotten pregnant within the first few weeks. Knowing he had a child on the way had changed Rafe in a profound way he'd never seen coming.

But Lynelle had never changed. Even after Ivy was born, she'd never even tried to tame the carefree spirit or wanderlust or just plain irresponsibility—whatever you wanted to call it—that drove her, seven years later, to tear out of their lives in a cloud of highway dust.

It struck him suddenly that from what Sophie had said back there, her ex had been no prize either.

Just drive, he thought. *Get her out of your head. Sophie McPhee, her ex, they're none of your business.*

The pale half-moon slipped behind a cloud as he stared straight ahead and drove toward the Good Luck ranch.

Sophie didn't want to think about what she'd felt when Rafe had reached for her hand. Or why he'd taken it. She pushed away the insane feelings that had tumbled through her out in the darkness with him back on that lonely road.

It had almost felt like they were the only two

153

people in Montana at that moment, as if the moon were hanging in the sky for them, as if the night were hiding them from everything and everyone. As if they could have done whatever they wanted out there in the cold, windswept darkness and no one would know, there'd be no questions or answers, no words or consequences. . . .

"Your ex." Rafe couldn't help it. He had to know. "Sounds like a real jerk. What'd he do to you? Or don't you want to talk about it?" he added, sensing her sudden tension beside him.

"What didn't he do?" Sophie stared straight ahead as Tidbit shifted on her lap and licked her hand. "He lied. Cheated on me with another woman. Made promises he didn't mean to keep. Sorry, it sounds like a bad country western song."

"What kinds of promises?"

She hesitated so long he thought she wasn't going to answer. Then she spoke, her voice quiet.

"I wanted a family. Ned claimed he did too. But he was just stringing me along while he was looking for a new job and sleeping with the woman who eventually hired him. Now"—she swallowed and forced herself to say the words—"he's with her. She's pregnant. His baby."

Rafe's eyes narrowed in the darkness.

"Sorry. I shouldn't have brought it up." He found himself wishing he could get his hands on Sophie's ex-husband for maybe five minutes. It wouldn't take any more than that to rearrange his face.

"The funny thing is," she said slowly. "I'm not. Sorry, I mean. Not anymore. I wasted too many days waiting for him, believing in him. At least now my life isn't on hold anymore."

Rafe knew what it was like to have your life on hold. In a lot of ways, his had been on hold since the day Lynelle left.

He hadn't allowed himself any involvements, any real relationships, other than his family. Keeping Ivy safe and happy and secure, running the ranch, and taking care of his family and his horses were his only priorities and focuses.

And he didn't regret it one bit. It was the way things were—and his choice that they be that way. But sometimes, at family gatherings, he looked at Lissie and Tommy, at his cousin Deck and his wife Leigh, saw the way they gazed at each other, and knew he was missing out on something. Something special. Something that with Lynelle he'd never known.

"It's hell when someone close to you lets you down," he said, glancing quickly at her profile.

Rafe turned onto Daisy Lane, drove toward the sprawling ranch house. The truck rolled past the spot where he'd let her off when she was fifteen, where she'd planted that kiss on him. And then his headlights caught a strange rig parked yards from the porch.

Who's here? Sophie wondered, her heart jumping. She leaned forward on the seat for a better look. *Could her mother and Doug Hartigan be back from dinner already?*

But as a man stepped out of the rig, she realized it wasn't Hartigan. Rafe's headlights illuminated a younger man, stocky, bull-necked, someone in his early thirties.

Roger Hendricks.

Even after all these years, Sophie recognized the playground bully.

"Oh, no," she murmured. "Crap."

"Hendricks?" Rafe frowned. "You expecting him?"

"No. God, no." She opened the door of the truck and stepped down, reaching for Tidbit. Rafe was out of the truck before she'd barely set the dog on the ground.

Roger started forward, smiling at Sophie—but his smile faded when he saw Rafe coming up to stand beside her.

"Sophie? I'm . . . uh, sorry. I thought . . ."

"What are you doing here, Roger?" Sophie asked, though she was fairly certain she knew.

"My aunt Dorothy . . . she suggested I come see you. She wouldn't give me your phone number, she just said something about you being back in town and—" He broke off, flushing. And glancing at Rafe, who was watching him in silence.

"Were you two . . . on a date?" Roger asked peevishly.

"That's none of your business," Rafe said.

"No, we weren't." Sophie shook her head. "I think there was a misunderstanding, Roger. I'm not dating. Anyone."

"Well, then, why did my aunt—" He scowled. Glanced again at Rafe, tall and implacable in front of him. Suspicion flickered in his square, pugnacious face. "If you weren't on a date, then why are you with *him?*"

"She doesn't owe you any explanations, Hendricks."

"We weren't on a date. I'm not dating," Sophie repeated quickly. "I think you should go, Roger. It's late."

He opened his mouth to argue, being a belligerent sort by nature, but one look into Rafe Tanner's eyes made his lips snap together.

"Fine. I'm gone. I was never here. Maybe I'll see you . . . in town, Sophie," he added. He gave her a smile, which Sophie was sure he thought charismatic, but it was a little too sure of itself and bordered on creepy.

The smile evaporated though when he glanced at Rafe. Turning on his heel, Hendricks stalked back to his rig and clambered in.

Rafe didn't take his eyes off the man until he disappeared inside the cab. "I'll walk you inside."

As Sophie and Tidbit crossed the porch and entered the ranch house ahead of him, Rafe held back, keeping an eye on the rig until Hendricks had backed all the way down Daisy Lane and roared off.

"What was that all about?" he asked as he followed Sophie into the brightly lit kitchen.

"My grandmother and her friends." She set a bowl of kibble on the floor for Tidbit. "They're pushing me to start dating. Apparently, they're determined to make my life miserable. Don't you dare laugh," she warned, as a grin spread across Rafe's face.

"The road to hell is paved with good intentions."

"Tell me about it." The faint melody of the wind chime tinkled its sweet music through the kitchen window. But all she could think of was Rafe.

He looked so good, standing there, all dark and rugged and male. She needed to fight the pull of attraction that was making her linger here with him, when she knew she should ask him to leave.

But he'd stopped to help her, given her a ride home, and yes, scared off Roger Hendricks by his mere size and presence.

She didn't want him to leave.

She wanted him to stay. . . .

Remember Ned. Remember how great things started out in the beginning, and then look what he did to you. You can't get involved with anyone, not again, not until you're Gran's age, or at least, Mom's.

The worst thing she could do was give in to the impulses that made her want to wrap her arms around Rafe's neck and kiss him again. Right here in the kitchen.

This couldn't be the same stupid pull of attraction that had betrayed her into kissing him all those years ago, could it? It had to be a new pull.

And she didn't want a new pull. Toward anyone. And especially not toward him.

"I don't suppose I could trouble you for a cup of coffee?"

He leaned against the counter, relaxed and gorgeous.

How could she say no after what he'd done tonight? It would be just plain rude to refuse the man a cup of coffee, kick him out the door.

"Of course. Sorry. Decaf or regular?"

"Loaded." His grin this time was slow, heart-stopping. "Hit me with everything you've got."

His words triggered a mental image of the two of them upstairs on her old bed, locked together in wild, frantic sex.

"You're on."

She busied herself measuring out coffee, setting out mugs and napkins on the table. Because she couldn't resist, she brought out the sugar cookies Gran had sent home with her this afternoon, setting them on a plate.

"Why'd you leave the hospital today without seeing Lissie?"

His question caught her by surprise and she turned to stare at him as the coffee brewed, the aroma filling the kitchen.

"I knew I'd see her tonight when I brought supper over. I wanted to give all of you more time to visit."

"Lissie loves you like a sister, Sophie. You weren't intruding." He eased away from the counter, ambled toward her. "I doubt you ever could."

What did that mean?

Rafe smiled at her questioning look. He forced himself to stop right in front of her, close but not too close. If he moved only a few inches closer, her breasts would be pressed against his chest. Their hips would be almost touching. He'd be able to smell the fragrance of her hair.

In that pale blue sweater and jeans, her toffee hair loose and flowing around her face, she looked more beautiful than ever, and damned kissable.

And ever since they'd rolled down Daisy Lane in his truck tonight, he'd had one thing on his mind. Kissing Sophie McPhee.

Don't do it, a voice inside his head warned. The smart, mature, post-Lynelle voice. But he was no longer listening. Maybe a part of the reckless boy he'd once been was back, haunting him, taking over the solid, sensible man he'd become. Instinct was taking over.

A raw primal instinct.

Every fiber of his male being was telling him to kiss this warm, beautiful woman who'd been right under his nose for most of his life.

"You fit, Sophie. Wherever you go. With the Tanners, with this town. There's something about you. You're easy to be around. To have around. In some ways," he added softly.

Her breath caught in her throat. "What's that supposed to mean?" she finally managed to ask.

He gently took her by the arms and backed her up against the wall. "It means I'm finding it anything but easy being around you right now. Without kissing you, that is."

Sophie stared into his eyes. Her heart began to hammer so loudly she was sure he could hear it.

"We don't want to go there," she whispered.

"Speak for yourself." With a grin that could have melted North Pole icicles, Rafe wrapped his arms around her waist. "I have to tell you the truth. Ever since I saw you at the Double Cross, I've been wondering what it would be like. To kiss you for real this time. Just one kiss. The last time, you were doing all the heavy lifting. This time will be different."

Will be? Sophie thought, dazed.

Just go for it, a tiny voice inside her prodded. *Rafe Tanner wants to kiss you. What are you waiting for? One kiss.*

It wouldn't mean anything and it wouldn't lead to anything and maybe if she just got it out of her system—got *him* out of her system—one kiss would be enough. There was nothing between them, of course, no feelings. And they weren't going to start having some crazy affair and bring full-blown sex in to complicate everything. It was just one kiss. . . .

"Do you always overthink everything?" Amusement tinged his voice. "You didn't when you were fifteen."

"I've changed a lot since I was fifteen. In case you haven't noticed." She tipped her head back, almost dizzy, and stared up into that wickedly handsome face she'd fallen in love with when she was a completely different person, a foolish young girl, knowing nothing of the world.

And listening only to the wildness of her heart.

One kiss. Get him out of your system. . . .

"I need to think. I *should* think, but I don't want to," she murmured suddenly. His midnight eyes lit with surprise—and laughter. She grasped his shirt front, yanked him closer. "Don't let me think, Rafe. I'm so damned tired of thinking. And I don't want to—not right now."

Rafe didn't need to be asked twice, having been brought up to oblige a lady.

His mouth brushed hers. Gently at first, then the kiss deepened as her lips parted, welcoming him, no, *beckoning* him, and he lost himself in the musky sweetness of her. It was a kiss of rose petals and dynamite. Softness and sex.

Her mouth was hot, willing, delectable. The peach-sweet taste and scent of her filled him, and a dark heat spread through him, wild as a mountain fire. When her arms encircled his neck, Rafe gripped her closer, angled his hips against hers, and slipped his tongue deeper inside her mouth.

He was met with a whimper of pleasure and a ferocious sweep of her tongue against his. She melted against him, and everything else faded away—the kitchen, the smell of fresh coffee, the solid old ranch house where they stood together in a whirlwind of heat.

He deepened the kiss, his hands roving over her body, slipping beneath her sweater. Inside her low-cut bra to cup her breast. She moaned in pleasure and he pushed her backward then, pressing her against the wall.

And that's when he heard the car door slam.

Sophie heard it at the same time. The sound ripped her from a daze of exploding pleasure so intense she could barely focus, but that thudding door, and one quick bark from Tidbit, had her cursing fate and shoving him away.

The sound of her mother's voice reached her . . .

and then she heard Mr. Hartigan. Gravel crunched—a car was backing out of Daisy Lane. . . .

Why hadn't she heard it coming *down* the lane? Never mind, she knew why.

"Oh, God." She yanked her sweater down, pressed her hands to her hot cheeks. With a low groan, Rafe made a beeline for the kitchen chair as the front door opened with a faint creak.

"Sophie?" As her mother sailed into the kitchen, Rafe stood up, as casual as if he'd been stopping by for years at the McPhees' to chat on a daily basis.

"Oh. Rafe." She stared at him in surprise. "You know, I thought that looked like your truck."

"Nice to see you, Ms. McPhee."

Diana glanced between Sophie and Rafe for three long beats, which made Sophie's nerves jangle, but her mother didn't say anything else, except to ask Rafe how Ivy was doing.

That's when Sophie trusted her voice enough to fill her in about Lissie spending most of the day at the hospital.

"But she and the baby are okay? Will she be up for the shower next Saturday?" She turned to Sophie, who was now pouring coffee into Rafe's mug. "Perhaps you and Mia should consider postponing it."

"She doesn't want anything postponed, Mom. And you know, Lissie. Once she makes up her mind, there's no changing it. Besides, the doctor says she'll be fine. Would you like some coffee?"

"At this hour? No, I'm going on up to bed. But where's your Blazer, Sophie?"

"Languishing on Squirrel Road. Waiting to hitch a ride with a tow truck."

It was Rafe who explained about the flat tires. Sophie could barely concentrate enough to remember to turn off the coffeemaker. Her lips still felt hot, and her entire body was jangling with sensation.

"Four flat tires?" Her mother frowned. "That's very strange."

"It was just some kid, pulling a prank, Mom."

"A pretty serious prank, if you ask me. Rafe, it's lucky you happened along."

"Always happy to help a lady."

Diana looked from one to the other of them. She suddenly turned toward the stairs. "Time for me to turn in. Good night, Rafe, Sophie. See you in the morning, dear," she added.

When her mother had disappeared upstairs, Sophie closed her eyes and sagged back against the counter.

When she opened them, Rafe was watching her, a grin on his face. He looked unruffled, handsomer than sin, and completely at ease.

"That was close," he said.

"You think this is funny?"

"Don't you?"

Not one bit. She had to break loose from the spell he'd cast over her, and she quickly moved away, gathering the coffee cups, bringing them to the sink.

Rafe had barely touched his coffee. He'd only touched her. The trouble was, she wanted him to touch her again. Touch her more . . .

"Shannon's folks will be dropping Ivy off soon." He sounded regretful. "I need to be home when she gets there. But for the record"—he moved close to her and lowered his voice—"that was some kiss." He couldn't help grinning at her. "I guess now we're even."

"Hardly." It took all of Sophie's willpower not to look away from those dangerous blue eyes that had the power to mesmerize her. "I can't believe you brought that up. Or even that you remember."

"Believe it. You're pretty unforgettable."

Rafe Tanner was flirting with her.

Sophie fought the urge to throw caution to the winds, twine her arms around his neck, and kiss him again. To seize his hand and run with him out to his truck. Or into the night.

And to do what? Strip off her clothes, then his? Have wild monkey sex with him beneath the stars?

She was crazy. She'd finally done it, she'd lost her mind.

"This isn't happening," she said suddenly,

panic rushing through her. She managed to speak calmly, though the way he was looking at her was setting her blood on fire. "I mean it, Rafe. We shouldn't do this—whatever *this* is. We have to forget what happened tonight."

"I'm not sure I can do that." His eyes glinted as he brushed a strand of hair from her face, studying her in silence. "Can you?"

"Yes." She said it too quickly though. He pulled her closer.

"I don't believe you."

"You should."

She stared into his eyes for a long moment. Rafe brushed his knuckles gently along her cheek.

"I won't push you, Sophie. You decide when—if—you want to do this—any of this—again." That heart-stopping grin that spread upward to light his eyes made her heart start to race. "But I can promise I'm going to try like hell to convince you."

Without another word, he walked out of the kitchen. She heard the gentle thud of the front door.

Chapter Eleven

Early the next morning, Sophie called for a tow truck. Then she let Tidbit out, poured herself a mug of coffee, and decided to go in search of her mother.

She carried the steaming mug with her as she stepped outside into a sharply cool day, which felt more like September than late August. But she barely noticed the chill as she made her way toward the old barn, now her mother's workroom.

Sure enough, her mom was there as she'd been most mornings, bent over her worktable, safety glasses engulfing most of her face as she drilled holes in hollow copper tubing. But she paused as Sophie entered, then set the drill and tubing down on the work surface crammed with hanging metal chains, drill bits, pliers, a wire cutter, glue, and a basket filled with glorious bits of stained glass, rose quartz, amethyst, shells, and beads of every color.

"Sorry to interrupt, Mom."

"Sophie? What is it?" Her mother lifted the safety glasses off and set them down.

"We need to talk." Sophie spoke quietly. "If you want me to, I can come back later, but . . . isn't it time for us to clear the air?"

"I'd say it's past time." Her mother came around the worktable, then leaned against it. "Let me start. I'm sorry I didn't tell you right away about Doug. What's that expression? He who hesitates, is lost."

Sophie moved closer, past the old wooden shelving where wind chimes were displayed on tiny hooks. "You don't have to apologize. You're free to date whoever you want."

Ted Bundy. Son of Sam. Doug Hartigan.

"What I don't understand, Mom, is why you want *him*. You can do a whole lot better. I bet Gran and Martha and Dorothy can make up an entire list."

Her mother's mouth twisted into a wry smile. "You don't know Doug," she said softly. "At least you don't know the man I do."

Moving forward, she snagged Sophie's arm. "Why don't we go back to the house? I could use some coffee myself."

When they were seated at the kitchen table with toast, cherry jam, and coffee, and Tidbit was noisily scarfing down his kibble, Diana looked Sophie squarely in the eye.

"I know you'll find this hard to believe, but Doug Hartigan is a good man. He's kind and he's intelligent. He tells dumb jokes, but they make me laugh. And you'll never believe this, but he plays the violin—beautifully. Math and music skills are closely linked, you know. You should hear him play sometime."

Sophie's fingers tightened on her mug. She wasn't about to dignify that with an answer.

"Sophie, you're not the same girl that you were back in high school," her mother pointed out with a shake of her head. "And Doug isn't the same man he was when he was your teacher either. He's been through some terrible things. He's different now than he was back then."

Sophie picked up a slice of toast, then set it down on the plate, no longer hungry. "What sorts of things?"

"His wife was sick. She had brain cancer. Since they lived in Timber Springs and Doug drove in every day just to teach at Lonesome Way High School, not a lot of people here knew him well, or had any idea what he was going through. His wife's surgeries, chemo, hospitalizations. They had no children, it was just the two of them. And he loved her very much. It was a horrible time for him, Sophie."

As Sophie started to speak, her mother interrupted. "I know, I know, it's not an excuse for how hard he was on you—and you're not the only one he treated that way. Doug has told me there were a half dozen students whose parents complained about him. He admits he was unfair, that he demanded too much. Especially from students who were struggling."

"Well, it's taken him long enough, hasn't it?" Sophie kept her voice level but still felt a twinge of remorse as her mother's gaze fell on her, looking chagrined.

"He's the first to admit he went overboard. He couldn't control what was happening in his own life—knowing he was losing Mary. But he thought he could control his classroom, the knowledge he was trying to impart to his students. And he took it much too far. He's retired now, you know."

"Making the school safe once again for Lonesome Way's teenagers."

"Sophie."

She sighed, reined in her anger, and took a breath.

"I'm trying to understand this, Mom. I really am."

Tidbit trotted over, looking up at her hopefully, and she scratched his ears. He rewarded her by looking at her with adoring dark eyes and relentlessly licking her arm.

Why couldn't love between humans be as simple as between a human and a dog?

Sophie read the distress in her mother's face. "What do you want me to say? I don't like the man and I don't trust him, but it's your choice, Mom." She took a breath. "I guess I can handle it. It's not as if you're marrying him anytime soon."

"N-no." Her mother's cheeks flushed. "Not anytime soon."

Whoa. Sophie stared at her. "So . . . he was telling the truth? This is *serious?* You're actually thinking about marriage?"

"Who's to say what's serious these days?" Her mother flushed a deeper shade of pink and took a quick gulp of coffee. "But you should know, we *are* going on a little trip together. There's a crafts show coming up in Helena. Doug's coming with me, to help me sell my wind chimes and some of my beaded purses and jewelry. We'll only be gone a few nights," she added quickly. As she watched Sophie for a reaction, her gaze was guarded but hopeful. "You . . . won't mind?"

Sophie bit back the truth. Yes, she damn well minded. What was wrong with her mother? The most grounded, sensible, practical woman she knew was making a terrible mistake.

"It's your life," she said at last, trying her best to hide the dismay flooding her. "Just . . . be careful."

It struck her even as she said the words that she should heed her own advice.

She'd slept fitfully, waking often in the dark quiet of the night, remembering every moment with Rafe in the kitchen last night.

The touch of his hands, the heat of his lips on hers. She couldn't believe she'd let things go so far—or that she'd wanted them to go further.

What happened to not getting involved with any man again? Not risking her heart?

She knew that theoretically she could have sex

with someone without giving her heart away. She just wasn't sure she was built that way. Or that she could pull that off with Rafe Tanner.

Having a fling with Rafe would be far too risky, since she obviously hadn't completely outgrown her adolescent fantasies about him.

Be smart, she told herself.

She tried not to think of those long, deep kisses, his hot tongue sliding along hers, whipping up sensations she'd thought were dead. Of the fire that had ignited inside her when he slid his hand beneath her sweater and cupped her breast . . .

She'd thought she'd melt. Or explode. *No.* She had to stay away from Rafe. He could ruin everything, destroy all her careful control, break down her walls with a kiss or a touch.

The man was just too damned dangerous.

She had to stay away.

"This job—Ms. McPhee, it would mean the world to me." Karla Sommers' afraid-to-hope gaze was pinned to Sophie's face.

They were seated on chairs in the bakery kitchen while Sam and Denny were on lunch break. The little boy Sophie had seen with Karla in Roy's Diner that first day was rolling a battered toy truck back and forth across the floor.

"Go fast, twuck!" he yelled, and Karla quietly shushed him.

"I'm sorry. He likes to talk. And yell. And run."

Sophie laughed. "No problem. What little boy doesn't? Tell me about your experience. Ever worked in a bakery before?"

It turned out, Karla had worked in a neighborhood bakery for three years when she was first married. The divorce had been a difficult one, and afterward her ex-husband had taken off for a job in Oregon, leaving no forwarding address and skipping out on his child-support payments.

"And you've also had waitressing experience at the Double Cross," Sophie mused, as Austin screamed "Cwash!"

The truck banged into the wall and fell over, wheels spinning as the little boy dove for it, shrieking.

"Sorry." Karla hurried to the boy and picked him up, trying to quiet him.

"No problem. He's just being a kid. I bet he'll love being with others his age when he's back in daycare."

"You're really going to hire me?" Karla looked like she was holding her breath, afraid to smile, afraid it might not be true. Sophie nodded, feeling almost as satisfied as she did when she pulled a pan of warm cinnamon rolls from the oven.

"I'll need you to start on Monday at eight A.M."

Sam and Denny returned just as Karla and

Austin were leaving. Denny held the door for them, then picked up Austin's truck and handed it back to him after the little boy dropped it right outside the bakery.

Sophie noticed Denny's face turn red as Karla thanked him. His cheeks were still flushed when he came inside.

"Do you guys know Karla Sommers and her son?" Sophie asked.

"Well, don't exactly know her, just seen her around," Sam replied, heading toward his tool kit.

"She's waited on me at the Double Cross a few times," Denny mumbled. Sophie remembered that Denny had never been married. He'd been shy growing up and had rarely dated in high school—or after, as far as she knew.

"I just hired her to work here. She's going to give her notice at the Double Cross," Sophie told both of them. She saw Denny register the information, and then turn, his big shoulders hunched as he watched Karla and her son disappear around the corner.

She caught herself smiling and closed her eyes. What was wrong with her? If she wasn't careful, she'd turn into Gran and Martha and Dorothy.

The one thing Lonesome Way definitely didn't need was one more matchmaker.

Chapter Twelve

The morning of the baby shower, Ivy chose her outfit carefully.

She slipped on her pale green and yellow print baby doll dress and her cutest flats, fluffed her hair, then swiped on a touch of the lip gloss she'd bought yesterday with Shannon and Val at Benson's Drugstore.

She'd picked the shiny raspberry gloss, Shannon had chosen whipped strawberry, and Val bought the sweet berry fusion.

Studying herself in her bedroom mirror, she thought she looked okay, but not great. She wished her boobs would start growing already, like Shannon's had. And she wished her chin wasn't so baby round, and that she was shorter by at least three inches. She bet she was already taller than nearly all the boys in her grade. Including Nate. Last year she'd been the same height as everyone else, but this year she was going to tower over them like some stupid giant.

Her stomach hurt just thinking about school.

Think about the shower, she told herself. *School doesn't start until Monday. And today will be fun.*

Not only would she get to help unwrap the

baby gifts and see all the cute presents for her new cousin, she'd finally have the chance to taste Sophie's famous cinnamon buns, the ones Aunt Liss had been raving about ever since Ivy could remember.

And tonight there was a sleepover at Val's. The last one of the summer.

Then her cell phone rang and she jumped. Even though she knew it might be Shannon or Val or one of her other friends, she rushed to grab it from the top of her maple dresser.

She'd been waiting and waiting for the next call, not knowing when it would come. Or if it would come.

What if Dad's around? she wondered the instant before she looked at the caller ID. *What if he wanted to know who she was talking to?*

She might have to lie and she didn't want to. Ivy never lied to her dad. Unless not telling him something this important about to happen in her life counted as a lie.

She was very much afraid that it did. Sometimes lately that thought kept her from falling asleep at night.

When she saw the now familiar number on the caller ID, her stomach clenched.

"Where are you?" she whispered into the phone. She was pretty sure her dad was still outside feeding the horses and working with Shiloh, like he did every morning, but he might've come indoors without her realizing it.

"Still in Texas, baby girl. I'm real sorry it's taking me so long to get to you."

She gripped the phone tight, listening to the quick, lilting, almost giddy voice of her mother.

"I can't come yet, but I'll be there soon, sweetie. Practically before you blink."

"When?" Ivy choked back the lump in her throat. She wanted to see her mother so badly the pain sometimes felt like it was slicing her in two.

Her friends saw their mothers every single day. Even the ones who were divorced lived in town. They got to hug them, ask them questions, talk to them whenever they wanted.

Ivy hadn't seen her mom in four years. But it felt like a hundred.

Sometimes it was hard even to remember exactly what her mother looked like. From the pictures she had, which she kept in a stationery box in the top drawer of her dresser, she knew her mother had very long, curly red hair—like hers, only darker and much prettier.

And her mom wasn't awkward or ugly, the way Ivy felt most of the time.

No, she was tall and glamorous and beautiful, and everyone used to stop and speak to her when they walked together down Main Street. Her mom had won the title Queen of the Rodeo back when she was fourteen—and held it for years and years.

She'd told Ivy all about how five different cowboys had begged her to marry them. That was the bedtime story her mom used to tell her before she went to sleep at night. How she had her choice of all five cowboys—champion bronc riders and bull riders and calf ropers—and even, once, the owner of the Silver Lake Rodeo in Wyoming, but she'd picked Ivy's dad instead.

Your daddy was the biggest catch of all, her mother had told her as she tucked the covers around Ivy and turned out the light.

All the girls in Lonesome Way wanted him for their own, but I'm the one who got him.

So why did you run away? Ivy had always wanted to know in the weeks and months and years after her mother left. She planned to ask her just that when she finally saw her again.

It was something she needed to know. She needed to know if her mom left because of her—because she was too much trouble or did something so bad that her mom couldn't stand being around her anymore and had to leave.

She didn't see how it could be because of her dad. There was nothing wrong with *him*. Out of all of her friends' dads—and there were some really nice ones—hers was hands down the best.

"Where are you, Mom? Right now, where in Texas are you?"

She hated that her voice quavered like she was going to cry. Okay, she *was* crying, a little. She sniffled as her mother ignored the question, just promised that they'd be together soon.

"You didn't mention anything to your daddy about me, did you, precious girl?"

"No." *But I want to,* Ivy thought miserably. She heard Bretta and Bonfire nickering in the corral.

"Why can't I tell him, Mom? He won't be mad that I'm going to see you," she whispered into the phone.

At least, she didn't *think* he'd be.

"Now you listen to me, Ivy Rose. No telling your daddy that I'm coming. Promise me."

"I already promised before," Ivy mumbled.

"You promise me again. C'mon now. If your daddy finds out, he won't let me see you. Is that what you want? For me to come all that way and your daddy says forget it?"

"N-no."

"Then promise. Right now."

Ivy squeezed her eyes tight shut. "I . . . promise."

"There's a sweet girl. Now I'll be there soon, so you just sit tight and wait to hear from me or Aunt Brenda, okay, baby?"

I'm not a baby, Ivy wanted to yell, but she didn't. If she did, who knew what would happen? Mom might get mad, hang up, never ever call her again.

"Wait a minute, Mom." *Mom.* The word tasted

strange on her tongue. Her friends said it all the time, talking to their moms, or about them. But Ivy didn't mention her mom to anyone, not even Shannon.

"When you get here, you're going to talk to Dad, aren't you?"

"Well, sure, precious, eventually. But not right away. He might get mad and not let me see you anymore at all. And that would just break my heart. But you—don't you worry about a thing. You just be ready. I'll call you again in a week or so. Let you know just how close I'm getting. I can't wait to see you, baby. You know that, right?"

Ivy wasn't sure, but she thought she heard some of the same longing in her mother's voice that twisted through her own heart. Her throat felt hard and tight, and she couldn't answer.

"We're going to have us a real happy reunion," her mother promised with all the confidence in the world.

Then there was silence. Her mother was gone. Just like the other times.

Ivy stared at the phone, and then tossed it down onto her bed. It sank into her cream and blue flowered comforter and she plunged down beside it, facedown, eyes closed, her cheeks pressed against the fluffy soft cotton.

As always, she tried not to think about the day her mom left. But memories of it continued to haunt her, even more so since her mother began to call.

She'd been seven when her mother left Lonesome Way, but she could still remember things about that day. How scared and alone she'd felt. The sun beating down on her, scorching hot. She had been wearing pink shorts and she'd felt like her legs were on fire. She had been thirsty from eating all those Doritos from the bag her mom pushed into her hand before she ran to that silver car and drove away.

Ivy remembered holding so tight to Peegee, her giraffe, that her fingers felt like they were going to fall off. And waiting, most of all, waiting for her dad to come and get her.

"You stay right here, darlin'. Peegee will keep you company. Your daddy's coming for you real soon. Don't you move now. Don't go with anyone except your daddy. Just sit tight, that's mommy's good girl."

Her mother had jumped into that car and sped away. Ivy didn't remember much about the man who was driving it, except he had slicked-back hair.

Ivy had waited and waited. Then waited some more.

Daddy's coming for me, she'd whispered to Peegee.

But he didn't come.

Finally, she'd started to cry, scared her dad wasn't ever coming for her.

Her mom had left. Maybe her dad had left too. . . .

"Ivy! Time to hit the road!"

When her father's voice boomed up the stairs and into her bedroom, Ivy's head jerked up.

She sprang off the bed, feeling like she wanted to cry, but forced herself to blink back the tears stinging behind her eyelids. Dropping her cell phone into her denim purse, she swiped on another dab of lip gloss and hurried downstairs.

"Feeling okay?" Her dad studied her, looking worried, which instantly annoyed her.

"I'm fine. Why are you all dressed up?"

He'd showered, his hair looked damp and freshly combed, and he had a tiny shaving cut on his jaw. And he'd changed from his blue chambray shirt and old Wranglers that he'd worn working in the barn with the horses earlier into a fresh black polo shirt and his nice jeans.

"Are you going somewhere?"

"Nope. Just dropping you off at Mia's house for the shower."

He winked at her and handed her the present she'd ordered online after Sophie suggested it— a baby mobile with tiny pink and silver stars dangling from it. She'd carefully wrapped the package in thinly striped pink and lavender paper.

"Are you staying for the whole shower, Dad? I don't get it. Why are you all dressed up?"

"I'm coming in to see Aunt Liss before it starts. Maybe I'll come back after if Uncle Tommy wants a hand loading all those gifts in the truck."

"Oh." But she studied him for a moment. It sounded fishy to her. Her dad dropping in at a baby shower? When he had a new horse that he was busy starting? And when Aunt Liss and Uncle Tommy had already said they'd bring her home?

Something was up.

But it was nice that he'd be there, she thought, following him out to the truck. Aunt Liss would be glad to see him. Uncle Jake and Uncle Travis hadn't been home to visit in a long time, though she and Aunt Liss had both talked to them on the phone after Dad called to tell them about the early labor. But ever since her grandparents died, she and her dad were the only family Aunt Liss had in Lonesome Way anymore. And vice versa.

She knew what it was like to want family around.

She didn't know if her mom would actually stick around this time when she came back, but every night Ivy said prayers that she would.

She prayed even harder that her dad wouldn't be mad at her when he found out all the things she wasn't telling him.

And especially what she was going to do.

Chapter Thirteen

Sophie arrived early at Mia's pin-neat little house on Larkspur Lane to help set up for the shower.

Mia had draped an exquisite cream-colored lace cloth across her oak dining table, and together they got to work setting out pretty flowered china plates and pale yellow cloth napkins. Sophie filled the punch bowl while Mia strung pink and silver streamers and balloons along the walls of the L-shaped living room, dining room, and even the kitchen.

Some high school friends, Becca Miller and Jess Blanchard, arrived even before the guest of honor, and pitched in to help arrange all of the food on pretty platters and serving bowls.

Becca, it turned out, had three-year-old twins, a boy and a girl, and Jess had a one-year-old named Evan.

"Everybody says he looks exactly like me," Jess babbled to Sophie, flipping open her phone and showing photos of a dark-haired little boy splashing in a bathtub. "But I think he's the spitting image of Dan."

"He has your eyes." Sophie was smiling as she glanced from the photo to the woman who'd been her lab partner in chemistry senior year. "But definitely Dan's nose and smile."

"My two look exactly like my side of the family. Look, Sophie." Becca held out her phone.

It was true—the little girl and boy in side-by-side swings on a backyard play set were like miniature versions of Becca, with her dark brown hair and doe-shaped eyes.

"Adorable." Sophie tried to ignore the empty ache in her heart as she handed back Becca's phone.

If things had been different, if Ned had been the man she thought she married, she'd have children of her own by now, with their pictures on her phone, their smiles and first words and bedtime giggles embedded in her heart.

"And how cute is Lissie's baby girl going to be, with those Tanner genes?" Mia sailed toward the dining room carrying the carved watermelon bowl filled with cantaloupe, watermelon, miniature marshmallows, grapes, raisins, and pineapple.

"Speak of the devil," Jess exclaimed as Lissie burst through the kitchen door, radiant in a silky blue top that flowed over chic black silk maternity pants.

"Who's ready to party?" Lissie's laughter bubbled through the kitchen. Then she spotted the cinnamon buns Sophie was arranging on a crystal platter.

"I need one of those, Sophie. Desperately. And I need it *now.*"

Sophie tossed one to her. Everyone cheered as she caught it and popped a morsel of gooey caramel and sweet dough into her mouth.

"This woman's bakery opens on Monday!" Lissie held the cinnamon bun aloft. "Baby and me will be the first ones in line."

There was laughter and a smattering of applause before Gran, Martha, and Dorothy arrived within moments of each other, and the kitchen crowd ebbed into the dining room to ooh and aah over the table settings.

Sophie was alone in the kitchen, sliding her pink-frosted cupcakes onto a white platter when Ivy came through the back door, with Rafe right behind her.

Ivy looked a bit withdrawn today but every bit as pretty as the cupcakes, with her wavy auburn hair glowing like a halo around her face.

And Rafe . . . well, Rafe made her pulse jump, the same way he had when she was eleven years old.

"Morning." Sophie's quick smile included both of them. She was pleased, thinking that she'd spoken with just the right tone of casual friendliness.

And then Rafe looked at her with those piercing eyes the color of a storm blue Montana sky, and she somehow knocked one of the cupcakes off the platter with her elbow. It toppled to the floor, the frosting shmushing against the planked wood.

"Let me give you a hand with that." He tore off a paper towel as Sophie knelt to gather up the splattered remnants.

"Where are we supposed to put the presents?" Ivy asked impatiently.

"In the living room. They're all piled up near the fireplace."

The words were barely out of her mouth before the girl darted from the kitchen to join the women gathered around Lissie, laughing and chattering. Sophie wondered what was wrong as she scraped up icing from the floor.

"It's a good thing I baked two dozen of these." She stood up, folding the gooey mess inside the paper towel.

"Even if you'd only made a handful, I can't see anyone going hungry today. Not with this spread."

It was true, there was enough food for double the number of women attending the shower. Besides the fruit, there was a fancy make-ahead French toast casserole, hash browns with mushrooms and sausage, and green salad with pine nuts, oranges, and strawberries. An egg and ham casserole, lightly browned on top, was ready to be set on the dining room table, as well as scoops of tuna salad in dainty lettuce cups and a wicker basket brimming with raspberry muffins, as well as the platter of cinnamon buns.

Which didn't even count the chocolate fudge cake with cream cheese icing Sophie had baked for dessert.

"Hungry?" The corners of her mouth turned up. "As the brother of the guest of honor, you're welcome to stay."

On the words, the front doorbell chimed, and still more women streamed into the living room. Sophie heard her mother's voice amidst the chatter.

"Thanks, but I know better than to let myself get outnumbered by a whole herd of women. I'll be back later though to pick up Ivy." His grin faded. "She's kind of down today. Moody or something. I'm not sure why. These days, I can't read her as well as I used to."

"She's growing up. Maybe she's nervous about school starting on Monday. Middle school is a big scary leap socially."

"Yeah, I know." Rafe looked thoughtful. "I guess it could be that."

His gaze settled on her. "Any more tire trouble?"

She shook her head. "I told you—it was just some silly kid."

"Ah-huh. Maybe." He looked doubtful. And deliciously ruggedly male in this little house decorated with balloons and streamers.

He was standing close to her in Mia's snug little kitchen, and Sophie couldn't help but remember what it had felt like when he'd backed her up against the wall of the Good Luck kitchen and kissed her dizzy. Waves of memory flowed through her. His raw strength as he held her, bending his head toward hers. Hot, deep, craving kisses that made her feel like her heart was going to fly out of her chest. His big hand sliding beneath her sweater . . .

"Penny for your thoughts, Ms. McPhee."

Heat rushed through her skin at his words, and that slow smile of his deepened. He might have been reading her mind.

"My thoughts'll cost you a lot more than that." She kept her voice light. But she felt her heart racing.

It would be so easy to lean into him right now. To wrap her arms around that hard-muscled body, lift her mouth to kiss him . . .

That way madness lies.

Or heartbreak.

She plunked herself back to reality, lifted the platter of cinnamon buns, and moved toward the dining room.

"Sophie. Wait."

She turned, gripping the platter.

"I was wondering . . . maybe you'd like to go riding later. And have supper at the ranch."

She was so surprised she nearly dropped the

platter. *Say no,* she told herself. *Right now.* But she wanted to say yes.

"Ivy has a sleepover. The last one before school starts. I could throw a few steaks on the grill, open a bottle of wine. Just as friends," he added. "I promise."

Unless you decide different. She could hear his thought though he didn't say it. It hung slender as a thread in the air between them.

Rafe found himself holding his breath as he waited for her to answer. He hadn't planned on extending the invitation. It had been spontaneous, but he didn't regret the words.

The only problem was that Sophie was looking at him as if he'd asked her to fly in a spaceship made of aluminum foil and mud to the outer reaches of the moon.

"Supper. Tonight," she repeated, obviously stalling, and he had to fight the urge to kiss her on the spot.

"That's right. Food. Drinks. Corn on the cob. The works."

More silence.

He usually didn't get hesitation when he extended an invitation to a woman. His chest tightened. She was going to say no.

"This isn't a date," she repeated cautiously. "Just a horseback ride and supper."

"You got it."

Date shmate. He wanted to spend time with

her. And there was no sense rushing into anything more. For one thing, she was nowhere near ready for anything more serious—not after the hell her asshole husband had put her through. And Rafe didn't *do* serious. Not with anyone.

Still, he had to be honest with himself. He wanted her. Bad. Raw physical need pulsed through him as he watched her face, lovely and thoughtful and filled with hesitation. In that strapless little peach sundress, her hair tumbling in soft waves around her shoulders, Sophie McPhee looked far more luscious than any of the desserts arrayed on that countertop.

But he had to be careful. She wasn't anything like the women he dated these days. They expected nothing more of him than a few drinks and a rollicking good time in bed. And that's exactly what he gave them.

He'd never invited any of them to the ranch, certainly not for supper. The thought had never occurred to him.

But Sophie was different. He couldn't seem to stop thinking about her. He was crazy attracted to her, even though he knew he had to tread carefully. Her husband had done a real number on her, and the last thing Rafe wanted was to risk her getting hurt again.

He didn't want to get into anything complicated himself—just the chance to get to know her better. But he needed to go slow. Maybe inviting her to supper wasn't his smartest, most thought-out move, he reflected. But it was too late to take back the invitation now. It had just sprung out of him with a life of its own.

"So what's it going to be? That platter looks heavy." He took it from her as she still seemed to be trying to make up her mind.

"I'll be there. What time?" She was smiling at him, and he loved the softness of her eyes when she smiled. If he was ten years old and not a grown man, he'd have pumped his fist in the air.

"How does five o'clock sound?"

"Perfect." She took the platter back and started toward the door. "I'm warning you though. I haven't ridden in a long time. I might be a little rusty."

"I'll find you my oldest, fattest, gentlest mare."

She shot him a look. "I've never been *that* rusty."

"Good, because I only have one old, fat, gentle mare, and no one over the age of eight gets to ride her."

"Great, you pick the horse, I'll bring dessert."

"Deal."

She was gone with a faint swish of that floaty peach skirt.

Rafe was whistling as he went out Mia's kitchen door, got in his truck, and roared off for Tobe's Mercantile to buy some steaks.

• • •

Perched on a folding chair in the living room filled with women of all ages, shapes, and sizes, Sophie tried to concentrate on Lissie, who was opening her gifts, and Ivy, who was assisting her, but instead, she found herself thinking about her "date" tonight with Rafe.

The word kept circling in her head. *Date.* Despite what he'd said, she, Sophie McPhee, was going on a date.

With Rafe Tanner.

She still couldn't believe she'd said yes. But she hadn't been able to imagine saying no.

As to where it would lead, she decided she'd figure that out later. For months she'd been living life cautiously. Boxed in by her anger and her fears. She was sick of it. Just for tonight, she wanted to have fun, let go, break out of the box Ned—no, she herself—had put herself in.

Rafe had invited her for a horseback ride and supper. How dangerous could that be?

It took a while, but gradually she began to focus on the tiny adorable dresses and sweaters and little matching socks Lissie was holding up for everyone to see. Sophie smiled in delight at the lace-edged denim skirt from the Gap in size three to six months, but a pang began to sear her heart. She kept the smile pasted on her face as Ivy, who seemed to have shed her sober mood, displayed the stack of receiving blankets and stuffed animals and dolls that were piling up in Mia's living room.

She'd always thought she'd have a baby of her own by now. As she listened to the talk of the other women at the shower, to the stories and laughter and advice offered to Lissie on everything from feeding schedules to diaper brands, she wondered with a stab of longing if she'd ever be part of that special sorority of mothers, the women who loved and nurtured and knew the joys of tucking a son or daughter into bed at night and wishing them happy dreams, teaching them to say please and thank you, and how to print their names, or helping them stir chocolate chips into a bowl of cookie dough.

She tried to ignore the ache deep inside her as Lissie exclaimed excitedly over each of the tiny outfits and fluffy stuffed animals. She told herself that having supper with Rafe tonight would be a good distraction. The pain of what she didn't have—might never have—still burned in her heart, but she wouldn't have to think about it for the entire rest of the night.

Then she felt her grandmother's gaze on her from the sofa where she sat knee-to-knee with Martha and Dorothy.

Bippity, Boppity, Boo.

While everyone else was focused on Ivy and Lissie strewing wrapping paper and opening gifts, Gran was waving a sheet of paper in the air, trying to catch Sophie's attention. She looked beautiful in a gauzy pink sweater and her best gray slacks, her white braid drifting serenely down her back. But it was the sheet of paper that made Sophie sigh.

The List, she thought grimly.

She was certain of it when Gran pointed at her and smiled.

Fortunately, everyone else in the living room was busy oohing and aahing over a tiny ruffled pink and white dress from Dorothy and didn't notice.

Except her mother.

Sophie saw her mom glancing between her and Gran. There was sympathy in her gaze.

But actually, Sophie thought wryly, her mom was the one who needed a list of new men to date.

Gran, Martha, and Dorothy wasted no time cornering Sophie in the hallway off the living room the moment the last of the gifts was set atop the pile and Ivy began collecting torn wrapping paper and stray bows.

"Dear, we've been meaning to talk to you," Martha began.

"We wanted to give you some space, like you asked for, but you've been home several weeks now and—"

"And we need to talk to you before the bakery

opens on Monday," Gran continued. "You'll be too busy for weeks after that."

"I want to make it clear that I didn't give my nephew your phone number," Dorothy piped up, her deep voice a little too loud for Sophie's comfort. "I did suggest he stop by and say hello sometime, but—"

"He told Dorothy you were out with Rafe Tanner." Gran's eyes were keen, watchful. Martha and Dorothy both stared at Sophie like hungry birds studying a worm. "Roger seemed to think you two were coming back from a date."

"There was no date," Sophie said firmly. "I had car trouble driving home from Lissie's. Rafe happened by and helped me out."

Which was the truth. Just not the whole truth.

"You should take a look at our list, Sophie," Gran urged, thrusting the paper at her.

"Hang on to it for me, Gran. I'll let you know when I'm ready." Gently she pushed the sheet back into her grandmother's hand.

Martha's lips pursed in disappointment. Dorothy blinked her round brown eyes and sighed. Both women turned toward Gran, waiting for her to do what was best for her granddaughter, and insist.

But for once Gran hesitated, searching Sophie's face. "Are you sure, dear? You don't want to take a peek, see what you think?"

"Mom." Diana came up, laying a hand on her

mother's arm. "Don't pester Sophie. She's a hostess today, remember? She needs to help Mia in the kitchen, and say good-bye to the guests. This can wait for another time, can't it?"

Way to go, Mom. Sophie threw her mother a grateful glance, kissed her grandmother's cool cheek, and escaped.

People began coming to her, saying their good-byes and streaming toward the door. She slipped into the kitchen and glanced at Mia's cheerful blue and white "coffee cup" clock as she began stacking dishes and platters in the sink.

She felt light, almost happy. And not, she told herself, because there were only three more hours until she'd be going riding with Rafe at Sage Ranch.

She was simply happy because, once again, she'd escaped having to deal with The List. And the shower had gone well. It had been wonderful catching up with old friends, Lissie had been delighted with all of the baby games, decorations, food, and gifts. And her mom had stuck up for her again when it counted.

It has nothing to do with Rafe Tanner, she told herself.

And she almost believed it.

Chapter Fourteen

Pulling on socks, jeans, and a sweatshirt later that afternoon, Sophie heard the sounds of wheels crunching on the drive. She zipped up her jeans and hurried to her open bedroom window in time to see Doug Hartigan climb out of an old Explorer.

He was wearing a crisp blue shirt and a pair of khaki pants and carrying a bouquet of daisies, asters, and miniature roses.

Give me a break.

But before she could turn away, the front door opened and her mother stepped out. Sophie didn't want to watch, but somehow she froze, unable to tear her gaze away as her mother walked straight up to Hartigan, cupped his face in both of her hands, and touched her mouth to his.

Eeeeuww.

Sophie's eyes narrowed. Was her mother really in love with this jerk? *How? Why?* If he hurt her . . .

She heard Hartigan say something, but the wind was rustling through the ponderosa pines and blew away the words, though she thought she caught one of them.

It sounded like . . . *anniversary.*

Was today some stupid dating anniversary? Had they been going out three months? Or five months?

Whatever.

She was about to spin away when she caught sight of her mother's face.

She was cradling Hartigan's flowers as if they were rare and precious gems. And her face was glowing.

Sophie forced herself to look at Hartigan. She'd never seen him smile before. He looked . . . almost human. It was a jolt. He was beaming at her mother and there was no trace of sourness in his face now. He looked . . . *they* looked . . . happy.

Moving away from the window, a strange feeling came over her. She dug an old pair of riding boots from the back of her closet and tugged them on, her mouth set as she tried to erase the expression she'd seen on her mother's face as she gazed at Doug Hartigan.

And the way he'd looked when he gazed at her.

She didn't want to think about any of that. She wanted to think about Rafe. About their date . . . or non-date.

About how she needed to be careful, guard her heart.

She needed to be smarter, more cautious, and more prepared than her mother, who seemed to actually believe she was in love with the teacher from hell.

Chapter Fifteen

Sunlight shimmered like gold dust above the mountains as Sophie pulled up before the sprawling two-story stone and timber house at the end of the long paved drive.

Sage Ranch.

For years it had been like a home away from home for her. And now the great house dominating the valley loomed before her in the sun-dappled haze of late afternoon, as lovely in its own way as the forests and meadows and streams that flowed in every direction across Tanner property.

A pair of hawks circled overhead in the cloudless sky. A horse whinnied from one of the corrals and was answered by another. In the distance, glowing foothills arced toward giant mountain peaks.

Memories washed over Sophie.

Sweet memories. All the happy times she'd spent here—riding around the big corral with Lissie, or galloping across the meadow beyond, racing down to the creek.

Rowdy family dinners with Lissie, her three brothers, and their parents in the spacious ranch kitchen.

Doing homework at the long cherrywood table as the Tanner boys roared like young bears, in one door, out another, sometimes laughing, sometimes arguing and tussling, always shouting.

For a moment, gazing at the house, even larger than the one her great-grandfather had built, she thought wryly of all the ways and times she and Lissie had bedeviled Rafe.

Never once had she ever dreamed that she'd be coming here on a golden afternoon to go horseback riding with him.

She lingered a moment in the Blazer, absorbing the familiar but still breathtaking surroundings. It wasn't only the weathered barns and paddocks and corrals, the outbuildings and sheds, that gave Sage Ranch the heft and dignity to match her own family's property; it was the thousands of acres of land that stretched beyond it as far as the eye could see.

While Sophie's mother had sold the Good Luck ranch cattle and leased most of the pasture to other ranchers after splitting from Hoot, Sage Ranch was still a highly profitable working horse ranch, and one of the most gorgeous properties in the state. Graced on one side by a craggy wood of stately ponderosa pines and on the other by pastures and gentle hills, the ranch boasted one of the most spectacular vistas in all of Lonesome Way.

Sophie drank in the sight of more than a dozen horses grazing in the white-fenced pasture. The meadow beyond the house was lush with wildflowers. And in the distance, the Crazy Mountains reared toward the sky, their dark silver peaks towering across the horizon.

She forgot all about the sight of those mountains though as Rafe walked out the front door and toward the Blazer.

Her pulse quickened. The man was pure cowboy. All tall, lean, and handsome, the brim of his hat partially shading his eyes. He looked perfectly matched to the rugged, dangerous beauty of his surroundings.

"I've been watching for you," he said easily.

The black mutt loping at his heels was more than twice as big as Tidbit, and quivering with excitement at the prospect of meeting a new friend.

"Any trouble finding the place?" Rafe grinned as he opened the Blazer's door for her.

"I think I could find it no problem blindfolded and upside down."

"Considering how much time you used to spend here, I'd be shocked if you couldn't." As he helped her step down, the touch of his hand set her heart bolting like a runaway train.

It was in that moment that she felt a twinge of panic.

She'd been telling herself all afternoon that she

203

could handle being alone with Rafe, that they were just friends.

But all he had to do was touch her hand, and little sparks seemed to burst through her. Unsettled, she glanced at him, then knelt to pet Rafe's wriggling dog—Starbucks, he told her—before she reached across to the passenger seat to remove a covered pan.

"What've you got in there?" Rafe asked, one eyebrow lifted.

"Dessert. Peanut butter cookies."

"Hey, my favorite." Then those cobalt eyes turned piercing as they studied her, and she knew he wondered if she'd remembered that from the Tanner family dinners. Sophie had—but she wasn't about to tell him.

Inside the house, Sophie set the pan of cookies on the kitchen countertop as Starbucks trotted over to a rag rug before the sink and curled up.

It warmed her to see that not much had changed in the downstairs rooms. Sage Ranch still felt cozy and homey, despite its size. It looked much as it had when Rafe's parents were alive—the handsome dining table and buffet was still there, as were the family portraits, the built-in mahogany bookcases, and the big overstuffed sofas in shades of cream, gray, and rose that warmed the open spaces of the high-ceilinged living room.

But some things were different, like the gaudy floral carpet in the little side parlor where Rafe's mother used to sew.

Sophie didn't like it nearly as much as the lovely faded needlepoint rug that had been there before.

Rafe followed her glance.

"My ex-wife added a few touches of her own." His mouth twisted. "I never changed things back, just haven't done much with the place since she left, except new windows and the granite countertops and backsplash."

"How long has it been . . . since she left?" Sophie asked quietly as they walked from the house toward the corral.

"Four years. Ivy was seven."

So young, Sophie thought with a pang of sympathy. *Too young for such a blow.* "I see. I'm sorry."

But she didn't see. She didn't see how a woman could leave a fragile young daughter, a husband, run off, and never come back.

She wished she'd asked Lissie more questions about Lynelle when they'd had lunch at Roy's.

Rafe had already saddled the horses and he gave Sophie a leg up onto the dappled Appaloosa named Belle he'd chosen for her.

As she slid into the saddle and adjusted the stirrups, she was surprised by how much at home she felt. She'd started riding when she was six, but she hadn't been in the saddle for years now, since she married Ned.

"Where are we headed?" she asked as Rafe swung up on his gelding, Deputy, with lithe grace. The powerful gray stallion pranced sideways, restless to be off.

"How about the creek? Too far?"

"You must be mixing me up with a tenderfoot," Sophie retorted. She touched her heels to Belle's flanks and the horse took off across the pasture at a trot. "Try to keep up—if you can."

She urged Belle to a gallop and laughed as they surged ahead toward the larkspur-studded meadow and the lush grass leading to Sage Creek.

Hidden in the shadow of the woods thirty feet from the main barn, Buck Crenshaw watched Rafe and Sophie ride out across the open pasture.

So that's how it is, he thought, and spat into the dirt.

He'd heard the low murmur of their voices and had seen Tanner, damn his hide, help the McPhee woman up into the saddle. But Buck hadn't been able to hear anything they said.

Didn't matter though.

He knew what was up. And what he was gonna do.

After the two of them set off, he waited until

they were specks on the horizon before he stepped out of the cover of the trees.

A quick glance reassured him that none of Tanner's wranglers were around. No other vehicles were in the drive, 'cept for the McPhee woman's Blazer. And no sign of Tanner's kid.

He had the place all to himself. Except for that dog inside the house that started up barking the moment he drew near the outbuildings. The dog didn't matter either though.

He had plenty of time to do what he'd come to do. Only now he could kill two birds with one stone.

Payback times two.

Chapter Sixteen

It didn't take long for Deputy to catch Belle. Sophie tossed Rafe a smile as the gelding pulled alongside her. She slowed her mare to a trot, and they crossed the meadow together, Rafe checking his horse's pace, matching Deputy's strides to Belle's so that he and Sophie could talk.

"Where are Jake and Travis these days?" she asked as they followed the trail through open land and a sky as big as the world.

He told her Jake was in South Dakota

somewhere on the rodeo circuit. And Travis was assigned to the FBI field office in Phoenix.

"Will they come visit after the baby's born?"

"They'd better, or Lissie's gonna kick their butts."

The trail dipped, twisting off between an outcropping of rocks and sagebrush. Rafe took the lead as they neared a grassy clearing less than twenty feet from the creek bank.

Rushing water tumbled over rocks beneath the branches of cottonwoods. The creek looked exactly as she remembered it. She breathed in the clean mossy scent of the clearing and the earthy creek banks as they tethered their horses by a clump of cottonwoods. Sophie flung herself down on the deep grass, lush with wildflowers whose names she'd forgotten.

Lying on her back, she gazed up at the sky.

"I've missed this," she breathed. "The peace of it. The quiet. I can almost hear myself think for once."

"What are you thinking about?" Rafe dropped down to stretch out beside her, close enough so that their hips were almost touching. She could see the five o'clock stubble across his lean jaw, and could almost feel the heat of his body.

You, she thought, intensely aware of him beside her. *I'm thinking about you.* But she just closed her eyes and murmured, "Stuff."

"You've been away a long time."

"Too long. On a day like this, I wonder why I ever left. Montana . . . Lonesome Way . . ."

She sat up, brushing a hand through the soft grass. "I didn't know how much I missed them . . . missed *this*"—her arm swept out to encompass the clearing—"until I got back."

"You're a Montana girl at heart."

"I guess I am. I'm beginning to think I always will be."

Rafe sat up beside her, his long legs stretched before him as he gazed into the distance. "We're the lucky ones. We can connect to a place, to people who're important in our lives. Not everyone can. Take my ex-wife—please," he added with a tight smile that never reached his eyes.

"I'm sorry. I . . . don't really know what happened." Sophie chose her words carefully. "Lissie mentioned something, but I didn't ask her the details."

A part of her hadn't wanted to know. Perhaps because knowing what Lynelle had done to hurt Ivy—and Rafe—might make her feel closer to them.

"Hard to believe no one's told you." Rafe shook his head. "It was the talk of the town for a long time, though it's pretty much died down by now."

"I'm guessing it was worse than leaving the front door open on her way out," she said, and saw the lines tighten around his mouth.

"You could say that. And a large part of it was my fault, for getting involved with Lynelle in the first place."

Sophie fell silent. She could hear the creek water rushing over rocks. A squirrel raced across a fallen branch, its feet making a skittering sound before it disappeared into the brush.

Rafe spoke into the quiet air. "I fell for Lynelle when I was twenty-two and stupid as a rock. It was the spring of my final year of college, and I thought I knew everything. Talk about being a dumbass."

She studied him, trying to decipher the distant look in his eyes. Was it there because he loved and missed Lynelle Tanner, or because he wished he'd never married her?

"She was a waitress at one of our campus hangouts—and she was good." Rafe sighed. "The best waitress I ever saw—fast and fun and flirty. There was something about her. Lynelle got more tips than everyone else combined. She had this great body, which seemed hugely important to me at the time, a stunning cover-model face, and a personality that screamed *look at me*. I looked. And unfortunately, I did a hell of a lot more than that. We went out and partied a few times, all within a couple of weeks. And I got carried away, decided I was in love with her—a woman I barely knew."

He thrust a hand through his hair and shook his

head. "She said she loved me too. So like a couple of fools, we ran off, rounded up a justice of the peace, and got ourselves married. Just the two of us, just like that." He snapped his fingers. "Several weeks later, when I finally started to realize the mistake we'd made—before I'd even brought her home or told my parents—we found out Lynelle was pregnant."

There was pain on his face, but also pride.

"I don't regret that for a second," he said quickly. "Because then I'd regret having Ivy. And I could never do that. She's the best thing in my life. Bar none."

"I know." Sophie's throat tightened. "I've seen you two together. It's clear how close you are."

He smiled and brushed a stray wisp of hair from her eyes.

"Sure you want to hear this story, Sophie? It wasn't part of the bargain. I promised you a horseback ride and a barbeque. Not a tale out of Dickens."

"I'm the one who asked. Tell me the rest."

The wind sighed through the cottonwoods, a low, lonely sound. Rafe was staring at the creek, his eyes seeing something she couldn't in the haze of the late-afternoon light.

"I had no idea how Lynelle had been raised," he said slowly. "That her father owned a small traveling rodeo out of North Dakota, and that every night from the time she was fourteen, she dressed up in some glittery costume and performed for the crowd. They called her the Queen of the Rodeo, and she sang, danced, rode—generally showing off and, as she got older, flirting with the crowd. She loved it. *Craved* it. Unlike her sister, Brenda, who was ten years older, and couldn't wait to escape the rodeo life, Lynelle grew up as a petted, adored little star, and she licked up all that attention on a spoon—like it was ice cream with caramel sauce. She was a natural-born gypsy, roaming from town to town, never sticking around longer than a month in any one place. It was the only way of life she knew, and for her, it was heaven."

"She had no home at all? Just the rodeo?" Sophie tried to take it in. "She must have been homeschooled."

"She was, until her mother died when Lynelle was sixteen. Then, around the time she turned twenty, her father took sick and he died too. She couldn't hold on to the rodeo—there were debts, injuries—she lost everything just a few months before I met her. So she started waitressing. What I didn't know," he added, as a late-afternoon breeze gusted through the clearing, fluttering the leaves of the cottonwoods and blowing Sophie's hair across her face, "was that she still couldn't stay in one place. Every few months she quit whatever job she had, moved away, started over. Found another job, another place to live, another man to sleep with and help her pay the bills. Lynelle didn't like being tied down any more than a mustang that finds itself roped and dragged and eventually saddled with a bit between its teeth."

Sophie's heart constricted. She was amazed that there was no bitterness in his tone. But beneath the evenness of his words, she thought she could detect pain—a long-ago pain that carried with it sadness and regret.

She knew about sadness and regret. And a marriage that didn't turn out at all the way you expected.

"The upshot is, after we found out she was pregnant, I brought Lynelle home—here to Sage Ranch to live with my parents—though not in the main house—in one of our cabins north of the creek. I figured she could use the family support with a baby on the way. And my parents, well . . ." He shook his head. "They were plenty upset at first about the way we got married, but then once they realized it was already done and there was a baby on the way, they were just plain excited at the prospect of a grandchild."

Rafe met Sophie's eyes. "You know how they were. They wanted to help in any way they could. Lynelle seemed to like that. But five months after Ivy was born, she ran away for the first time."

The first time? How many times did she run?

Sophie wondered. "She couldn't take it," he continued, his expression grim. "She couldn't take any of it—the responsibility, the work of caring for an infant, the sameness of life lived day to day on a ranch. She took off three times during the first few years of Ivy's life."

A frisson of sadness touched Sophie. "That must have been . . . a nightmare." Her eyes were wide with shock. "I'm so sorry, Rafe. Did she come back on her own, or did you bring her back?"

"Well, I didn't drag her back by the hair or anything like that," he said ruefully. "Each time I caught up with her, Lynelle cried like a baby herself. She swore to me she wanted to come back."

He scrubbed a hand through his hair. "She was screwed up. I realized it by then. But we were married, and we had Ivy. So we tried couples therapy, but Lynelle refused to stick with it. I never knew what the next day would bring, Sophie. If she'd be there or take off again. There was an engine revving inside her, and it was as if she couldn't control it, much less turn it off. Then my parents died in that plane crash, and I moved us into the big house."

She could picture it—Lynelle, flighty and beautiful, wanting to run. Rafe trying to take care of his family, take care of the ranch. And Ivy, a very young child, at her most vulnerable.

"It was just the three of us in the house then, and it suddenly felt huge and empty. Jake and Travis came home for the funeral, of course, and popped in now and then. But I think being home at Sage Ranch without Mom and Dad was hard for them—it brought their deaths home to them more somehow. So for a few years, it was just the three of us, and for a while, Lynelle seemed better. I think she understood that Ivy needed her and she stuck it out, stayed put, and seemed happy most of the time. We were making it work."

"And you . . . you loved her?"

The question just slipped out and Sophie wished she could grab it back. She wasn't even sure why she wanted to know. But she did.

He didn't answer at first. When he looked at her, his gaze was somber. "I *thought* I did in those first few crazy weeks after we met. And I tried to before Ivy was born—and after. After that first heady rush when we met, I wanted to love her and keep loving her. But I didn't," he said quietly as the wind picked up, whistling through the cottonwoods. "I wish to hell I had. Maybe then, somehow . . . Hell, I don't know. Maybe things would have turned out different."

The words hung between them.

Rafe cleared his throat. "One day when Ivy was seven, I was at a meeting in Livingston with a rancher who wanted to buy two dozen horses for a guest ranch he'd invested in. We'd just got down to talking terms when I got a call from Sheriff Hodge. He'd come across Ivy."

"*Come across* Ivy?"

"She was in town. Alone. Sitting all by herself on a bench in the hot sun."

The chill that blew through Sophie started at her scalp and tingled all the way down to her toes. "I don't understand."

Rafe hadn't had to tell anyone the story in a long time. It didn't ever get easier though.

"Lynelle brought her to Lonesome Way and left her. She sat Ivy on that bench right in front of the Laundromat, and she skipped out. Ivy told me later that a man in a car stopped and her mother got in. And blew her a kiss out the window as the car took off."

Sophie couldn't speak. She tried to take in the thought of a seven-year-old girl, with bright wavy hair and eyes too big for her face, abandoned on a bench in Lonesome Way.

"Apparently Lynelle decided it would be safer to leave her on her own in town than at the ranch. I guess she figured someone in Lonesome Way would come along before too much time passed and take care of her, then get in touch with me. That Ivy would be fine."

Sophie realized her hands were clenched, and carefully relaxed them. She could only imagine how frightened Ivy must have been. It was unbearable to even think about.

Did Lynelle have any idea how lucky she was that her daughter hadn't been found by a stranger passing through town, someone who'd prey on a vulnerable child? The newspapers were full of such horrors.

Or Ivy could have wandered away, gotten lost, or run into the street, been struck by a car. . . .

What kind of woman would take a chance like that with her child's life?

"How long did she sit on that bench?"

"We've no way of knowing. But she was crying, sunburnt, and dehydrated when Hodge happened by—and still crying when I got there. I held her in my arms for hours until I could get her to calm down."

The tension in his lean jaw made her want to wrap her arms around him. Instead she reached out, touched his hand.

"I'm . . . sorry. It's awful."

"Almost as bad is the fact that Ivy hasn't seen Lynelle since that day. Neither have I—which is fine with me." His eyes were cold. "She sent Ivy a couple of notes, a birthday card here and there. And let me know where she was long enough so that we could get our divorce. She didn't fight me on full custody, didn't want a penny. Just her freedom, apparently. And now . . . who knows if Lynelle even remembers she

217

has a child, much less ever thinks about her."

"What about Ivy? Does she ever ask about her mother?"

"She had nonstop questions at first. That ended a few years ago. Now she never mentions Lynelle—in fact, she changes the subject if anyone else does. The last time Lynelle sent a birthday card, Ivy read it, tucked it in a drawer, and didn't say a single word about it. At least, not to me."

But she must think about her mother, Sophie realized. She tried to imagine what it would feel like to have a mother who ran off and never looked back. Who'd leave her child alone and vulnerable on a town bench and desert her husband without a word. She thought about her own mother, who'd brushed her hair until it shone every morning when she was small, and taken her to the library whenever she wanted to go, and read her stories for nearly an hour at bedtime each night. Who'd somehow always known when she most needed a hug. Who'd made Halloween costumes for her and Wes, and smoothed things over when Hoot was at his most critical. Who'd gone to bat for her when Doug Hartigan was the bogey man making Sophie's life miserable.

And who had welcomed her back to Lonesome Way with open and supportive arms.

She swallowed. Ivy had Rafe, and she was far

luckier than she knew, but Sophie's heart grieved for everything the little girl had missed out on.

And at the mountain of hurt that must still ache inside her.

And Rafe? Did he miss Lynelle too? It didn't seem so. He claimed he'd never loved her, but he'd never married again. . . .

"More than you wanted to know, I'd bet."

"No, I'm glad you told me."

"You sure?" His lips curled in a rueful grin. "It's a lot more than you bargained for. You must be wondering what kind of a date this is."

"This isn't a date, remember? You said so."

"Did I?" The heaviness seemed to have fallen from his broad shoulders. With that grin spreading across his face, Rafe looked suddenly much more like that mischievous young cowboy she remembered. Only harder, tougher, and if possible, sexier than he'd been back then. His eyes glinted beneath that shock of dark hair, and he suddenly rolled over and swept her beneath him on the grass.

"We need to lighten things up," he said softly, bracing himself above her. "Have some fun. For the rest of the day, we're concentrating on us."

"Us? There's an us?" She tried not to stare at the bulge of impressive chest muscles beneath his white tee. And instead found herself staring at his mouth. Equally dangerous. Feeling breathless, she pushed herself up on her elbows, trying to regain her equilibrium, but that only brought her closer to his mouth—and to that powerful chest. She was in trouble now.

She wanted to kiss him.

"There's definitely an us." Rafe's smile could've melted rock. Shifting, he smoothed a wisp of her hair back from her cheek, his touch gentle, but the look in his eyes would make any woman moan in anticipation. She knew everything, what he wanted to do, what he was going to do . . . unless she stopped him.

But she didn't want to stop him.

A fire started deep inside her, and she knew if it wasn't banked soon, it would go out of control. . . .

"I'm going to kiss you now, Sophie. More than once. Just so you know. If you have any objections, speak now or . . . you know the rest."

Maybe she should listen. Maybe she should push him away. But she didn't. Wouldn't. Couldn't.

Just for a little while, she'd pretend not to hear the warning voice telling her to keep him at arm's length. . . .

"Go for it, cowboy," she heard herself dare him breathlessly, her hands digging into his shoulders, pulling him down toward her because she not only wanted to kiss him, Sophie knew she *needed* to right that very minute.

Tingles raced through her as he brushed his

mouth against hers. His lips were firm and warm and they felt just right, molding against hers as if memorizing them for all time.

It was a long kiss, deep and slow. Excruciatingly sexy.

Besides the kiss in the kitchen at the Good Luck ranch, it was the best kiss she'd ever known. But the next one took her under. It was even deeper, softer and somehow more intimate than the one before.

"You . . . taste so good." Rafe's voice was rough as he came up for air, staring into her eyes with a dark intensity that might have scared her if she didn't feel so safe lying here with him.

"Don't stop now, cowboy. Don't you dare stop."

She pulled his head down as he grinned. She needed to kiss him again, but even as her mouth clung to his, she knew *she* should be the one to stop. She should be careful, stay in control, but she couldn't. Not yet. It felt too good. Too right. Completely right.

"Not a chance of that," he whispered, his hot mouth against hers. "Not unless you tell me to."

The way he kissed her next left her no breath or will to tell him anything.

She was dizzy, breathless as his hands explored her body. She stroked her fingers across the muscles of his back, down to his taut butt as their tongues circled and danced, and a crazy warmth spun through her.

They were both breathing hard as his hands roamed over her, slid beneath her sweatshirt and lace bra, and found her breast, even as he tasted her mouth again, his tongue and teeth rougher this time.

Sophie moaned, drowning in a haze of pleasure. Then she was clutching at his shirt, her fingers flying at the buttons. The next thing she knew, they were locked together on the cool thick grass and her sweatshirt was somewhere, tossed aside. So was his shirt. *What was she doing?*

He flung off her bra and stroked her breasts, caressing her as raw heat tore like wildfire through her.

"Rafe, this is . . . crazy," she gasped, then gave a quick, intake of breath as he thumbed her nipple. "Completely . . . crazy," she breathed. Her hands had stilled upon his broad, strong back.

"But good crazy," he whispered with a grin, drawing back to look into her eyes. "God, Sophie, you're so beautiful."

Her hair spilled like wild honey across the grass, and her face was flushed the most delicate seashell pink he'd ever seen. He was hard and wanted her so much. He'd been wanting her since that night at the Double Cross, not admitting it to himself. But every time he saw her, he thought about her more. He hadn't felt this way about any woman ever. He didn't just want to have sex with her, he wanted to spend time with her, look at her, listen to her. And yeah, have sex with her.

She was gorgeous and kind and sweet in a way that drew him in no matter how much he tried not to get attached. There was a quiet strength about her that was every bit as alluring as those green eyes and the way she smiled and the faint huskiness of her voice.

He noticed a faint sheen at her hairline and her lips were red and moist from his kisses. He wanted to take in, breathe in, all of her. Now.

He pressed his lips to the hollow of her throat and felt her tremble.

His mouth trailed lower, until his tongue flicked at one lovely nipple, licking and swirling and teasing its nail-hard peak with his teeth until she gasped and her hands fisted in his hair.

Sophie was losing all control. She opened her eyes as Rafe's hand slid to the button on her jeans, flicked it open. He started working the zipper down, and she realized suddenly that if they didn't stop now, there'd be *no* stopping. . . .

An oh-so-tempting thought, but . . .

Sanity was flooding back like a waterfall unleashed. She shifted suddenly, panicking, and put a hand on his arm. "No. W-wait . . . stop."

His finger paused on the zipper. He drew in his breath.

"I don't think . . . We shouldn't. . . ."

"Yeah, we should, baby. We really should.

But . . . it's okay." He shifted away from her, managing to smile though the tension searing him was almost unbearable. She looked stunned, panicked. *Too much, too soon,* he thought. He should have known better.

But man, he'd lost track of everything for a while there. How recent her divorce was . . . how much she'd been hurt. Even how careful he always was about who he slept with and why, and how it was just sex and laughs and maybe friendship, but nothing more. . . .

This was nothing like he'd ever done before. He'd never had these intense feelings or this sense of loss as she quickly fastened her bra and pulled on her sweatshirt.

Damn, his blood was still pounding. She was killing him here. But he took a deep breath and fought down the need and the tension so close to exploding inside him as he pulled on his shirt.

Her cheeks were bright pink as she fastened her jeans and scrambled to her feet.

"This was . . . It was great, don't get me wrong, but I . . . I'm not ready for this . . . for more . . . for anything, really . . . not yet, and I don't know when . . ." She drew in her breath, hoping she sounded calm and logical and in control, even though she was struggling for composure.

The truth was she liked him too much. *Much too much.* She had to find her equilibrium again, the careful self-possession that got her through the days and nights since the divorce. Rafe Tanner had all but destroyed it with his kissing and touching and tasting, with the way he grinned at her and looked at her. And with the way he made her feel.

To her surprise, he reached out and smoothed her tangled hair back from her face.

"Don't think I don't want you right here, right now, Sophie, because I do. More than you know. I want to do things to you—with you—but you need to do what *you* have to do and"—his voice was quiet—"I'll wait until you've figured out exactly what you want."

"You'll . . . but . . . who knows how long that will be?" She was muttering half to herself. She sounded like a lunatic.

"I'm counting on it not being *too* long." Smiling, he traced a finger over her lips. "In the meantime, I'll wait."

"Why?" Sophie stared at him. Her heart skipped a few beats under that piercing midnight blue gaze.

"A few things are worth waiting for in this world," he said quietly. "And something tells me you're one of them." The flash of his smile felt like dynamite under her skin. She couldn't think what to say.

"Come on." He took her hand, pulling her toward the horses. "It's getting late. It'll be dark soon and I promised you a barbecue."

Chapter Seventeen

The sun was melting in a lilac and rose sky when they reached Sage Ranch, and from inside the house, Starbucks was barking furiously. Hoarse, frantic barks, Rafe realized. Not his usual welcoming ones.

Just as the first trace of uneasiness hit his gut, he spotted the smashed corral fence.

"What the hell." He was out of the saddle and running in a flash. Fury tore through him.

A good chunk of the north side of the fence was down. It looked like someone had taken an axe to it. Weathered white rails lay in splintered heaps in the dirt, and the horses were running restlessly back and forth in a cluster at the far end of the corral.

Thoroughly spooked. And who could blame them.

Sliding off Belle, Sophie raced after him, a chill wiggling down her spine as she reached his side and stared at the savaged remnants of his fence.

"Who would *do* this?" Dismayed, she watched Rafe crouch down to more closely examine the damage.

"Damned if I know. But then, I wondered the

226

same thing about whoever let the air out of your tires."

As his words sank in, her gaze flew to his face. "You can't believe the same person is responsible?"

"I have to think it's a possibility, Sophie. There's not a lot of vandalism in Lonesome Way. Don't you think it's strange that first you were targeted and now me? My ranch?"

Frowning, he stood, his tall frame tense. Narrowing his eyes against the setting sun, he scanned his property, his careful gaze scoping out the barns and sheds and outbuildings, then settling on the ranch house itself, where Starbucks was stationed at the window, his barking nearly hysterical now.

"I need to check everything out. And I need you to come with me."

"You think whoever did this could still be around." She was unable to stop a shiver at the thought of someone even now watching them, waiting. . . .

"Probably not. I doubt the coward who did this has the guts to hang around, but I'm not taking any chances." *Not with you,* he thought.

"Rafe, you need to call Sheriff Hodge."

"That's the first order of business once we get Starbucks calmed down. Then we'll take a look around. Unless you'd rather wait in the house— after I've checked it out."

"No way. I'm coming with you."

Dusk was tiptoeing in from the mountains, and with it came cooler air. Sophie found herself shivering in her sweatshirt and jeans as she helped Rafe tend to the horses and as they made a quick but thorough search of the ranch buildings while waiting for the sheriff to arrive.

It wasn't the encroaching cold of night that made her shiver though—it was the knowledge that someone had been here at Sage Ranch, hacking away at Rafe's corral, while they were down at the creek coming *this close* to making love.

But they found nothing further amiss. Until they circled around to check out the front of the house and the long paved drive.

Starbucks had raced nervously ahead, on full alert, barking suspiciously at every rustle of the leaves as a chill wind whined through the pines. But it was Sophie who first spotted her Blazer and gasped.

Following her gaze, Rafe swore under his breath.

"Shit. Wait here. You don't need to look at this."

But she did. She had to see. Had to know.

Her stomach churned as they approached the Blazer and saw in sickening detail the dead squirrel crumpled on the hood. The animal's body had been split in two, its blood smeared across the windshield. Both side windows had been smashed in—there was shattered glass everywhere, and the shards glinted like crystals in the fading light.

Rafe's brows were drawn together in concern as he surveyed the vandal's handiwork. Starbucks whined, scenting blood and death.

Those flat tires weren't a prank, Sophie thought, feeling queasy. Deep down, she'd wondered, but hadn't wanted to acknowledge, the possibility that someone had done it out of malice. Now there was no way to deny it. This was the second time her car had been damaged. And the same person had wrecked Rafe's corral.

"We don't have enemies, Rafe, neither one of us. Who'd do this? Any of this?"

He met her eyes in the fading daylight. "I'm not sure, but believe me, Sophie, we're damn well going to find out."

"You say you two were out riding when this happened. How long would you guess you were gone?"

Sheriff Teddy Hodge leaned back on one of the sofas in the Sage Ranch living room and stretched his legs out in front of him. His small shrewd gray eyes flitted back and forth between Sophie and Rafe, both seated on the opposite sofa. He was a big man with a wide girth, the shoulders of a football player, and a methodical mind. His big fingers dwarfed the pen in his hand, which he kept flicking reflexively.

Hodge had taken note that Sophie McPhee and Rafe Tanner had been out together—and that young Ivy was nowhere around. *Interesting. Not relevant to the case, of course, but from a personal standpoint . . . interesting.*

These two were sitting a few feet apart, hardly looking at each other, but they'd spent the past few hours together—riding, they said—and hanging out at the creek.

It didn't take a cop to figure out something was going on.

If he were the gossiping sort, his wife would have an earful to tell her friends tomorrow. But Hodge wasn't.

If Joanie was to hear about this, it wouldn't be from him.

But oh, wouldn't she just love to know.

Of course, Rafe Tanner and Sophie McPhee could just be friends, but Tanner would have to be dead not to notice a woman as pretty as Sophie. And Tanner was anything but dead. Especially where women were concerned.

Right now, he looked tough and calm and ready for a fight. Hodge sensed his determination. The man was ready to take on the devil himself if it meant protecting his family and property. And Hodge couldn't blame him.

But this was a matter for the law.

"We weren't gone more than two hours," Rafe replied as the dog next to him gave a low, uneasy growl. "We got back shortly before dark."

"And you didn't hear or see anything unusual before you left?"

"Nothing. Nothing at all." Sophie managed to speak with a calm she didn't feel.

"But someone could have parked up on one of the side roads off Eagle's Bluff, then come through the woods to the ranch once we were gone," Rafe pointed out.

Even saying the words, he felt his stomach clench.

Nothing like this had ever happened on the ranch before. The idea that someone had been hiding out there, possibly in the woods that flanked the drive, just waiting for a chance to slither out and do damage, slid along his skin like a long rusty nail.

Ivy was at the age where she could almost be left home alone for a short time, if need be—but not now. Not after today.

Someone out there was sending a clear message. Someone meant harm to Sage Ranch. And possibly to the people who lived here. And that same someone had already targeted Sophie twice.

Rafe wished like hell he'd caught the bastard red-handed. The very thought of Ivy and Sophie being upset by this was worse than a kick in the gut. He didn't want any of this to touch them again. Hodge had to get to the bottom of this before it came to that.

As Starbucks let out another low growl, Rafe set his hand lightly upon the old dog's head. The mutt had been so wound up when they came into the house, Rafe had been worried, wondering if dogs could have heart attacks. Starbucks must have seen whoever had wrecked the corral fence and he hadn't been able to do a thing about it.

He was slightly more settled down now, but every once in a while, his head jerked up, his ears pricked as if hearing some remote sound, and another growl rumbled in his throat.

Almost as if he was expecting whoever had smashed the fence and the Blazer's windows— and left that dead squirrel on the hood of Sophie's rig—to come back.

Which makes two of us. Rafe's instincts all told him that whoever was behind this wasn't done yet.

"Well, I didn't see much out there before it got dark, but I did manage to get some photos," Hodge rumbled. "'Fraid you'll have to leave your car here overnight though, Sophie, until the state police boys get a chance to come take their crime scene photos. I'll be back first thing in the morning too, for another look around.

"You know," the sheriff mused, "it's possible

kids were behind this. Teenagers, looking for mischief. The Fletcher twins got themselves drunk again last month and shot up Marv Peterson's barn. Fools didn't even remember doing it once they slept it off. Marv didn't press charges, because those boys agreed to patch up his barn. And that's about all they're doing these days," Hodge added.

"Mary and Jack grounded those kids for three months—they can't go anywhere but school and to Marv's to make up for what they did."

"You think they might have done this too?" Sophie wasn't buying it.

"Nope. Not really." The sheriff sighed. "But I'll drop by and have a word with them, just in case. Could be some other fool teenagers might have had a hand in this though."

Rafe thought the Fletcher twins sounded like a pretty big long shot to him. He was silent as Hodge fixed those penetrating gray eyes of his on Sophie.

"You don't have any guesses who'd have let the air out of your tires that other night? Anyone mad at you since you came back to town?"

"No one. Up until a few hours ago, I'd convinced myself it was a prank." She hesitated. "I'm sure this has nothing to do with it, but you've probably heard that I'm opening a new bakery where Roy's Diner used to be. A few people are bothered by that, so I've been told. I guess just because I took over so soon after Roy's closed."

"Seems to me I've heard a little grumbling along those lines. Some folks get petty now and then." Hodge pursed his lips, scribbled something on his notepad. "Downright silly thing to grouse about, it seems to me."

"And it's hard to imagine anyone would let the air out of my tires because of that—or kill a squirrel," Sophie added quickly. "I just can't see it. But it's the only thing I can think of."

"Sure seems like a stretch, doesn't it?" Hodge shifted on the sofa, his face thoughtful. "The thing is, you never can tell. Strange things go on in people's heads sometimes. You learn that on this job pretty damn quick."

His bushy brows drew together as he eyed Rafe. "Any problems with neighbors, ranch hands? Anyone in town? Did some horse sale go wrong, or did you fire anyone recently? Any kind of dustup come to mind?"

"There's been nothing like that, Teddy." Rafe thrust a hand through his hair. "All my wranglers have been with me for years. I haven't fired anyone since—"

He broke off, frowning. "Last winter, damn it. Crenshaw."

"Buck Crenshaw? He's working for the Hanging W now, isn't he? You telling me you fired him?"

"He was only hired to fill in while Rowdy was down with pneumonia and I was short-handed. I had to let him go, though, even before Rowdy came back. The man was careless and didn't know spit about barn safety. Or couldn't be bothered. But there's something else, Teddy." Rafe met the sheriff's keen eyes.

"He and I had a little run-in at the Double Cross recently."

"Let's hear it."

As Rafe explained what had happened, Hodge scratched notes on his pad.

"No punches were thrown, but Crenshaw was pissed. And pretty damned drunk."

"In that case, reckon I'll need to talk to him." The older man turned to Sophie, who was trying and failing to think of any way that Crenshaw could possibly blame her for the incident at the Double Cross. It made no sense.

"Crenshaw nearly shoved Wade Holden into you, is that right? But it was an accident. He didn't single you out?"

"It was definitely an accident. I'd only just arrived—was barely in the door."

"Did you know Crenshaw before this happened?" the sheriff asked.

She shook her head.

"Ever run into him again after that night? Any other contact with him anywhere—anytime?"

"No—never. He has no reason to be angry with

me. I can't imagine why he'd want to let the air out of my tires—or leave a dead squirrel on my car—or do any of this." She swallowed, and Rafe reached over, clasped her hand.

Hodge refrained from smiling at the gesture. Had he called it or hadn't he? "Well, it doesn't seem to make much sense, does it—him going after your car." He pushed himself to his feet. "I'll run a background check on him, then see what he's got to say."

Rafe walked the sheriff to the door.

"I've got Ivy to think of, Teddy." Rafe's voice was low, serious. "You need to find out who did this and soon."

"Oh, I'll find out. Don't you worry." The sheriff tucked away his notepad as he stepped over the threshold. "In the meantime, you keep your eyes and ears open. Both of you," he said, glancing back at Sophie.

He stopped again and turned back once more on the way to his cruiser. "It's possible, if we're lucky, this could be the end of it, you know. Whoever's out there nursing a grudge, there's a chance he just got it out of his system."

Sophie's chest felt as tight as hardened wax. Then Rafe voiced the exact same thought that was circling in her head.

"Or maybe he's just getting started."

Chapter Eighteen

The night glowed with a thousand stars by the time Sophie and Rafe finished supper at the kitchen table. She had tossed together a salad while Rafe grilled the steaks and corn on the cob. As the moon edged out from behind a filmy cloud, bathing the mountains in a pale silver sheen, she tilted her wineglass and drained the last drops of her merlot.

Crazily, despite everything that had happened, she felt oddly relaxed. *Merlot helps,* she thought, as the gentle warmth of the wine slid through her and she remembered she was on her second glass.

"Ready for dessert?" she asked.

"Always. What've you got in mind?"

She smiled. An image of the two of them in bed flew into her mind, and she had to blink to force it away.

"Peanut butter cookies, remember?"

"Definitely my second choice, but I'll take what I can get."

It was strange, she thought later, as they munched cookies and sipped hot coffee, how much she'd loved this simple meal, this quiet dinner with Rafe at Sage Ranch.

It surpassed all of the elaborate gourmet meals she and Ned had ordered at fancy restaurants and the excitement and energy of San Francisco's legendary nightlife.

Sitting here in this kitchen with Rafe, a platter of cookies and two mugs of hot coffee between them, she felt something she couldn't remember feeling in a long time.

Happiness.

Even what they'd discovered when they returned from the creek today couldn't touch the calm that had come over her as they fixed supper together and talked about the bakery, the new horses he'd recently acquired at auction, and Ivy.

And it wasn't only the wine that made her feel this way, Sophie realized.

It was everything. It was Rafe.

A girl could get used to feeling . . . happy.

Sophie met his eyes. She felt the pull between them, stronger than ever, and she suddenly had to fight the urge to reach across the table and touch his face. She wanted to slide onto his lap and kiss him, to stroke her fingers through his hair. To lead him up the stairs to his bedroom and melt with him as one down onto the bed. . . .

It's too soon, she told herself, a rush of panic skittering through her. *Too risky.*

But was it really? Or was she simply stalling for time because she was letting fear run her life, make all the decisions?

When was she going to trust herself—trust her heart?

She stood up from the table and began stacking the dishes, wondering if this was just the remnants of the wine talking—or if she was seeing the truth. For months now she'd been clinging to the memories of her own hurt, using them as a shield against life, love, hope.

In the kitchen, Rafe switched on the radio on the counter and joined in the cleanup.

First Waylon Jennings serenaded them. "Mammas Don't Let Your Babies Grow Up to Be Cowboys." An Eagles song came on next. "Take It Easy."

Rafe took away the last plate Sophie had been about to set in the dishwasher and laid it on the counter, then swung her into his arms, grinning at her gasp of surprise.

C'mon, baaaby, don't say maaaaybe . . .

His arm was snug around her waist, his other hand clasped hers. The music filled her soul, her heart.

So did the smile in Rafe's eyes as he held her close.

I gotta know if your sweet love is gonna saaaave me. . . .

He spun her around, drew her back against him, and she laughed as he dipped her. They kissed just as the song ended.

"Nice," she murmured. She kissed him again.

Rafe kissed her back, a longer, slower kiss this time. A serious kiss. The music had ended, and a commercial was squawking, but they were still dancing, still kissing, their mouths seeking with a need of their own.

"I want to show you something."

She opened her eyes, tilted her head. "I'll just bet you do."

"It's not what you think."

On the words, he pulled her toward the back door. They stepped around Starbucks, sound asleep finally on his soft rug in the corner of the kitchen, and emerged into the brilliance of the starlit night.

She breathed in cool crisp mountain air as he led her away from the house. Not to the new modern pole barn he'd built ten years ago, but to the old barn now used as an extra tack room, temporary bunkhouse, and storage area for feed and supplies, as well as a place where the wranglers could take a break in the middle of the day, sit at the old wooden table, and eat a sandwich, drink some coffee, or catch a few z's if they needed a place to sleep.

Drawing her inside, Rafe switched on a light and a yellow glow banished the shadows.

"Remember this place?"

Sophie laughed. "I'd say so." She'd never forget this barn. Here was where she and Lissie had hidden in the hayloft one afternoon, knowing

240

Rafe and his girlfriend of the week would be sneaking in here after they got back from chowing down on French fries and Cokes at Roy's after school.

This was his favorite make-out spot.

Until that day he came here with Colleen Finch, who'd lasted longer than most, and who had a reputation as a girl who was working her way through every cute boy in Lonesome Way High.

Colleen, giggling, had dashed straight to the ladder and started climbing, with Rafe right behind her. It had all happened so fast, and there'd been no place for Sophie and Lissie to hide. Upon reaching the top of the ladder and stumbling into the loft, instead of finding soft hay and darkness, Colleen had spotted an embarrassed Sophie and Lissie crouched in the shadows, and had let out an ear-piercing scream. Behind her on the ladder, Rafe glared at them in fury.

Then he leaped into the loft and started to yell.

Somehow they'd managed to scramble down the ladder without falling, and even though Rafe had chased them out of the barn, he hadn't come after them, but had closed and locked the barn door.

"I haven't been back in here since that day," she murmured.

Being here now with Rafe brought back a flood

of memories. All of the feelings she used to have about him collided with the feelings she had for him now.

It dawned on her that she, Sophie McPhee, could now be the girl in the hayloft. All she had to do was climb.

"I was so mad at you and Lissie that day. But afterward I had to laugh. The looks of fear on your faces was better than anything I could have done to you two."

"We were utterly mortified."

"And now?"

"Now," Sophie said, tilting her head up to look into his eyes. "I'm wondering why you brought me here."

He backed her up against the barn door and braced his hands on it, just above her shoulders. A slow smile softened the intensity of those deep blue eyes.

"Because the past is over. You're not that bratty little kid anymore and I'm not that wild jackass of a guy. We're not who we were back then. We're who we are now. I thought being here might help bring that home to you."

She slid her arms around his neck and drew him closer. He smelled so good, like saddle leather and sagebrush and spice. Her heartbeat quickened as those hard-muscled arms swept tight around her waist.

"I like us better now," she whispered.

She'd been secretly in love with him back then, and also scared of him. But she wasn't scared of him now at all. She felt safe here with Rafe in this big old barn. Safer than she'd felt in a long time. And braver.

She'd been busy protecting her heart, but somehow it had opened to him anyway. She could deny it all she wanted, but she wanted him and she wasn't afraid.

Her lips parted as she kissed him, inviting him in. She didn't try to resist the delightful sensations that swept her as his kiss intensified and he pressed her back against the barn door. Sophie's eyes drifted closed as his mouth explored hers, as their tongues sparred in an erotic secret battle.

His teeth caught her lower lip—gently—then grazed lower. She drew in her breath as his mouth skimmed across her jaw, nibbled at her earlobe. His tongue began tracing a slow, moist path around the delicate shell of her ear.

She felt herself sinking into a haze of heat and pleasure. They held each other, touched each other, and sank to the floor. Their kisses were slow and deep and sexy. An ache started deep inside Sophie, an ache for this man, this night, this moment.

In between kisses, she unbuttoned his shirt, pulled it off his broad shoulders, ran her hands over his chest. Rafe drew her sweatshirt over her head and tossed it down beneath her, making a pillow for her as he pressed her against the ground. Her bra went sailing, even as Sophie slid her hand to the taut zipper of his jeans.

He was hard, his eyes gleaming into hers with so much need and hunger she was breathless. This time his kiss was filled with a rough urgency that made her heart jump.

"Quick," she gasped, working the zipper. She didn't want to wait any longer, to risk changing her mind or getting interrupted. "I want you so much, Rafe. I want you right now."

"Not a quarter as much as I want you."

"We need . . . protection. . . ."

"No fears, I've got it covered. But what's the hurry?" He pinned her hands on either side of her head and bent to kiss her again, devouring her until they were both out of breath. Sophie quivered all over as he moved lower, his tongue flicking over the pulse at the base of her throat.

"You're so incredibly beautiful." His voice was low and rough. "And there's so much I want to learn about you, Sophie. And do to you."

"It almost scares me how much I want you." The words rushed out before she could stop them. She could barely breathe as no-holds-barred desire seared her. "I . . . know I should wait . . . think . . . but . . . I don't want to . . . I don't want to wait another second, Rafe."

"You're sure?" Releasing her hands, he stared

at her, his eyes keen and searching. "I can't believe I'm saying this, but we can stop right now, Sophie. It damn well won't be easy, but . . ."

"There's no stopping, cowboy. We're at the point of no return." She laughed breathlessly and got him out of those jeans so fast he chuckled. He was so gorgeous, bronzed and muscled, that her blood pounded. "I want you, Rafe. Here. Tonight. Now."

"You got me, sweetheart. All of me. No turning back." His mouth drove against hers, taking her to a hot, shivery place she'd never known. Not with Ned, not with anyone. Not like this.

"I've been wanting to do this since that night I first saw you in the Double Cross Bar and Grill," he breathed in her ear.

"I've been wanting to do this since that day I was fifteen when you picked me up on Squirrel Road," Sophie gasped. "Maybe even before." Her mouth clung to his. "And I'm not of a mind to wait any longer."

"Far be it from me to keep a lady waiting," he drawled, which made her laugh.

And then he made her gasp again and fist her fingers in his hair as he began to kiss her breasts. His tongue flicked at her nipple, first one and then the other, licking and teasing, even as he worked her out of her jeans.

Then his mouth slid lower. Down her belly. Past her hips.

She was trembling with need when he finally freed her of that fragile wisp of a pink thong. And he himself was more than ready to roll.

She wasn't just beautiful, she was exquisite. And so sensitive to every stroke of his tongue and every brush of his lips.

Her skin was smooth and softly fragrant. *Like an exotic flower,* Rafe thought. And he was losing himself fast in the taste and scent and sweetness of her. Her hands clutched at his back, her hips moved desperately against him, and need vibrated from every single beautiful pore.

He wanted to tell her that he hadn't been able to stop thinking about her, that he'd never felt this way about any other woman, not Lynelle, not anyone who had danced in and out of his life.

But he didn't. He didn't know yet what all this meant, where it was leading. And he didn't want to promise more than he could give.

So instead he thought about protection. He couldn't forget that.

But soon he forgot damn near everything else. The old barn just faded away. So did the cool, star-bright night and all sense of time. There was only the two of them and the fire inside them.

His muscular body covered hers and Sophie wrapped her legs around him. Sanity slipped away as he filled her, thrusting deep and hard and then deeper still. They swept together to the edge and then over, and she cried out against the heat of his lips.

There was only the two of them in the whole wide world. Night and fire. Soaring flight and explosive release. Bodies clinging, seeking—and finally shattering as they fused into one.

Then at last a shuddering peace—and Sophie. Rafe kissed her throat very gently, stroked her hair, and gathered her close against his sweat-slicked body in the silence of the old barn.

Chapter Nineteen

"Big day today, Tid," Sophie whispered the morning of the bakery's opening.

It was an hour until dawn and her feet had just hit the floor. Tidbit had lifted his head from the foot of her bed, his tail immediately wagging when she glanced at him.

"I'll fill you in on how it goes tonight," she said softly, and slipped down the hall to shower. She was on her way to town a scant half hour later, even as the last few stars clung to the sky. Instead of her Blazer, which was in the shop getting its side windows replaced, she was driving a rented Jeep, and the weather guy on the radio informed her it was going to be a sunny day with a high of around sixty-two degrees.

She let herself into A Bun in the Oven at five A.M., switched on the lights, and moved swiftly past the tables and the counter, the display shelves and booths, back into the kitchen. Her home away from home.

Yesterday she'd come with her master list in hand and done a meticulous final check of the sacks and tubs and tins and barrels of ingredients all neatly stacked in the storage room on floor-to-ceiling shelves.

Sugar, *check*. Raisins, almonds, butter. *Check.* Honey, yeast. *Check, check, check, check, check.*

When she'd turned her attention to the ingredients for the cafe side of the menu, where she'd be serving a soup, two sandwiches, and a specialty salad daily, it had hit her.

This was really happening. A Bun in the Oven was finally opening.

Nerves had fluttered through her like a million insect wings flapping in her blood. She'd felt this way when her very first Sweet Sensations opened too. And that had been a huge success, she'd reminded herself.

Now as she stood in the empty bakery, the long first day ahead of her, she wondered.

Could she do it again? Here, in Lonesome Way?

She closed her eyes for a moment. It would be awful to fail in her home town. Rumors persisted about certain people boycotting the bakery because it opened so quickly after Roy's closed up.

But she couldn't allow herself to dwell on that. There was too much to do. And an ever dwindling amount of time in which to do it.

Get to work, she told herself, and turned her attention to the first order of business—baking bread. When the bell chimed over the front door at six A.M., she hurried out front in time to see her grandmother padding toward the counter holding a white and blue milk pitcher brimming with spray roses, fluffy pink carnations, asters, and daisies all clustered around a sunflower.

Gran held the flowers out toward her with the same sweet smile she wore when she pulled a pan of brownies from the oven.

"These are for good luck. Not that you need any, dear. You know how to make your own luck."

"Oh, Gran. They're gorgeous." Flooded with a rush of emotions, she pressed a kiss to her grandmother's cheek, which, as usual, smelled of Pond's cream and gardenias.

"I'm so proud of you," Gran whispered.

Sophie hugged her, then straightened, the butterflies returning to her stomach as she set the milk pitcher on the counter. "Don't be proud yet. See if I survive today. And if any customers return tomorrow. That's the real test."

"Oh, you'll survive. You come from a long line

of strong women. It's in your blood." Gran's sneakers made a soft squeaky sound as she walked behind the counter, glancing this way and that, missing nothing as she took in all the changes to Roy's Diner. Her smooth white braid trailed down her back, gleaming against her bright blue sweater.

"Look how much you've already accomplished." She waved a hand at the cheery freshness of the bakery, the gleaming glass shelves waiting to be filled with pastries, the antique cash register polished and glinting in the afternoon light, the cappuccino machine installed behind the counter.

"You're going to need to hire more people besides me and Karla, that's my prediction. A Bun in the Oven is going to draw folks in droves."

Then her gaze paused at the pictures framed on the walls.

Sophie had kept the same prints and paintings that had been here when the place was Roy's. She'd re-matted and reframed the scenes of cattle, horses, and weathered old cabins in shiny black metal frames. They were familiar and nostalgic, summoning up images of Montana life, yet the frames made them fresh and contemporary.

"What a lovely idea." Gran nodded approvingly. "Like keeping that old cash register. Mixing the old with the new."

"Some connections are meant to be continued, not broken," Sophie murmured.

She'd thought about it often as she'd worked on the redesign.

How the past and the present were inextricably linked, for better or worse. This new space she'd created, this bakery, had its roots in the long-standing diner that held warm memories for everyone in town, herself included. She wanted something of Roy's to remain—even as A Bun in the Oven tried to carve a place for itself.

Maybe the homey spirit of the diner could live on within these walls. Sophie had given them new life and her own touch, but she hoped some of the love and energy Lil and Roy had expended here would remain.

Gran headed toward the kitchen, her face beaming. "It's charming. Just the way a bakery should look."

The next few hours were a blur, and later, Sophie would barely even remember filling the cases with loaves of sourdough and honey whole wheat bread, raspberry Danishes, blueberry pies, chocolate chip pecan cookies, crunchy almond bars, and thick slices of lemon pound cake.

And cinnamon buns. Trays and trays of cinnamon buns.

Karla arrived at 8:50 and the first customer came through the door at nine A.M. on the dot just as Sophie hurried out from the kitchen.

He was tall, dark, and handsome and regarded her seriously from beneath the brim of his hat.

"Morning, ma'am. I'll take five of those cinnamon buns there, and a dozen of those cookies. Got myself some hard-working wranglers with a sweet tooth, every one of 'em."

"I'll handle this," Sophie told Karla, without taking her eyes from Rafe. Karla glanced back and forth between them with a dawning smile, and then busied herself setting out cream and skim milk in clear pitchers beside the cappuccino machine.

"My very first customer," Sophie murmured as she counted out the fragrant cinnamon buns and cookies into white paper sacks.

"And your favorite one, I hope."

"You're definitely in the running." She met his eyes and smiled as the now familiar tingles shot through her. Rafe always looked good, but today he looked especially good in a navy polo shirt and jeans, his dark hair almost touching his shoulders, his eyes warm and amused on hers.

When she looked at him, she remembered the way that magnificent rock-hard body felt beneath her fingertips, the way she felt when he touched her, but she carefully pushed away the thoughts.

Today was not a day to be distracted. Rafe could distract her without even trying. But she needed to be sharp, cool, professional.

His next words, quietly spoken as Karla

disappeared into the kitchen, captured her attention, though in a completely different way.

"I just came from meeting with the sheriff."

Her heart jumped. "He talked to Crenshaw?"

Rafe nodded. "Crenshaw claims he was at a casino over in Bozeman Saturday night. From five o'clock until after ten, playing poker. But so far, Hodge hasn't found anyone to confirm it. The manager, the bartender on duty that night, the waitresses, and the regulars—not one of them remembered seeing him."

"So what happens now?"

"Hodge says he'll dig a little deeper on Crenshaw, but . . ." He shrugged. "There's no other suspects. No evidence. So unless someone can place Buck in Lonesome Way that night and prove he's lying about being in Bozeman, Hodge doesn't have much to go on."

"I still can't think of any reason he'd slit my tires. Or why anyone else would. But it can't be a coincidence that someone's gone after my car twice now—"

She broke off as she saw several wranglers in chambray shirts, jeans, and worn, dusty boots; Lissie, Martha, and Dorothy; and several other women she recognized from the library fundraiser meeting headed toward her door.

"I do believe my morning rush is about to start."

Glancing over his shoulder, he turned back

with a smile. "Catch you later. How about supper tonight, you, me, and Ivy at the Double Cross? We can celebrate your first day."

It took her by surprise, but in the best possible way. "You're on," she heard herself say before the bell tinkled over the door and customers began to stream in.

After that, the day flew by like a spinning kaleidoscope. At lunchtime, there was actually a wait for tables and booths, and the chatter of customers mingled with the aromas of the bakery to create a pleasant hum of activity centered around people, coffee, food.

Naturally, Doug Hartigan came in when things were at their most hectic. Sophie was giving Karla a hand at the counter, since there was a line outside the door. She watched Hartigan avidly scan the contents of all of her glass cases as if looking for something in particular—and not finding it. He placed an order for a turkey sandwich on sourdough and a slice of blueberry pie.

"Sophie, do you have any brown sugar chews?" he asked quietly as she was ringing up Erma Wilkins from Top to Toe.

Idiot. If she had them, wouldn't they be on display?

"No." She handed Erma her bowl of soup and a cinnamon bun and gave her change back from a twenty-dollar bill.

"My great-aunt Deedee used to make brown sugar chews when we visited her in Tennessee." The man sounded wistful. "They were always my favorite. I was wondering if you ever plan to have them on the menu."

Not a chance in hell, Sophie thought. "Not planning on it." She kept her voice as neutral as she could. "Will there be anything else?"

"No, uh, nothing else." She saw disappointment in his eyes before he lowered them and dug out his wallet. *Perhaps not only about the chews,* Sophie thought, but she couldn't be sure. Then she forgot all about Doug Hartigan and his brown sugar chews as a rowdy family of six, all tourists, stepped up to the counter and placed the biggest order of the day.

When there was a small lull at two o'clock in the afternoon—only one customer in a half hour —she forced both Gran and Karla to sit down at a table for their sandwiches and bowls of hearty bean soup. She, in the meantime, grabbed coffee and, later, a roast beef sandwich, in between whipping up more cookies, almond bars, and with Gran's help, another cake.

"Middle school and high school lets out at two forty-five." Gran's braid had a few loose strands, but other than that she looked calm and together and totally in her element. "If I don't miss my bet, a lot of those kids—the ones who would have normally gone to Roy's for Cokes, fries, burgers, or pie, will head over here and check us out."

I hope so, Sophie thought. Not just because it would be good for business. She wanted to see Ivy, see how her first day of middle school had gone. It was a big step, and to Ivy, still a child, but tilting toward tweendom, it probably felt huge. It would take a while before she learned that every step in life, both big and small, was filled with both pitfalls and promise.

As Sophie crossed the bakery to the front door a short time later, stepped outside a moment into the sunny September air, and gazed up Main Street toward the middle and high school, she hoped that Ivy had found her first day filled with more of the latter than the former.

A horde of middle schoolers were tramping along Main Street with their backpacks and roller blades and athletic shoes, their voices shrill as they called to each other and swarmed toward A Bun in the Oven in noisy groups of twos, threes, and fours.

She scanned them more than once, searching for a certain slender eleven-year-old with a mop of bright curls, but there was no sign of Ivy.

Chapter Twenty

Sixth grade sucked. There was *so* much homework—more than she had in a whole week of elementary school. The teachers were a lot stricter than they'd been in fifth grade. And she and Shannon had only two classes together out of the whole day, though at least she had three with Val.

Still, thank heavens for *lunch.*

Ivy was rushing to meet Shannon and Val after the final bell rang, but she'd lost her locker combination somewhere in her backpack, and she couldn't find it for ten whole minutes.

She texted Shannon to wait for her—they were going to A Bun in the Oven, and she couldn't wait to see Sophie and how the bakery looked and everything—but just as she grabbed her history book from her locker, her cell rang and she knew—not that she knew how she knew, she just did—who it was going to be.

"Baby, I'm going to be another couple of weeks," her mom said, without even saying hello first. Disappointment stabbed through Ivy.

"It can't be helped," her mom continued quickly. "I need more money to make the trip, so I gotta work another few weeks is all. I don't want you to worry, baby. Just wait a little longer. You haven't told your dad anything, have you, sweet girl?"

"No." She'd almost said "No, Mom," which would've been a big mistake, because Susie Tyler was only two lockers away and she'd have noticed that Ivy said "No, Mom" on the phone and she'd tell everyone and everyone would be talking about it, because they all knew Ivy didn't have a mom. At least, not a mom who lived in Lonesome Way.

"Why so long? I mean, can't it be sooner?" How much money did it take to drive to Lonesome Way? She couldn't believe she'd have to wait *weeks,* and keep the secret even longer. It felt like a big iron anchor around her neck, keeping this secret from her dad, from everyone. And she was annoyed about the timing of the phone call too. Right now, when she was late and had to meet her friends, and maybe they wouldn't wait for her, and it was hard to talk when other kids were around. . . .

Why couldn't her mom have called when she was in her room alone doing homework or mucking out stalls or someplace where there weren't a bunch of people around?

"I'm not real good with money, and to tell you the truth, I lost a lot of what I had," her mom said real fast, sounding defensive and a little bit desperate. "I had a lucky feeling and so I sat down in this private backroom poker game run by a guy I know. But it didn't work out and I lost three hundred and forty bucks. Because that's just the way my luck is rolling these days, baby girl." Lynelle sighed.

"So now I gotta earn it back and I'm stuck in this dump of a town a little longer. But I'll call you again right after I get to Aunt Brenda's house. Just make sure you don't say one word to your dad, okay? And, baby, I can't wait. I bet you're such a big girl now and I know you're beautiful!"

No, I'm not. I'm okay, Mom, maybe not butt ugly, but I'm nowhere near beautiful.

What if she's disappointed when she sees me? The thought stabbed Ivy like a thorn as she stuffed her phone in her backpack. For a moment she had to bite her lip to keep from crying.

Which would be a total disaster.

Everyone around would think she was a baby. Worse, a loser.

But all this time she'd waited to see her mom again and now she had to wait longer. *But she's coming,* Ivy reminded herself. That's the important part.

But what if she doesn't like me?

Ivy's stomach gave a sudden lurch as she rushed down the hall. Her mom hadn't liked her all that much anyway—or she wouldn't have left, right? What if she expected her to be this gorgeous, perfect kid? Her mom had been gorgeous. She'd been Queen of the Rodeo when she was fourteen. She'd had five marriage proposals, and that didn't count the one from Dad. She was almost famous, at least on the rodeo circuit.

And me . . . I'm not anything like her, Ivy thought, suddenly panicking. She took deep breaths to try to calm herself down, feeling almost as upset as she had at the hospital when Aunt Liss thought the baby was coming early.

She wished she could be more like Sophie. Sophie always managed to seem calm and not afraid. Her dad was the same way. Solid, in control. Lately, never knowing when her mom was going to call, if she was really going to come back, and if her dad would find out she was keeping secrets from him, made Ivy feel scared and worried and guilty all the time, but there was nothing she could do about that.

She didn't want to get her mom mad at her. Or hurt her dad's feelings. Or make him think seeing her mom was more important than him.

She hurried outside, relieved at least to see there were still a ton of kids around. But no Shannon and Val, she realized after a moment, weaving her way through the kids still milling around on school grounds, searching through all their faces, still not seeing her two best friends.

Didn't Shannon get my text?

Maybe they got tired of waiting. I'll catch up to them at A Bun in the Oven.

A big group of kids were way up the street, laughing and shoving each other, maybe going to the bakery too.

WHERE R U? Ivy texted Shannon, then slung her backpack over her shoulders and started to run toward Main Street.

"Hey, wait up, you dropped this."

She skidded to a stop and spun around in response to the voice behind her. Nate Miles was holding up a copy of Lois Lowry's *The Giver.* In chagrin, Ivy realized it must have fallen out of her backpack when she slung it over her shoulders. She had to read the first three chapters tonight.

"Thanks. I'd be dead if I lost this." She took the book from Nate, hoping she wasn't blushing. He was just so cute, with his shaggy brown hair and golden brown eyes and that way he had of smiling kind of crookedly. She had one class with him. Science.

Today they'd sat in different rows, but she'd noticed when he came into class a minute after the bell that she wasn't taller than him this year after all. Nate had shot up too over the summer. He was at least an inch taller than Ivy, so she didn't feel like the jolly green giant standing next to him right now. She relaxed a little.

"Who do you have for English?" she asked. Since she was holding her English homework, it was the first—and only—thing that popped into her head.

"Johnson." He shrugged. "She's making us write some lame essay tonight about—"

"Hey, Miles," someone yelled. "You coming or not?"

Nate's best friend was Jack Parrish. He and another, chunkier boy who looked like a seventh grader were staring at them.

"Tryouts in ten! Come on!" the other boy shouted, and then he and Jack took off at a jog back toward the gymnasium.

"Gotta go. Football tryouts." Nate shrugged again. "See ya around."

He was gone just like that, racing after the other two boys. But not before he gave her another one of those lopsided smiles.

Ivy stared after him, holding the book he'd touched in her hands, not ready yet to stuff it in her backpack.

Maybe today hadn't been such a *totally* horrible day after all.

Chapter Twenty-one

"I can't believe it." Sophie felt both drained and exhilarated as she sank down in a booth at the Double Cross opposite Rafe and Ivy. "We sold out of nearly everything."

"That's great." Ivy leaned back in the booth.

"Now you just have to do it all again tomorrow. And the next day. And the next."

Rafe's brows lifted. "Let her enjoy the moment, will you, Ives? Sophie's probably exhausted."

"I am. But I'm also very happy." She had to look away from Rafe, because he looked so good, and she wanted to kiss him in celebration, but she couldn't. For one thing, Ivy was here. And for another, someone else might see.

No one actually knew about them, not just Ivy. Sophie kept telling herself that anyone who saw them together here would assume they were just friends.

But, of course, kissing him in public would definitely take care of *that*. And she wasn't sure she was ready to take that step. Or any step.

To be honest, she didn't know where they went from here. She'd never been very good at just letting things happen. Sophie liked to plan, to think, to shape her future. But this—whatever it was she had with Rafe—was new and different from anything else. She didn't want to spoil it or sabotage it by analyzing too much or making it more—or less—than it was.

Ever since Saturday night, she'd been telling herself to take it day by day. Because for the first time in a very long time, things were going more right than wrong in her life. And she was almost afraid to trust that.

They ordered chicken wings, burgers, fries, and coleslaw. The Double Cross wasn't crowded this early—there were only a few families seated in the booths and some tourists and wranglers sitting at the bar. But the jukebox was already blasting. Clint Black's voice shook the rafters.

As soon as the waitress brought Rafe's beer, Sophie's glass of wine, and Ivy's Coke in a frosted glass, Rafe had them all clink and toast to Ivy's first day of middle school and the opening of A Bun in the Oven.

Then his cell phone rang and it was the horse breeder in North Dakota he'd been trying to reach for nearly a week. Apologizing, he excused himself to take the call in the relative quiet outside.

"So day one—good, bad, or indifferent?" Sophie asked as Ivy sipped her Coke through a straw.

"Could've been worse. I only have two classes with Shannon, which sucks. Thanks for the cookies though," Ivy said suddenly, a genuine smile breaking across her face. "Shannon and Val said they were the best."

Despite that smile and her easy stream of words, Sophie again sensed something shuttered about Ivy tonight. As if she was holding something back. Or holding it in.

It's probably just adolescence, she told herself. *That's all.* But a part of her wondered if something else was bothering the girl. A bit uneasily, she hoped it wasn't that she was joining Ivy and Rafe for dinner.

She'd barely had a chance to speak to Ivy when she'd run breathlessly into the bakery this afternoon. The girl had sent her a quick wave and a smile—looking sort of stressed, Sophie remembered—then immediately joined Shannon and Val at their table.

But Sophie had sent Karla over with a plate of fresh-from-the-oven chocolate chip cookies for all of them on the house, and had received a broad, happier smile from Ivy as the girls all squealed and grabbed for the cookies.

By four o'clock, the three of them had left to walk to the library together to do their homework.

Maybe she just has a ton of homework. Or friend issues, Sophie thought. *Par for the course in middle school.*

But she couldn't resist saying casually as she set down her wineglass, "So overall it went pretty well? First days of anything can be tricky. And middle school's a big deal."

"Yeah. I'm cool with it though. Sorta." Then Ivy paused. She glanced over her shoulder—making sure Rafe wasn't on his way back? Then turned to peer at Sophie, those lovely indigo eyes serious and intent.

"School wasn't awful. It wasn't great either,

265

but . . . the thing is, I think I can handle it. It's just . . ." She studied Sophie a minute, weighing something in her eleven-year-old brain, then she took a breath.

"Can I ask you a question?"

Sophie braced herself, suddenly wondering wildly if this was a question about sex or drugs or something else big. Something Ivy needed to discuss with Rafe. What if she wanted to know how babies were made? But surely Rafe . . . or Lissie . . . would have told her all about that by now. . . .

"I can't ask my dad about this." Ivy spoke quickly now. "And Aunt Lissie has enough on her mind with the baby coming so soon and all. So I . . . I'd just like your opinion," she said carefully. She took a breath, then peered anxiously at Sophie.

"Is it wrong to keep a secret?"

Sophie absorbed the words with a tiny shock. They weren't what she'd been expecting. Not at all.

"Well, that depends." She hoped her concern didn't show on her face. "If someone's in trouble, you need to tell. If it could save a life, or keep someone from getting sick or hurt or putting themselves in danger, you need to tell a grown-up and get help. And that includes if you need to protect yourself—Ivy, do you? Are you in trouble, do *you* need help?"

Her heart was beating fast now as she searched the girl's pretty, serious face, wishing she knew what this was about, but Ivy's lids lowered so Sophie couldn't see her eyes.

"Ivy? You can tell me," she said quietly, even as a knot of worry locked around her heart.

Ivy looked up then. Shook her head. "It's not that kind of a secret. It's not dangerous. It's just . . . someone's feelings might get hurt."

Relief rushed over Sophie. *Feelings. Very middle school. Very normal.* Still, she searched the girl's face. It sounded as if this was a friendship kind of secret. Something along the lines of liking someone else's boyfriend or knowing that somebody had talked behind someone's back or whatever other kind of drama went on in middle school these days. Not life or death or drugs or anything ugly or dangerous.

Still . . .

"Who's feelings? A friend's?"

Ivy shook her head. "I can't tell you."

"Maybe you can tell your dad. Or Aunt Liss. I must have told Lissie a hundred secrets when we were in middle school and she kept all of them. She's a great person to talk to. Sometimes it really helps to talk things out."

"I know, but it's not about me . . . I mean, not exactly."

Sophie thought she saw a flash of misery for an instant, then it was gone.

The next thing she knew, Ivy had a smile on her face. *Did it look a little forced?* Sophie couldn't be sure.

"It's not that big of a deal, Sophie. Honest. Everything's fine."

She slurped more Coke through the straw, then her gaze shifted toward the double doors.

"Dad's coming. I just remembered—I need to ask him—"

She turned to her father as he slid into the booth beside her. "There's a field trip next week. You have to remind me to give you the permission slip when we get home."

"Here's a better idea. Hand it over now, Ives, then we won't have to worry about it later." Rafe's gaze rested on Sophie as his daughter began rummaging inside her backpack. His smile was warm enough to almost make her forget about middle school secrets and field trips and the fact that she needed to be rolling out of bed again in eleven hours.

"Sorry that took so long."

His words were casual, but his eyes held an intimacy that for that one moment made her feel as if they were the only two people in the restaurant, maybe in all of Lonesome Way.

I missed you, his eyes said. *I want to kiss you. And do about a dozen other things to you as soon as we can be alone together again.*

"No problem," she murmured as Ivy surfaced

with the permission slip. "It gave Ivy and me a chance to catch up."

Then their waitress skidded to a halt and began unloading a tray piled with food, and they were once again three people sharing dinner and talking about school and classes and homework. The moment was lost. But not before giving Sophie more of those tingles.

Chapter Twenty-two

Sunday morning several weeks later dawned wet and rainy. But Sophie didn't care.

Life was good.

The bakery was closed all day on Sunday. No one had vandalized her car since the day she'd ridden to the creek with Rafe. And she had a man in her bed.

A rugged, giving, sexy man.

"Stay awhile," Rafe urged, yanking her back onto the pillows when she started to slide her feet to the floor.

"I thought you'd fallen back asleep."

"Who can sleep when there's a beautiful woman driving you absolutely crazy?"

Laughing, she snuggled against him, closing her eyes as he rolled atop her and nuzzled her neck. Tidbit and Starbucks, who'd both already been let out once, snored from opposite corners of her bedroom. Chill September rain splashed against her window.

But she felt safe and warm and wanted as she and Rafe kissed and caressed and took their time making love again beneath her old faded comforter.

Afterward they pulled on T-shirts and jeans and padded downstairs barefoot, trying not to trip over the dogs both lunging past them at the same time. She melted butter in a skillet and scrambled eggs, while Rafe poured juice and brewed coffee, and the dogs crunched over separate bowls of kibble.

Glancing at the stove clock, she felt a stab of disappointment. It was ten o'clock and he'd have to leave soon to pick Ivy up from her sleepover at Val's house. Sophie's mother and Doug Hartigan would be home later this afternoon from the crafts fair in Helena. They'd been gone the past three days.

That meant tonight she'd be sleeping upstairs alone.

"Something wrong?" He set down his coffee cup, watching her face. "For a minute there, you looked sad."

"I'm not. I'm happy. Happier than I've been for a long time."

"Know the feeling." He smiled. He was the picture of relaxed masculinity in those snug jeans and a black T-shirt. His jaw was dark with stubble and his eyes glinted a far deeper blue than the cup in his big hand. He was the sexiest man she'd ever laid eyes on.

But that wasn't what made her heart suddenly tremble.

Sophie lifted her cup, took a sip, trying to keep her hand from shaking. She hoped the cup would hide the emotions written in her face. The same emotions that made her heart feel like it was going to burst from her chest.

She *was* happy. Because of Rafe.

The realization terrified her. How had he come to mean so much to her in such a short time? How had she let herself get so involved with him when she'd known how important it was to be careful? Careful with her heart, which had already been thoroughly stomped on and couldn't survive another frontal assault.

She and Rafe saw each other whenever they could, and up until now, it had been enough. At least, that's what she'd been telling herself.

The bakery had taken off in a big way, and she'd focused her thoughts on that, not on what was evolving between her and Rafe.

She had regular customers now, those who made stopping at A Bun in the Oven part of their daily routine—like Martha, who bought donuts or cinnamon buns or Danishes first thing every morning for her manicurist and Ina

Miller, who did the shampooing, and for all the customers who wanted a sweet treat with their coffee in between haircuts and manicures and gossip.

Mia and nearly a dozen other teachers from both middle school and high school came nearly every day after classes let out, and so did a lot of the kids. Denny McDonald popped in regularly, though more, Sophie suspected, to exchange a few shy words with Karla than for the slice of pie and icy lemonade he always ordered.

Even Georgia Timmons had finally broken down and come in last week, ostensibly to discuss plans for the fund-raiser with Sophie, since it was only a week away—but she'd bought an éclair and three slices of cinnamon coffee cake before she left.

"I'm thinking I should get my own place," Sophie said slowly, and her words seemed to echo around the walls of the kitchen. "You know that little cabin near the woods a half mile away? It's on Good Luck land and it's been in my family for generations."

Rafe looked startled. "I know it. The old place off Timber Road."

"My grandmother moved there for a time after my grandfather passed away, until she decided to take an apartment in town. But that was years ago. No one's lived there in ages." Sophie set her cup down and folded her arms on the table. "I was thinking . . . I could fix it up. It would be fun and I—we"—she smiled at him—"would have more privacy. And so would my mother—and Mr. Hartigan," she added dryly.

The idea didn't seem to sit well with Rafe. "That cabin's pretty isolated." He frowned. "Do you really want to live out there all . . ." He paused as his cell beeped.

"Ivy," he muttered in the instant before he answered the call. "Hey, Ives—"

A moment later he sprang out of his chair.

"Okay, honey, calm down. I'm on my way. Be right there."

"What's wrong?" Sophie asked quickly.

"She woke up feeling sick. Just a sore throat and a cold, but I've got to go pick her up. Sorry."

"Don't be, it's all right. Go." She watched him take the stairs up to her bedroom two at a time to get his boots and jacket, and then she wrapped a couple of brownies and pecan cookies she'd brought home from the bakery yesterday in plastic wrap and gave them to him when he returned.

"For Ivy. And you. Want me to make some soup and bring it over later?"

"You're incredible, you know that? That would be great." He took time to kiss her warmly enough to make her want more.

"I don't know what I'd do without you, Sophie." Tracing a finger along her cheek, his lips brushed against hers. "And I don't ever want to find out."

The words reverberated through her. Before she could fully absorb them and frame a lighthearted response, Rafe had grabbed up the little bundle of pastries, called to Starbucks, and was striding toward the door, the mutt bounding at his boot heels.

"I'll call you later," he promised over his shoulder as he opened the door.

Sophie missed him the moment his truck rumbled up the road. Rafe Tanner was an easy man to miss. And an easy man to love . . .

Love?

No. It's too soon to fall in love, she told herself quickly.

But whoever said love came with a timetable?

She sank into a kitchen chair, feeling dazed. And a little bit like she'd been punched in the stomach.

Do you fall in love by the calendar? she wondered, trying to stay calm. It's been *this long* since my divorce, now I can fall in love again. It's been *this long* since Ned broke my heart, now I can open it to another man.

Was there ever a good time, a safe time to fall in love?

She hadn't thought much about Ned these past weeks. But did that mean she was over him? Over the hurt?

Was she in love with Rafe?

A seed of panic took hold inside her, and she needed to take a couple of deep breaths not to lose it completely.

What happened to being careful, guarding her heart? One night making love with Rafe in a barn had pretty much blown everything else from her mind—all of her wariness, common sense, and defenses. She was in deep here, about as deep as she could get.

Sophie went still as a sparrow on a tree limb as she realized the truth.

It had sneaked up on her. They had fun and laughter, not to mention incredible sex. She loved his smile and all those muscles, and the way he touched her. How he looked at her with those magnetic blue eyes she could get lost in.

But she didn't just love those things about him. She loved Rafe. As a man, a friend, a lover. The sum of all those things and so much more. Her whole heart belonged to him. The power of what she felt for him hit her all at once, and left her stunned.

Her feelings for Ivy had deepened too, without her even realizing it. Somehow she'd begun to lose her heart to Rafe's daughter. Ivy was so vulnerable, so cautious, walking the tightrope of adolescence one small scary step at a time.

How had they both become so important to her? And, she wondered, springing out of the chair and pacing around the kitchen as she fought a new wave of panic, what were the chances Rafe felt the same way about *her?*

I don't know what I'd do without you. And I don't ever want to find out.

She didn't want to find out what she'd do without him either. The very thought felt like a blow to her ribcage.

Shaken at finding herself vulnerable again, she tore furiously into cleaning the kitchen and then, with Tidbit at her heels, hurried upstairs to shower and dress. Her mind whirled in turmoil. She actually felt a little sick. As she stepped out of the shower, nausea rose in her throat, and for one horrible moment, she thought she was going to throw up.

Bracing herself against the bathroom sink, she sucked in deep breaths. And as the rain pattering against the bathroom window slowed to a soft drizzle and the clouds muddying the sky began to break, she suddenly realized that it was the end of September.

And she'd missed her period. By more than two weeks.

Sophie clung to the sink as the realization settled into her.

She was as regular as the sunrise. She never missed.

But this month she had.

We used protection. Always . . . or nearly

always. Didn't we? She thought back quickly, her heart racing, memories quivering through her. Had there been one time when they'd been in too much of a hurry, too caught up in each other? That night in Rafe's bed when Ivy was away on her field trip? Had they used a condom then?

Or had a condom simply failed . . . ?

The nausea was still there. But suddenly she felt a smile spreading across her face. She must be crazy, but she felt the smile on her lips, felt it beating in her heart. Despite everything, joy flooded her like sunshine after weeks of gray.

A baby was growing inside her. A small, beautiful, innocent life. A tiny person to be nurtured and cherished.

And loved.

She looked down, touched her belly with wonder, and suddenly she was filled with a rush of hope and delight and anticipation—and an excitement she didn't dare believe in all at the same time.

Chapter Twenty-three

The morning of the fund-raiser dawned cool and clear a week later. A perfect golden September day.

It was chilly enough for Sophie to shiver in

her leather jacket as she unlocked the bakery door and stepped into the dim interior of A Bun in the Oven. But by eleven o'clock, when she and Karla and Ivy had finished packing up box after box of rhubarb cherry pies, double fudge brownies, chocolate chunk cookies, and cinnamon buns, it had warmed up to a mellow sixty degrees, and the sun glimmered like a ball of butter in the sapphire sky as they loaded the boxes into her Blazer and in the trunk of Karla's Chevy.

Gran was meeting them at the high school, so Ivy rode beside Sophie as they ferried the food over to the grounds. Rafe was waiting for the vet to come take a look at one of his horses, but Ivy had offered to help Sophie set up the baked goods on the long tables arranged around the grounds of the high school, so Sophie had picked her up on her way to town.

But Ivy seemed completely distracted today. Sophie had to repeat herself several times before Ivy seemed to hear her, and even when she'd been busily packing brownies in pastry boxes, she'd seemed lost in her own world.

She looked especially pretty though in a soft pink pullover, jeans, and sneakers—she was even wearing tiny silver star earrings, but she kept checking her phone and didn't seem much interested in making conversation.

"Expecting a call?" Sophie asked at last as she parked the Blazer on the far outskirts of the high school lot. It wasn't even noon yet and the place was already packed.

"No. Well, yeah." Ivy's cheeks flushed a delicate seashell pink. "Shannon and Val. They're going to call when they get here so we can walk around together and hang out."

"Are you entering the raffle drawing for that mountain bike?" The bike was one of the big-ticket items of the fund-raiser. She'd heard dozens of kids at the bakery talking about it yesterday.

"Maybe . . . I guess."

Ivy was already springing out of the car, ready to unload.

Something's definitely on her mind, Sophie thought, and wondered if it could be a boy.

She sure didn't sound very interested in the bike. But then, Ivy was into horses. Just like Rafe.

At the thought of Rafe, Sophie felt a quiver. She wasn't sure if it was a nervous quiver or not. She hadn't told him yet about the baby.

She hadn't yet figured out exactly what words to say or when was the best time to tell him. How would he react? What if she saw consternation in his face?

The very idea of that made her heart drop.

She was brimming with a happiness that seemed to shimmer from the deepest core of her soul. She was having a baby. Rafe's baby. It was all she could do not to sing it out and whirl around like Julie Andrews in *The Sound of Music*. And she wanted Rafe to be as overjoyed as she was. But what if he wasn't?

The pregnancy test she'd driven all the way to Livingston to buy had finally made it feel real. There was no way she could have bought that test at Benson's Drugstore. If she had, no doubt Lila Benson would've kept a straight face all the while she was ringing Sophie up, but before the traffic light on Main Street had changed four times, every shop owner on Main Street, including Martha—and, of course, everyone who worked at the Cuttin' Loose or who was getting a haircut or a manicure that day—would have known that Sophie McPhee just purchased a pregnancy test.

"Hmmm, where to start?" Lissie mused a short time later as she approached the tables laden with baked goods. Her due date was less than a month away, and she looked beautiful, but uncomfortable, her belly as huge beneath her yellow maternity top as if she'd swallowed a giant balloon.

"Can I have one of each, Soph? I'll have the pie now and the others to go. Since I've already passed the elephant stage, I'm now going straight for hippopotamus."

Sophie laughed as she handed over a slice of the rhubarb cherry pie, a napkin, and a fork.

"Well, no fears, you'd be the prettiest hippo ever, but this baby's going to pop out of you before you even get close."

She'd wanted to say, "I'm pregnant too. You're going to be an aunt again. And I hope I look as great as you when I'm in my third trimester." But she couldn't do that yet. Not until she'd told Rafe.

"You know"—Lissie speared a forkful of pie —"I hear you and my brother have been spending *a lot* of time together. Mmmm." Lissie closed her eyes appreciatively as she tasted the pie, then opened them to study Sophie's face. "It's no use trying to deny it. So what's up with that? Is this serious?"

"We're seriously good friends." Sophie struggled to sound impassive and hoped she wasn't blushing. But she couldn't keep from smiling, and Lissie pounced on that like a bird spying a berry.

"What does that smile mean, Sophie McPhee? Do you expect me to believe that you're only friends with my brother?"

She waggled her plastic fork. "I knew you back in the days when you'd cry if you colored outside the lines, and I know you had a thing for Rafe ever since you were Ivy's age. Not that you ever told me, but I knew. I thought it was icky at the time, but now I can't help hoping. . . ."

She deliberately let her voice trail off. Her

eyes were sparkling and expectant, but Sophie wasn't prepared to talk about Rafe, or the baby, or what the future might hold, not with anyone yet, not even Lissie.

"I'm just hoping your brother makes it here today." Sophie kept her tone light. "He's waiting for the vet to come check out one of his horses, but he's one of my best customers for these chocolate chunk cookies. Ivy's around here somewhere too," Sophie added, hoping to distract Lissie by mentioning her niece.

"I saw her with Shannon and Val about ten minutes ago. They're over by the basketball court, where the band is setting up. They looked all googly-eyed over the guy setting up the sound system. But you're changing the subject."

"You think?"

Lissie's rich laugh rang out, and then Gran arrived, and Tommy, who wanted a cinnamon bun. Sophie busied herself setting up a folding chair for her grandmother and selling brownies to some high school boys eager to go buy raffle tickets for the bike.

Karla was cutting a big piece of pie for Denny McDonald, who stepped aside reluctantly when Georgia bustled up to the table and reminded everyone in a voice that no doubt carried to the parking lot that every person working the tables was to remind folks to buy raffle tickets for the mountain bike, the free haircuts and perms and manicures offered by the Cuttin' Loose, and the free dinners being raffled off by the Double Cross Bar and Grill, insisting they hammer home the point that all profits would go to the library.

Lissie and Tommy wandered away to browse the wind chimes Sophie's mom was selling at a table near the bike racks. Sophie saw Doug Hartigan standing beside her mom's table too, talking to her mother, making her laugh whenever she wasn't busy selling a wind chime or some beaded jewelry.

"Sophie, we're getting low on brownies and cinnamon buns." Gran frowned after counting what was left after Dorothy bought a box of each to take as a gift to the women working at the daycare center—who'd volunteered to work for free on a Saturday so that other women with young children could work the fund-raiser.

"There's a half dozen more boxes in the Blazer, Gran. You and Karla hold the fort. I'll run out and get them."

She crossed the grounds quickly, greeting those she knew, pleased by how many people had gathered here today as a community to raise funds for the library. For a moment, she felt almost dizzy with happiness. She was exactly where she wanted to be.

And she wouldn't choose any other place in the world right now—except perhaps lying in

Rafe's arms. *Preferably in his king-sized bed at Sage Ranch,* she thought dreamily.

She smiled to herself as she threaded her way through the cars jamming the parking lot, away from the noise and the laughter and the music as the band began to play. Amidst a riff of guitars and drums and banjos, the lead singer was whomping out a rowdy crowd-pleaser loud enough to get everyone stomping and clapping.

Through the clamor, she was trying to remember exactly where she'd parked, and it wasn't until she cut around a dusty pickup and past a black Explorer that she spotted her Blazer.

And the man bending down beside it.

Sophie's first thought was that he'd noticed something amiss. *Had someone let the air out of her tires again?* Her steps quickened, but as she reached the Blazer, the man straightened and spun toward her. And she saw his face.

Buck Crenshaw.

She froze, fear lodging in her throat as she saw the pocketknife clenched in his hand and the three deep scratch lines gouging the Blazer's driver's-side door.

"Now that's what I call real bad timing." Crenshaw's raspy voice sounded slurred. He'd been drinking. Dear God.

"Bad timing for you." On the words, Sophie whipped out her cell phone and hit nine and one.

But before she could complete the call,

Crenshaw was on her, wrenching the phone from her hand. He threw it to the ground and stamped on it, his dust-caked cowboy boot grinding the metal into the cement.

Her heart pounding, Sophie whirled and tried to run, but Crenshaw grabbed her arm and yanked her roughly back. Shoving her up against the Blazer, he pinned her there, staring into her face with a smile that reminded her of a reptile's grin, the pocketknife still clenched in his hand.

"Go ahead and scream. A lotta good it'll do you."

Fear spiked through her as Sophie realized he was right. The parking lot was deserted. If she screamed, no one on the school grounds would hear, not with the heart-pounding volume of the band cranked up, not until the throbbing blare of music ended.

"Too bad you had to see me." Crenshaw ran his tongue across his lips. "Should've stayed where you were."

"Why . . . are you doing this?" She tried to keep her voice calm, but it rose in barely contained panic. "I don't even know you. I've never done anything to—"

"Shut the hell up! I'm trying to think!" His grip tightened on her arm until she winced.

"If you let me go right now, I won't press any charges—"

"I said *shut up!*"

Now she saw not only anger but hatred flame in his eyes. Desperate, Sophie tried to twist away, but he was too strong and he shoved her back against the car and leaned in closer. The blade of the knife glistened in the sun.

She forced herself to go still, to meet those dark furious eyes. What she saw there terrified her.

He was a man pushed to the edge. A man capable of anything. The world stilled around her as she thought of the tiny life growing inside her. The life she had to protect.

"I won't scream . . . or file charges." Her voice quavered, but it was low and calm. "I promise. If you let me go right now, I promise I won't tell anyone I saw you. You only scratched my car. It's no big deal. All you have to do is let me go."

It was a lie, but she'd say whatever she had to say to protect her baby.

"You think I'm dumb enough to believe you, you little bitch?" Crenshaw's sneer twisted his face. "You're as big a liar as your father. I wouldn't trust either one of you as far as I could throw you."

Ice-cold shock coursed through her. She felt his fingers biting into her flesh, and her breath came in short gasps, but as she tried to steady it, to take a deep breath, all she could think of was what he'd just said.

"You . . . knew my father?"

A furious smile contorted Crenshaw's lips. "Yeah, Miss Fancy Pants Spoiled Brat. You bet your ass I did." The whiskey on his breath made her want to gag. "You think you're the only one who knew ol' Hoot? I know a helluva lot more about your old man than you do."

Chapter Twenty-four

So far it had been a hell of a day, Rafe thought as he vaulted into his truck, gunned the engine, and took off down the long drive, then made the turn on Hickson Road toward the high school.

He'd woken up to the bad news that Shiloh, his new gelding, had colic. Will Brady had become alarmed when he noticed the horse sweating, trying to roll and to nip his own belly. When he'd checked Shiloh's pulse and found it accelerated, he'd notified Rafe, who immediately called Doc Weatherby and had then gone out to check on the horse himself.

There were all different kinds of equine colic, and some were minor and treatable with medication and exercise. Others could swiftly turn serious—even fatal—if surgery wasn't performed at the earliest stages. So the vet had come fast. After a series of examinations, he'd reassured Rafe that the gelding wasn't in any imminent danger.

But Rafe had been distracted with worrying about the horse and had burned Ivy's eggs this morning, had to start breakfast over.

The only bright spot so far had been when Sophie picked Ivy up on her way to the fund-raiser. They'd only had a moment together, and Ivy had been there all along, so he hadn't been able to do more than drink in the sight of her while Ivy climbed into the Blazer.

But he couldn't help smiling now in his truck, thinking about the two of them heading off to the fund-raiser together. The two most beautiful females in Lonesome Way. Hell, in all of Montana. What was he talking about?

In the whole damned country.

Rafe grinned wider. He had the rest of the afternoon to spend with them. But it would go by pretty quickly. He was getting tired, though, of having to say good-bye to Sophie all the time. Leaving her at the Good Luck ranch. Or watching *her* drive away from Sage Ranch. Even knowing she was only a few miles away didn't help. That was a few miles too far. Out of reach, out of his home, out of his bed.

Before now, he'd dated sporadically and nonexclusively. He had fun and satisfying sex with several women who enjoyed the freedom of friendship with benefits, but when he didn't see one of them for a few weeks or months, it was no big deal. But with Sophie . . . it was different. Everything was different.

She plugged up all the holes of loneliness that had taken over his life. She made him feel something deeper than he'd ever imagined before.

He missed her like hell when he wasn't with her. Missed her smile and the way she melted into his arms. He missed the way he could open up to her about Ivy, about anything. And the way she listened, really listened. Sophie stayed calm and thought things through, she didn't just toss off superficial advice.

There was a texture, a depth, a realness to her. She *cared*.

And . . . he cared about her. More than he'd even known—up until this very minute.

We need to be together, he thought, his hands tightening on the steering wheel. *Me, Sophie, and Ivy. A family,* he realized.

Suddenly he felt as if he'd just climbed out of a mine shaft into sunlight.

The pieces were all there. They'd been there for a while now. The laughter. The closeness. *The love.*

She'd mentioned moving into that cabin—he knew she was thinking that would give them more privacy, without having to worry about when Diana McPhee and Hartigan might be around, or when Ivy was coming home.

But he hated that idea. He had a much better one. Now he just had to find the right time and place to tell her. He needed to pray real hard that he was right, and she'd want the same thing he did.

It was becoming difficult to remember what he'd done with his life before Sophie came back into it. Now he thought about her every night when he went to sleep—when she was with him, and when he was alone. He thought about her when he opened his eyes in the morning, when he was out in the corral working with his horses or meeting with a potential buyer or broker.

He thought about her scent, softer than flowers on the prairie. And that way she had of tilting her head when she smiled. Even the calm, cool sound of her voice when she was waiting on someone in the bakery turned him on.

Rafe was stunned to realize he'd only been going through the motions of his life all this time—until Sophie came back to town. *Had he ever once told her that?*

No. Not yet. But it suddenly occurred to him as he took the turn on Lonesome Gulch, and caught sight of the two-story brick high school building ahead in the distance, as he heard the raucous music pounding from the grounds and through the open window of his truck, that he needed to.

He needed to tell her everything and make sure she believed him.

Chapter Twenty-five

"Hoot McPhee was banging my mama. You didn't know that, did you? There's a shitload of crap you didn't know about your old man."

Sophie felt the blood drain from her face. "He . . . I . . ." She gritted her teeth as Buck Crenshaw laughed, deriving an ugly pleasure from her confusion.

"Who was your mother?" she demanded more strongly.

"She was the one you never met. Probably never even heard of." His voice was low now, shaking with anger. "She wasn't from this damned town. We lived outside of Billings and we weren't rich and we didn't own any fancy property. But he used to visit us a lot. Well, *her,* anyway. She used to lock me in my room when he came calling. Said he didn't want to see me. But I saw him out the window every damn time he showed up—and when he left. I saw how she got herself all gussied up when he was coming. How she always had money to buy steak and whiskey and cigarettes and nice perfume after he'd been there. He was the only thing in this world other than booze that made her happy. Until he didn't."

I need to get away from here. Sophie felt sick. Her mind was reeling from the revelation that there had been yet another woman she, her mother, and most likely Wes knew nothing of.

What's one more? a bitter voice inside her mocked.

But it made her stomach twist like a washing machine, just as finding out about all the other women her father had cheated with had.

And there was something else. She didn't like that look in Crenshaw's eyes. The anger dead in the center of them hardened when he talked about Hoot and his mother.

She had to fight him, get away. Hurt him if she could, do whatever she had to.

She stomped down on his instep with all of her strength and broke free for one frantic instant as he grunted in pain. But he recovered too quickly, his hand clamping into her arm, yanking her backward against the Blazer. He used his body to trap her, his fingers tightening cruelly until she cried out.

"I thought you wanted to hear how I know your father? There's more to the story. A lot more."

"I . . . get the picture. I do. Let go. You're . . . hurting me." The band had finished one song and, over the thunder of applause, had rolled right into another. The grounds of the fund-raiser, the people who cared about her, felt miles away.

"Too bad. You're going to hear about your precious Hoot. You're going to hear all about how that bastard killed my mother."

Killed? Sophie shook her head without even realizing it.

Her father had been a demanding son of a bitch, but he was no killer. He'd been judgmental, set in his ways, and certain he was always right. He'd cheated on her mother with countless women, including the mayor's wife, but she knew he'd loved his family in his own rigid, hard-headed way. He'd never laid a hand on anyone that she knew of and he'd certainly never killed anyone.

Crenshaw was lying.

And she told him so.

But the anger flashing in his eyes only darkened. Deepened. She felt the rage vibrating off him, like heat off summer pavement. It seemed to pulse, to burn even through the grip of his fingers.

"Hoot killed her all right. Same as if he put a gun to her head. Only he didn't do it that smooth and clean. Oh, no, he just broke it off with her. Told her he was tired of her. Done with her. Told her he wasn't ever coming back." He yanked Sophie closer, right up to his face.

"My mama took it bad. Kept crying, saying she loved him, that he was the only good thing in her life. Guess *I* didn't count." Crenshaw's voice was like glass shards scraping over her skin.

"A week went by," he continued, ignoring her gasp of pain. "And she was always late to work. Cried and drank the cheap stuff all night long, so no wonder she couldn't drag herself outta bed. Then you wanna know what happened next?"

"I *want* you to let me go. Now!"

"I found her on the floor in the morning." Crenshaw's voice trembled with rage. "I thought at first she'd just passed out. But she wasn't breathing. You hear that? *She wasn't breathing.* She'd taken a fistful of sleeping pills, washed 'em down with a pint of whiskey. She went to sleep and she never woke up. All because of Hoot McPhee."

"Oh God, no. *No.*" Horror engulfed Sophie. She shook her head feebly. But even as she tried to deny it, she knew it was true. The truth glittered in Crenshaw's eyes. In the hatred she saw in them. And in what she already knew of her father.

The truth shivered in her heart.

"You know what happened to me, after she died? After that bastard killed her? I got sent away to my uncle's house in Missoula. They didn't want me there much, 'cept to work around the place every minute I wasn't in school. My uncle liked to beat on me whenever anything didn't go his way. And things didn't go his way a lot of the time. You know what I mean, Miss Filthy Rich Spoiled Rotten Sophie McPhee?

294

Do you?" His voice rose to an enraged roar, dulled only by the throb of the music.

"Guess that's a dumb question, huh? How would you know?" he shouted, with a derisive snort. "You grew up on that big ranch, had everything handed to you on a solid-gold platter. I reckon no one ever screamed at you, much less smacked you around. But I spent five years getting the shit beat out of me because of what your daddy did to my mama. You don't think ol' Hoot deserves a little payback for that?"

"Slitting my tires—that's how you're paying him back? Smashing my car's windows . . . gouging my Blazer? That's crazy. He's dead and I never did one thing to you."

"Well, Hoot ain't here, is he, so you're the next best thing. And you know what? He's probably rolling in his damned grave because I'm messing with his precious little girl. The one who grew up at that big important ranch, who got to have anything her little heart wanted. Hoot's probably madder'n fire that I'm getting back at *you* and there ain't a damned thing he can do about it! And if you're smart, you won't tell anyone about any of this—"

"Hey! Take your hands off her. Right now!"

A man's voice, breathless, shouted from behind her, and she heard pounding footsteps over the hammering of her heart. They got louder as Crenshaw stared past her in sudden alarm.

"Help me!" she yelled at the top of her lungs, and then gasped as Crenshaw shoved her aside and took off running. She caught herself against the side of the Blazer in time to keep from falling, and managed to straighten just as Doug Hartigan skidded to a stop beside her.

At the same moment, she heard brakes screech from somewhere nearby.

"Sophie! Are you all right? Your mother sent me to look for you—" Doug Hartigan was breathing hard, his face flushed in the bright September sunlight.

"He . . . didn't hurt me. But we need to call Sheriff Hodge right now—he broke my phone—"

Hartigan was no longer listening. He was bolting after Crenshaw, his boots slamming against the pavement.

Suddenly Sophie realized that Hartigan wasn't the only one giving chase.

Rafe's truck was at a standstill twenty yards away, the engine still running, the driver's door wide open. Rafe was barreling toward Crenshaw with fast, powerful strides, closing the gap and heading him off as he dodged between cars.

Hartigan ran to the right, Rafe slightly left, and Crenshaw was cornered between the two. With a desperate burst of speed, Crenshaw tried to make a break for his rig, but Rafe hurtled toward him like a torpedo. He dove at him in a flying tackle perfected at football practice at

Lonesome Way High and knocked him to the ground with a sickening *thwack*.

Crenshaw groaned and tried to roll free. Rafe slammed a fist into his jaw, then hit him again, this time in the eye. Crenshaw's head lolled to the side just as Hartigan reached them.

"Rafe, don't. Stop!" Sophie had been rushing toward them, but she faltered to a standstill as she saw Buck Crenshaw sprawled on the pavement. Out cold.

"Calling . . . the sheriff," Hartigan panted, quickly punching buttons on his phone.

Scrambling off Crenshaw, Rafe ran to Sophie and pulled her close. "Are you all right?"

He held her as if she were made of fragile china, his handsome face pale beneath his tan. "Did he hurt you?"

"N-no. I'm not hurt. I'm—" She buried her face in his chest, struck by the huskiness of his tone, but mostly thankful to have his arms around her. "I caught him keying my car with a pocketknife . . . and he told me why." She leaned back, looked up at him with dismay. "Rafe, it's horrible."

His arms tightened around her and she rested her head against his chest, so hard and solid and comforting. She was dimly aware of Hartigan on his cell phone a few yards away and knew she'd have to thank him later for coming to her aid. She owed him that much.

Probably more. *Perhaps even an apology,* she thought, as something that might have been forgiveness opened like a flower in her heart and pushed the old weeds of anger away.

She looked straight at Rafe.

"It was my father," she said quietly. "Rafe, it was all because of my father."

Diana hovered over her, looking worried, but Sophie continued setting out brownies and cinnamon buns.

"Are you *sure* you're all right?" her mother asked. "You must be in shock or something."

"I think you should sit down and take a break," Gran suggested, watching her with concern.

Martha and Dorothy bobbed their heads in— for once—silent agreement.

"Not a bad idea," Doug Hartigan put in mildly, but Sophie shook her head.

"I'm fine."

They were back at the bakery tables, and she was dealing with what had happened in the only way she knew how—by throwing herself into work. Teddy Hodge's deputy had handcuffed Crenshaw in a police cruiser while the sheriff had taken Sophie's and Doug's initial statements, then the wrangler had been hauled off to lockup.

We don't need to worry about him anymore, at least not for today, Sophie thought. *With any luck, we won't have to think about him again until his hearing and his trial.*

"I'm all right, everyone. You can stop looking at me like I'm going to disintegrate. I'm just sorry that . . . well, I thought we knew everything there was to know about my father . . . and now this," she muttered, meeting her mother's eyes.

"Nothing about Hoot surprises me anymore." Diana's face was pale, but set. "Nothing about him hurts me either," she added unexpectedly, as Hartigan slipped an arm around her waist.

They looked so comfortable together. Easy. Close. For once, Sophie found herself feeling happy for her mother and, to her surprise, couldn't muster even the slightest whiff of resentment toward the man at her side.

"I'm only sorry your father still has the power to hurt *you,*" Diana told her softly. "You and Wes both."

"Well, maybe what Wes doesn't know can't hurt him. We don't exactly have to call him up and tell him about this, do we, Mom?"

Sophie watched Karla hand over cookies and napkins to Lila and Tom Benson, then slide the money Tom handed over into the cash box. "No," her mother replied. She looked relieved. "Right this minute, no, we do not."

"Where did Rafe go?" Gran asked Sophie. Boppity and Boo exchanged knowing glances.

Great, does everyone know now about me and Rafe? They've probably known for weeks, ever since Roger Hendricks claimed we were out on a date. Even though we weren't.

But somehow the thought of people knowing about the two of them didn't bother her anymore. In fact, she'd been hard put lately not to want to shout it from the bakery rooftop.

Sophie and Rafe. Sitting in a tree. K-I-S-S-I-N-G.

Lame, she thought, deciding she was turning into a mushy-headed idiot. But there was a warm glow inside her as she realized that baby made three.

Or, actually—even better—with Ivy *and* the baby, they would be four.

Or possibly two . . . and two.

She swallowed. She had to tell Rafe. And then deal with his reaction, whatever it might be.

"Rafe went to look for Ivy," she told Gran. "He wants to make sure she's okay—and to let her know about Shiloh. But she's not answering her cell phone."

"The music was so loud for a while, she probably couldn't hear it," Gran suggested.

"Or she's too busy with her friends to bother answering." Dorothy nodded sagely, drawing on her extensive knowledge of young people as a former school principal.

"The last time I saw her," Martha put in, "she and a bunch of other girls were gathered near where the band was setting up. From the way those girls were looking at the boys and their guitars, you'd think every one of 'em was Elvis returned to life."

But the band was taking a break now, thankfully. And in another few hours, Sophie realized, the fund-raiser's decorating committee would be frantically setting up in the gymnasium for the dance tonight and Lee Ann Hollows' performance, followed by the singer personally auctioning off Brad Paisley's cowboy hat.

She pictured herself dancing on the crowded wood floor with Rafe, the gymnasium bright with candles and streamers and balloons. Maybe after a little while they'd duck out alone under the stars and she'd slip her arms around him, tilt her head back, and tell him about the baby. . . .

"Well, now, there's Shannon and Val, right over there." Her grandmother pointed toward Ivy's best friends. "But I don't see Ivy with them."

Shannon and Val were flipping through the stacks of donated CD's on sale beside the booth where lemonade, coffee, bottles of water, and soft drinks were on sale. And Gran was right. Ivy was nowhere around.

"I'll be right back." Slipping from behind the table, Sophie skirted Martha and Dorothy, and dodged through the throng of people toward the girls.

But when she asked them if they'd seen Ivy,

Shannon glanced quickly over at Val in a way that stirred a tiny sense of unease in Sophie.

Then they both shook their heads.

"Her father's looking for her," Sophie told them. "We heard she was hanging out with you earlier."

A frozen pause. Sophie thought she saw panic in Val's eyes before the girl dropped her gaze.

"She was—but she left." Val shrugged.

"We . . . we're not sure where she went," Shannon added quickly.

A little too quickly.

What middle school drama was this? Had the girls gotten into an argument, and Ivy had gone off on her own? Was she upset, alone somewhere? *Crying?* Sophie thought, her heart constricting.

These two were definitely holding something back. She spotted Rafe making his way back toward the bakery table and saw with dismay that Ivy wasn't with him.

"Listen to me, both of you." She kept her voice as calm as she could. "I'm very worried about Ivy right now, and her father's going to be too. He's on his way back from searching for her and he's going to want to talk to you. You need to tell me if something happened. Where did Ivy go?"

Val's face flushed bright pink. "We promised we wouldn't say anything."

Tears sparkled in Shannon's eyes. "Please.

Don't make us tell. She doesn't want to hurt her dad's feelings."

Hurt his *feelings?*

Something echoed in Sophie's brain. The Double Cross. Ivy mentioning a secret. Worried about hurting someone's feelings.

Oh, God. Her fingers shook. How bad was this going to be?

"Tell me . . . right now." The sternness of her tone startled them. Both girls stared at her in panic. But not as much panic as was flooding through Sophie.

"Tell me this minute," she ordered.

"We only found out today." A lone tear slid down Shannon's cheek. "I swear, we didn't know before this. She's . . ."

"She's okay," Val interrupted on a gulp. "She's not doing anything wrong. We promise."

Sophie saw Rafe looking toward her from the far side of the grounds and waved her arm frantically at him. He started toward them.

"Not good enough." She turned back to Shannon and Val. "Her father wants to know where she is, and I suggest you tell me right now before he gets here—"

"She's with her mom!" Shannon blurted. Tears were now flowing freely down her cheeks.

Her mom? Sophie felt her body go rigid with shock. "Lynelle?" she gasped in a voice that sounded nothing like her own.

"Ivy doesn't want her dad to know. She just wants to talk to her mom by herself." Val tried to look defiant, but her confidence was fading fast.

"Where? Where are they meeting?" For a moment Sophie had a horrible vision of Ivy hitchhiking on the highway to get to her mother. "Please tell me she's here—in Lonesome Way."

It was Shannon who answered, her words tumbling now. "Yeah, she's here. They're meeting in town."

"*Where* in town?"

Val spoke up just as Rafe reached them. "They're at A Bun in the Oven. Right this very minute."

Chapter Twenty-six

"Ivy? Is that you?"

Slowly, her mother moved from the kitchen doorway into the front part of the bakery, flashing a nervous smile.

She's limping, Ivy noticed with a shock. Carefully, she closed the door to Main Street behind her.

And she looks . . . different. Different from her picture.

"Come on back here, honey, into the kitchen, where no one can see us from the street." Lynelle's voice was high-pitched, almost breathless. "Hurry, baby girl." She waved a hand with nails painted purple with tiny pink stars on them. "C'mon, what are you waiting for? I don't bite."

Was she trying to make a joke now? Ivy didn't think anything was funny, not at this moment. Her heart felt like a huge weight taking up all the space in her chest as she scurried around the counter and past the booths into the bakery kitchen.

The only thought spinning through her mind was that this woman with the straggly, nearly waist-length blond hair and huge dangling onyx earrings didn't look at all like the vibrant red-haired mother she remembered. The woman now facing her, standing beside Sophie's long spotless worktable, looked like a stranger, a hollow-cheeked, nervous stranger who might have been a tourist passing through town. Her big blue eyes looked sad beneath their generous frosting of lavender eye shadow and dark black mascara, and her smile was so big and toothy beneath bright pink lipstick that it seemed fake.

As Lynelle took a step toward her, Ivy fought the urge to shrink back. She couldn't really see any resemblance to the beautiful, exuberant woman in the photograph she took out of her dresser drawer now and then and studied when no one was looking and she was missing her mother.

But this weary-looking woman *was* her mother. And she should be feeling . . . what?

Love? Joy? Closeness? The kind of closeness Shannon had with her mom when they both laughed at something at the same time? That Val had with her mom, even though they argued a lot?

Ivy was sure that the feelings roiling through her were too huge and strange to be normal. They scared her. Longing and anger all twisted together, forming a huge tight knot right in the center of her throat, making it hard for her to even swallow.

She stopped short of her mother and stood there, trying to think what to say or do. Her mom was skinny, but her jeans were so tight they looked like they were a size too small for her hips, and her lime green sweater with its bracelet sleeves was cut *way* too low.

No one else's mother dressed like that.

"You look different than I . . . remember," Ivy murmured, not knowing what to say and wondering too late if that had been a rude comment. She'd never dreamed she'd have trouble talking to her own mother, but she wasn't sure where to start. What do you say after someone left you on a bench with just Peegee and a bag of Doritos?

"Yeah, I'm different, baby girl. Old and washed up." Lynelle gave a sad-sounding laugh, as if she hoped it wasn't true and wanted Ivy to protest and reassure her. "I dyed my hair blond because it's supposed to make you look younger. Not sure it really did that," she added with a rueful smile.

Then she studied Ivy, top to toe. "But you look different too, sweetie pie. My heavens, you're so grown up and beautiful. I'd give up ten years of my life just to be eleven or even twelve again and look like you, with everything in front of me. You're so lucky—look at you, even prettier than I was at your age. And I was Queen of the Rodeo."

Was her mom bragging? Or regretful? Or was she sad? It was hard to tell. There was a wistful look on her face, a longing in her voice. But Ivy flushed. She wasn't beautiful. She was gawky and plain and she'd never been queen of anything.

"I didn't tell anyone I'm here," she offered at last.

"That's good, sweetie, that's real good. Your dad, well, he'd probably yell his head off if he knew. I'm positive he's still pissed—I mean, mad—at me, not that I blame him. I probably shouldn't have up and left the way I did, he has a point, but I just couldn't stay on that ranch one more hour, much less one more day. I had to go, you understand that, don't you, baby?"

Lynelle had taken a step forward, but she paused as Ivy stiffened.

"I mean, it wasn't because of *you,* of course—I love you from the bottom of my heart, precious girl. And you were always so good. Not a crier or a clinger, like some of them, you know? But I just . . . I needed *more.* You'll understand some day."

No, I won't understand. Not ever. I'm not like you.

A flash of something tore through Ivy like a tiny jolt of lightning. Her chest felt like it was going to burst wide open and her heart with all its fury would fly out.

But she forced herself to take a step, and then another one, closer to her mother. She had to, she didn't know why. Her mom wasn't quite as tall as Sophie, and beneath her makeup, she looked kind of tired. She was holding a big shiny silver purse and she set it down on the floor as Ivy approached her, then threw her arms around her and hugged her tight.

Uncertainly, Ivy hugged her back. She tried not to breathe in the smell of her mother's perfume. It was too strong, too sweet, and it made her nose itch.

"Listen to me, Ivy, honey." Her mom pulled back but held on to Ivy's hands, clutching them tightly. "I had this great idea. I want to make things up to you. I want us to get to know each other. What do you think about coming to live with me at Aunt Brenda's for a while? You've had all this time with your dad. Years! I want my turn now. What do you say?"

"I . . . you . . . want me to move to Forks Peak?" *To leave Dad?* Panic rushed through her. "But . . . you . . . you were the one who left *me*," she blurted.

Her mother flushed, then tossed her hair back. "Things were different then. I couldn't stay, I just couldn't, baby girl. But last year, something happened."

Ivy stared at her, not saying anything.

"I had this accident, honey. A real bad one. First time in my life—I was performing in this rodeo in Fort Worth—owned by this man named Harlan Cooper. And a horse threw me, and my leg got broke, and my back was messed up real bad. I couldn't walk for a long time, months and months. I went through physical therapy and rehab . . . it was awful, baby, but Harlan paid for everything and I learned to walk again. And you know what? I got kinda used to staying in one place and it . . . it wasn't so bad. Harlan took real good care of me, until he dumped me for that scheming little buzzard Billie Jean Maple."

Ivy was silent. Her stomach felt awful, like someone was pinching it all over. She shifted from one foot to the other, suddenly thinking how empty the bakery felt with only her and her mom there. It didn't seem right to be here without Sophie.

"Billie Jean didn't know a thing about riding or performing," Lynelle went on, "but she knew how to do Harlan's books. I think he just got tired of paying someone to do them, you know? Anyway, he married Billie Jean, and she couldn't stand having me around, so I hightailed it out of there soon as I could. But the thing is, I got to thinking. I miss you and I want to be a mama to you again. So since I got better, I've been waitressing, bartending, you name it—just to get enough money to come here and start over. I didn't figure this was the kind of thing we could plan on the phone. You know? So here I am."

She smiled, an eager, uncertain smile. "So how about it, baby girl? Tell me you'll come live with me at Aunt Brenda's. Just for a while, until I can save enough for our own place. Don't you want to give us another chance?"

Ivy felt a ripple of panic. Leave her dad? And Sage Ranch . . . Starbucks . . . her *horses?* Like Mom had left Misty Mae? She didn't want to leave them, or her room, her friends, Sophie. . . .

"I . . . can't. I have school," she said quickly.

"Well, that's no problem. You could transfer, couldn't you? People do it all the time. For a semester, maybe two. Think, honey, we could spend so much time together. We could even share a room at Aunt Brenda's. And then, if you want to transfer back to your school in Lonesome Way after Christmas or maybe in the spring, you could. But think of all the fun we'd have living together. We'll be best friends. I want that, Ivy, I want that so much. We have so much time to make up for."

But that's not my fault, Ivy thought, her stomach dropping at the pleading hopefulness in her mom's eyes. She couldn't seem to stop the flow of questions circling through her head. *How long do you want to be best friends, Mom? Until you're ready to take off again? Until you're tired of Forks Peak? Of me?* She felt guilty for thinking that way, but she knew the scared voice inside her head had a point.

"You said I'd understand." Ivy swallowed. "But I . . . I don't."

"What don't you understand, baby?"

Ivy's hands were clenched. She'd thought she'd be happy once she actually saw her mom again. Instead she felt like she was going to cry. But no. She wouldn't. She couldn't let herself. No matter how many times her mom called her baby, she wasn't a baby anymore.

"You left me on a *bench,* Mom." She hated that her voice trembled, but she couldn't help it and plugged resolutely on. "You left me all *alone. I don't understand.*"

Lynelle stepped back. Her mouth opened and then closed. Like a fish, Ivy thought. Then she snapped her lips together for a moment.

"Well, that's just crazy, honey. You weren't all

alone. Not exactly." She shook her head, and her long blond hair swirled. "You were in the middle of *town,* for Pete's sake. There's lots of people in Lonesome Way, and everyone takes care of everyone else. That's how these small towns work. I knew you'd be fine. I mean, people here don't even lock their doors, do they? Look how whoever owns this bakery left it unlocked while everyone's at the high school. It's the way small towns work. I knew that. So I knew someone would find you soon and your dad would come for you and—"

"I was scared, Mom!" The words flew from her, sounding high-pitched, foreign, as strange as the squawk of a startled wild bird. They might have come from some creature Ivy didn't even know. "I was so scared! Don't you even care?"

"Baby . . . honey . . . there's no reason to cry now. It was a long time ago. You're *fine.* I knew you'd be fine." Tears filled her mother's lake blue eyes. "I knew your father would take care of you and I had to—"

Lynelle broke off as behind them the bell tinkled over the door. Ivy whirled. And there was her father, tall, strong, handsome, running across the bakery toward her, looking a hundred times more tense and worried than he had even this morning when he found out Shiloh was sick.

Anguish clutched at her heart. She'd done this

to him. Scared him, hurt him. Would he ever be able to forgive her? she thought, a sob rising in her throat.

Then she knew the answer as relief flooded his face. He drew a deep breath right inside the kitchen doorway and managed to smile at her as Sophie rushed in right behind him. She was pale, but she smiled too, an encouraging smile that said, *It's okay, you're not in trouble, we're just happy we found you.*

Ivy tried to choke back her tears. They seemed stuck on her eyelashes. She couldn't even speak. There were too many feelings welling up inside her, and they were all tangled up, rushing to get out.

When the sobs finally burst from her, they were hard and painful and wracked her throat.

"D-Dad!" It was the only word she could force out.

The next thing she knew, she had flung herself into his arms and he was kneeling beside her, gathering her tight against him. As she buried her face in his shoulder, she felt his strong arms tighten around her, and finally, finally, with her eyes closed hard against his shirt, she let the tears fall.

Chapter Twenty-seven

The first snowfall of the season blew in with a flurry of clouds a week later.

It was a fluffy, luxuriant snow, distinguished by flakes as thick as feathers. They dusted the foothills and coated the back roads and carried with them a fierce wind rushing straight down from the mountains to usher in the first icy taste of the long Montana winter.

Sophie and Ivy and Rafe ate grilled cheese sandwiches on sourdough rye and drank hot chocolate at the kitchen table at Sage Ranch on that Sunday afternoon. They were waiting for Shannon and Kate Gordon to pick up Ivy. The girls were going to the library to do homework together—according to Ivy, she had a *landslide* of homework.

"Calm down, you two," Sophie admonished in amusement as a horn tooted in the driveway and Tidbit and Starbucks went nuts, barking in frantic tandem. Of course, both dogs ignored her, continuing their racket even after Ivy raced outside in her parka and scarf and bundled into Kate Gordon's Explorer. They barked like maniacs until the SUV disappeared from view. Then as calmly as if nothing had happened, they trotted over to the warmest corner of the kitchen, curled up together, and went to sleep.

"Now *they've* got the right idea." Rafe came up behind Sophie, wrapped his arms around her waist, and dropped a kiss to the back of her neck. "Proving dogs are a lot smarter than most people think."

Grinning, he led her into the living room, tugged her down onto the sofa with him, and pulled her close. She laughed and wiggled closer. They stretched out like spoons in front of the fire while snowflakes kissed the windowpanes.

Listening to the snap of the logs, watching the flames dance hypnotically before them, Sophie thought: *Now. Tell him now.*

She hadn't found the right time to tell him about the baby since the day of the fund-raiser —at least that's what she'd tried to convince herself. Deep down she'd been delaying sharing the news as long as possible. For one thing, he'd been plenty busy sorting everything out between Lynelle and Ivy. For another, she knew in her heart that once she told him, everything between them would change. For better or for worse— this carefree, sexy, no-strings *thing* between them would evaporate forever.

And Rafe would feel either trapped, guilty, obligated, or . . . dare she even hope for it? *Happy.*

She *needed* him to feel happy, even one

hundredth as happy as she was. And she knew she'd be devastated if he reacted with dismay or a sense of obligation, especially if he tried to hide it. She'd know. And there was no reason to think that dismay and obligation wasn't exactly what he would feel. She knew he enjoyed her company and they had great sex. She knew Rafe was an honorable man.

But he'd never told her he loved her. Never spoken of a commitment. Never made her any promises.

She didn't want a husband who didn't need her with his whole heart. She'd already had one of those, and she wasn't going down that road again.

So she'd been reminding herself over and over, she didn't *need* a husband to raise this child. She'd love it enough for two parents easily, effortlessly, even though she was certain Rafe would want to be involved.

But involved didn't mean married. It didn't mean love.

So she'd been clinging to these last sweet, uncomplicated days, to the joy she felt when she was with him. She didn't want this to end. But it had to. Today.

It wasn't fair to either her or Rafe not to tell him, so she braced herself and twisted around in his arms so she was facing him.

Her throat went dry as she kissed him one

last time, savoring the taste and scent and warmth of him.

But before she could gather breath to speak, his cell phone rang.

"Damn, I hate this thing." He sighed against her lips.

Not as much as I do, Sophie thought. Her heart was pounding. Now she just wanted to get it over with. Face the music, whatever happened.

"Dad." Ivy's voice was breathless and clearly audible to both of them. "I forgot, what day is Mom coming over?"

"Two weeks from today, Ives, why?"

Rafe tensed. Ever since Lynelle had reappeared in their lives, he'd been worried about the repercussions on Ivy. She'd seemed okay with everything up until this moment. Now he braced himself, wondering if she'd changed her mind and wanted to see Lynelle sooner than he'd arranged—or not at all. "It's okay if you've had second thoughts about wanting to see your mother," he said. "Because if you don't, I'll—"

"No, it's not that. I want to see her, I guess. But Winnie Chandler's birthday party is in three weeks. It's at the bowling alley in Bozeman. She's here at the library and she just invited me and Shannon. I wanted to make sure it wasn't the same day I'm supposed to see Mom. That's all. So I can go, right?"

"Winnie's parents will be there?"

"Of course."

"Are boys invited to this party?"

"Well . . . yeah." Ivy spoke quickly. "It's just bowling, Dad, no big deal. You have to let me go."

No, I sure as hell don't, was his first thought. Hearing the urgency in his daughter's voice though, he swore silently. Sophie's gaze was trained on him, and she looked sympathetic but amused as she pulled back and they both sat up.

He could guess what she was thinking: that he couldn't stop Ivy from growing up, liking boys, going to parties—*supervised* parties, he reminded himself. That it was all natural and normal. He knew all that. Recognized the logic of it. But he'd seen things from the other side, and it scared the hell out of him to see his daughter entering this new phase of life. He knew those boys without having met them, knew their instincts, their hormones, what they wanted, because he'd been one of them way back when. Maybe the worst of the bunch. And it wasn't daisies and rainbows and horseback rides into an innocent sunset that they were looking for.

Ivy was vulnerable. Young. She ought to still be playing with Peegee and Hawaiian Barbie, not going to bowling parties with boys. He needed to protect her as long as he possibly could.

Like until she was forty.

"Dad?" Her voice sounded plaintive. Almost desperate. "I can go, can't I?"

Rafe let out his breath. "After I talk to Winnie Chandler's parents and check this all out, and *if* they're going to be there the whole time, you can go."

"You're the *best,* Dad! Bye, gotta study."

He heard the sound of girlish giggles as his daughter hung up on him before he could take anything back.

"Boys." His mouth grim, he tossed aside his phone. "Suddenly I have to worry about boys."

"You knew this day was coming sooner or later," Sophie pointed out.

"And later's always better. Between this and that deal I worked out with Lynelle to visit Ivy here once a month, I'm not sure how much more I can take."

Ordinarily she might have smiled at the scowl in his eyes, but inwardly she was thinking that depending on how he took the news she was going to impart, his day might be getting a whole lot worse. Still, she clung to the hope it would instead get better.

"You'll get used to it," she said quietly. "The boys, I mean. Ivy's eleven, almost twelve. It's just the start." She touched his hand. "The good thing in all this is that you handled the Lynelle situation brilliantly. You have it all under control."

"Right." Pulling Sophie onto his lap, Rafe wrapped his arms around her. "Until she up and leaves again and doesn't bother to say good-bye to Ives."

He'd made it clear to Lynelle that the only way she was going to see Ivy until her eighteenth birthday was under *his* terms. That meant one afternoon a month for the time being, and only at Sage Ranch, and only when he was present. They'd see how things went after that. Take it or leave it.

Ivy herself had been relieved almost to the point of tears at this laying down of the law. And after a bit of yelling and then weeping, Lynelle had capitulated. There wasn't much else she could do, especially after what she'd pulled with all those secret phone calls and a covert meeting at the bakery.

Rafe had gone to court after she first disappeared, and along with his divorce, he'd been granted sole custody of Ivy. Lynelle didn't have a prayer of getting legal visitation rights now after having abandoned her daughter and virtually disappearing from her life for the past four years. She'd have to take what she could get and rebuild any possible relationship with Ivy gradually.

If that was really what she wanted and if she was capable of it at all.

"We'll see how long she sticks around this

time." Rafe shook his head. "But if she hurts Ivy again . . ."

"Ivy seems to have her mother's number," Sophie said. "Her guard is up, sad as that is to say. It's amazing that she's even willing to give Lynelle a chance." She smiled at him. "You should be proud. Your daughter has a heart as big as all of Montana. And whatever happens, she knows you're there for her. That'll see her through whatever comes."

"I hate what she's been going through all this time. All those lies and secrets. It tears me apart to think she'd been carrying this around for so long."

Sophie met his eyes. "I only wish I'd realized sooner. When Ivy told me she was keeping a secret, I had no idea—"

"Hey." He kissed her quickly and traced a finger gently down her cheek. "Don't apologize. We've been through this already. You couldn't possibly have imagined what Lynelle was up to. What she was putting Ivy through."

She'd told him the day of the fund-raiser, after they'd discovered Ivy and her mother meeting in the bakery, of how Ivy had confided she was keeping a secret, but Sophie had thought it was some fleeting tween drama.

"No way in hell you could have known, Sophie," Rafe had told her at the time.

Now, as the fire crackled and the wind whistled

through the pines outside the ranch house, he cupped her face in his hands. "You can't beat yourself up over this. I won't let you."

His kiss almost made her forget what she still needed to say.

"Maybe things will work out better than you think with Lynelle," she murmured. "Sometimes people really can change."

"Yeah?" Rafe grinned. "Anyone in particular you're referring to?"

"We both know who I'm referring to." Sophie's mouth curved as she pushed back a lock of his dark hair. And thought about Doug Hartigan.

Her mother had told her only a few days ago that she and Hartigan had secretly gotten married in Billings during one of their long weekend trips to a crafts fair. They'd been waiting for the right time to break the news to Sophie, and finally, after the events of the fundraiser and the debacle with Ivy and Lynelle, they'd decided to come clean.

They wanted to start living together as husband and wife, and had told her they were planning to move into Doug's old house in Timber Springs.

But Sophie knew how much her mother loved the Good Luck ranch. Like Sophie, she'd grown up there, and so had Gran. Her mom shouldn't have to leave the home she loved just because she didn't want to force Sophie to live under the same roof with her former teacher.

"I don't hate him anymore," she'd told her mother, and was surprised to find that the words were true. "He's good for you, Mom. I see that now. And . . . I'm beginning to see the person you see when you look at him, instead of the one I remember."

Doug Hartigan made her mother happy in a way she'd never been with Hoot. There was no doubt of that. If Ivy Tanner could give Lynelle a second chance, as wary as she might be, Sophie knew she owed Hartigan one too.

But she drew the line at living under the same roof. She, her mother, Hartigan—and her baby?

No.

"I went to the cabin yesterday and checked it out," she said slowly, just as Rafe was about to kiss her again.

Pausing, he stared at her. "Yeah?" His voice sounded wary. "How was it?"

"Not as bad as I thought. All it needs is a really good cleaning, some paint, new appliances. I'd order a new bed, of course, but there's a pretty antique cherry table and some lovely chairs— I'd just need new cushions, perhaps some window treatments—"

And a crib and changing table, diaper pail, rocking chair . . . Now is the time to tell him, Sophie thought. Right now. She'd been waiting all week, hoping for the perfect moment, but it suddenly dawned on her that there *was* no perfect moment. You just had to take the plunge.

"I have something I—"

"You really think it's a good idea, living in that isolated cabin all alone?" Rafe interrupted her.

"It's no different from staying at the Good Luck ranch all alone. And now that Crenshaw's locked up and it looks like he'll be serving time, I can't see what there is to be afraid of. Rafe, I need to tell you—"

"I don't want you living in that cabin, Sophie." Rafe's gaze locked on hers. Her heartbeat quickened at the intensity she saw in his eyes.

"I want you living with me. With *us*. Me and Ivy." His thumb brushed her cheek. "I want us to be a family."

She stared at him, unable to speak. But that was okay, because he was on a roll. "Sophie, I love you." His voice thickened. "I want a life with you more than anything in this world. I want to marry you, spend every day and every night with you, have a dozen babies with you. I want us to be together for the rest of our lives."

He kissed her long and deep and decisively, tangling his hands in her hair. "Sophie," he muttered, reluctantly pulling away from her lips, gazing into her eyes. "Sophie, I have dreams now, dreams about the future. And they're all because of you. They all revolve around you."

"Did you say . . . a dozen babies?" Her heart was soaring.

"Yeah. I did." He chuckled. "But that's open for discussion, of course. We could start with just one."

"As a matter of fact," she whispered, "we *are* starting with just one." Happiness spilled through her and her heart felt ready to burst. "One baby, Rafe. Coming right up. Well, in about eight months," she added very softly, watching his eyes.

She saw stunned bewilderment. Then a rush of joy.

"Eight months." He looked dazed. Then he grabbed her suddenly and kissed her with such fierce joy she felt it penetrating right through her skin, piercing her heart. His arms were tight around her, but not too tight. They circled protectively. His strong mouth lifted from hers. "And you were going to tell me when?" he demanded.

"As soon as I worked up the courage. I . . ."

She broke off with a yelp as he scooped her off the sofa and into his arms and spun her around until she was dizzy.

"We're having a baby!" he shouted, and the dogs, startled, came racing from the kitchen, staring at them both and wagging their tails.

"We have to tell Ives first. Then Lissie. Or your mom if you want. No, your grandmother,"

Rafe said, laughing as she stared at him as if he were a crazy man. "That'll be the quickest way to get it all over town. I want the world to know that I'm marrying Sophie McPhee and she's—" He broke off. "You didn't say yes yet."

"You didn't give me a chance—"

"Don't say another word." He set her down very gently on the sofa, kissed her, then strode to the desk near the window, yanked open the top middle drawer, and snatched something from it.

She stared at the dark blue velvet jewel box nearly swallowed up in his big hand as he came toward her.

Sophie jumped up from the sofa, but she sank back down again immediately as he dropped to one knee. He caught her hand, cradling it in his. His fingers wrapped around hers felt warm and strong and exactly right.

"I hadn't planned on doing this today, but I got this thing five days ago. I've been searching for just the right time. But if this isn't that time, I don't know when would be better—" He broke off, took a deep breath, and popped open the box.

"Sophie McPhee," he said.

Rafe Tanner, former bad boy of Lonesome Way, smiled into her eyes.

"If I have to ask you a thousand times, I will, but it would be a whole lot easier if you'd just say yes right now. Will you marry me?"